T0196642

In 15th Century England, alliances can be deadly for a Knight of the Swan. Especially those made in the heat of passion . . .

Fleeing for her life after a savage attack on her homeland, Lady Sabine of Clearmorrow finds sanctuary on the windswept shores of southern England, praying that her family reaches her before her foes. When Sir Darrick of Lockwood shows up in a swirl of raging wildfires, Sabine is not willing to trust the dark knight, though he may be her last hope. And when she learns of his urgent quest to locate his sister, she realizes she may be his, too . . .

Lady Sabine is the last woman who saw his beloved sister alive, which is the only reason Darrick demands she join him on the perilous journey to bring Elizabeth home. But even as he shelters Sabine from their powerful enemies—and savors the sweet passion between them—he wonders if the brave beauty will bring him all that he desires, or draw him deeper into danger . . .

Visit us at www.kensingtonbooks.com

Books by C.C. Wiley

Knights of the Swan
Knight Secrets
Knight Quests
Knight Treasures

Published by Kensington Publishing Corporation

Knight Treasures

Knights of the Swan

C.C. Wiley

LYRICAL PRESS
Kensington Publishing Corp.
www.kensingtonbooks.com

This story is dedicated to Harley. My big darling dog—You will always live in my heart, and now you will be able to run through these pages forever.

Acknowledgments

I would like to thank Kimberley Troutte and Susie Fourt for their continued support and helpful comments. Their careful reading brings insight and clarity to the tale. I would like to also express my gratitude to my editor Tara Gavin at Kensington Publishing for giving me the opportunity to share my stories. Finally, my thanks go to my copy editor for proofreading with passion and wisdom. I am eternally grateful.

Chapter 1

The biting wind, heavy with moisture from an approaching storm, tore at Sabine's hair. She swiped at the bits of dried vegetation stuck to her cheek and drew the bundle closer to her chest. As she wove her way through the stand of trees, she prayed the thin woolen cloak would muffle the babe's cry.

Fear that she had waited too long deepened with every step that brought her closer to the hermit's cottage. Lady Elizabeth must have led Vincent DePierce's mercenaries to the tiny island. How else would they have found this deserted pile of rocks hidden off England's shores?

Sabine stopped in front of the gnarled bushes. There in the shadows, hidden by brambles and twisting branches, stood the entrance to the cottage she had called her home for nearly a year.

She waited in the storm, listening for a careless hunter's footsteps, and checked the many traps set around the building. After making certain she was not being watched, she slipped inside and kicked the door shut.

Exhaustion turned her trembling legs to water and she slid down the door.

How had it happened so quickly? The men must have known Elizabeth was there and lay in wait, stalking the new mother until she was alone.

Sabine rubbed her forehead. She should have followed closer. Found a way to stop them.

The scene exploded behind her eyelids. A flash of lightning. Shadows reaching from behind. A cry for help. And then the babe's mother disappeared over the cliffs.

Despite the slippery footing, Sabine had tried to see over the edge. The crashing waves had pummeled the shore below. Watching for signs of life. No matter how long she stared into the blackness, the rocks and water refused to release their hold. Elizabeth was gone. And the newborn baby remained hidden in the brush, out of sight and protected from DePierce's mercenaries.

Sabine pressed her palm to her forehead and tried to erase the horrid memory. To no avail. Her thoughts returned to the cliffs and the lives that had been destroyed in an instant.

* * * *

Sir Darrick of Lockwood bunched his fists in frustration. Their travel from France to England's southwest coast had cost them precious time. He had prayed that when he arrived at the cottage near Balforth Castle, that Elizabeth would run out to greet them, her laughter ringing out at the lark she had played on her older brother. 'Twas as their mother feared: his sister had disappeared somewhere between Lockwood lands and Balforth Castle. His heart clenched. Elizabeth was in trouble.

He stared down at the injured man lying on the bed. The villagers said the clergyman called himself Rhys and they placed little trust in the man of the cloth. Although there were few signs that he'd been beaten, he had yet to stir from his deep sleep, not even when Darrick and his soldiers rode in that morning. But his mother, Lady Camilla of Lockwood, was confident Rhys had vital information about Elizabeth.

The longer they waited, the colder the trail.

Darrick swatted his gauntlets against his thigh. He needed the answers to Elizabeth's disappearance. How was he to awaken the clergyman from his deep sleep?

Darrick turned as Sir Nathan Staves entered the musty room. Nathan's massive body, formed from years swinging a battle sword for King Henry, blocked what little light the torch produced. He bent, narrowly missing the low wooden beam hidden in the thatched ceiling.

"Sir Vincent DePierce, Lord of Balforth, insists Elizabeth never arrived at his castle gate," Nathan said. "He professes that his men scoured the countryside searching for signs of his nephew's wife. Claims they returned empty handed. She has simply vanished."

Darrick grunted, not bothering to voice his disgust with DePierce's ridiculous story. Instead, he voiced his own theory. "A few of the servants hiding on the neighboring lands say that when Hugh left for France, he took with him a vast number of soldiers still riding under the old Lockwood banner."

"That would leave Lockwood and Elizabeth virtually unprotected."

"Unprotected and without an heir. I'm told a recent missive reported Sir Hugh's disappearance from his command."

"And there were orders from Hugh that should harm befall him, Elizabeth was to make haste to Balforth. To his uncle, DePierce," Nathan added.

"Someone used Hugh's death as bait to draw Elizabeth from Lockwood's safety?" Darrick nodded as if answering his own question. "We find the one who did this, we find Elizabeth. Then we grind him into the ground."

Nathan's green eyes shimmered with vengeance. Darrick could almost see the plans forming inside his friend's head. He would do well to keep his tall friend out of trouble and still manage to find his sister.

"What of the runner we intercepted?" Nathan asked.

Darrick placed a hand over his heart, quoting the missive they had taken from the messenger. "'After a lengthy search, it is with our deepest regret that we failed to find the remains of Sir Hugh DePierce, Lord of Lockwood.'" He paced the confining cottage. "My God! Vincent DePierce's nephew, Hugh, now Lord of Lockwood. Indeed, it still burns my throat to speak of another man's name attached to my ancestor's home."

"I fear it will not bode well for the servant who misplaced his lordship's body."

"A man of Hugh's ilk will turn up, whether you like it or not," Darrick said with a thin smile.

"You doubt his death?"

"Until I see his body, I advise we embrace caution while we travel upon these lands."

Nathan nodded at the wizened lump lying motionless in the bed. "What of that one? Have you been able to shake him awake? Question him about what he knows?"

Darrick straightened his shoulders. "'Tis useless. For now, we'll put the hounds on the trail again."

Nathan scrubbed at the stray whiskers on his jaw. "Did you note the fear in the villagers' eyes? None would mention your sister's name. Perhaps if I speak with them without the Lord of Balforth by my side, we will discover where he has hidden Elizabeth."

"'Tis imperative we find her. Without Elizabeth to claim Lockwood from the king, DePierce may stand to receive all the lands held in Hugh's name."

"You're in Henry's good graces. Surely Elizabeth's rights as heir to Lockwood will hold."

"Unless DePierce claims Elizabeth as his latest wife and declares Lockwood as his own," Darrick said.

He leaned forward and pressed his ear close to Rhys. Nothing more than the sound of labored breathing came from the clergyman's cracked lips. Darrick spoke over his shoulder as he continued to watch the little man. "Would that I could leave this bedside and join you, Nathan. Once again, I must ask you to put yourself in danger and see what you can learn from the people of Balforth."

Nathan flexed his shoulders. Restless, he strode to the window and looked out. "You know I stand for you. Have done so since we were children playing as knights protecting our king."

"In truth, you are part of my family," Darrick said. "More so than those of my blood."

Nathan nodded. "Knights of the Swans until the day we die."

Darrick's gaze shuttered. "Perhaps those are memories left for another time. You know the consequences."

"Let us away from these lands," Nathan said. "Ignore those who've turned their backs on you. An eye for an eye. Turn away from the lot of them."

"You know I could never do that," Darrick said. "'Tis certain DePierce has drawn Elizabeth into his greedy clutches. I am honor bound to find her and ensure her safety. Try as I might, I cannot ignore my family's call for help. His need for power continues to grow. No longer can I let the threat to Lockwood run free."

"So be it," Nathan relented. "I honor your decision."

Darrick frowned. "Be safe, my friend," he warned.

Nathan moved to carry out his orders. He paused in the doorway. His indecision apparent, as he wrestled with his thoughts. "You know Elizabeth already may have succumbed to his treachery."

"We must continue to hold the hope that she will be found alive and well," Darrick said. "I'll have the men prepare to ride as soon as we learn anything new." He paused when he felt a tug on his sleeve.

"I must know," Rhys whispered, his voice as hoarse as flint scraping across a rock. "In truth, do you intend to help the Lady Elizabeth?"

Awash with relief, Darrick leaned forward and pulled the little man upright. "Tell me what you know."

Rhys stared into his face. "I see now that you, too, have your father's eyes. The bards didn't exaggerate their tale when they likened them to the strength of steel." He stopped his efforts to pry Darrick's hands from his clothes. "Be a good soul. Pour me a drink from yon jar. See there. Sitting on the shelf..."

Darrick unlocked his fingers and let Rhys fall back to the straw mattress. He snatched the jar with one hand, grabbing the wooden vessel that stood beside it with the other. Thrusting it into Rhys's hands, he waited impatiently for the man to continue.

After sipping the elixir from the wooden cup, Rhys spoke slowly. "I arrived at Balforth after I left your father's side. They had need of both healer and clergy at the castle."

Darrick waited as Rhys took another slow, laborious swallow. The little man made a show of letting the soothing liquid trickle down his parched throat. Testing Darrick's patience further, he took another drink before continuing.

"Unfortunately, the wives of Lord Balforth have been beset by poor health."

"Plague?" Darrick asked.

Rhys looked up from under a ragged hank of hair. He took a deep, rattling breath, and added, "Nay," he said. "The marriage bed."

"You forget, old man, Elizabeth is not Lord Balforth's wife."

"Not yet," Rhys mumbled under his breath. "When I heard your sister was widowed, and traveling to Balforth, I tried to watch over her. As a favor to your father."

Nathan returned to the cot. "How did you know of Hugh's death so soon? 'Tis only recently that official notice was delivered."

Rhys glanced back at Darrick. Shrugging, he waved aside Nathan's question with a pale hand. "'Tis of no importance. Perhaps a loyal retainer came with the report. I don't recall."

"Quickly, old man, where is she?" Darrick asked.

"Vincent DePierce was most displeased when your sister arrived at Balforth Castle. You see—"

"You saw her?" Nathan pressed closer. "She arrived at Balforth?" He turned to Darrick. "I knew it. We'll tear Balforth apart."

"Please continue with your tale. Where is my sister?"

"She hides on a small island off the west coast. Few people know of its existence." Rhys hesitated before continuing, "Should have found safety there. Until today. No one knew where she was. Save myself and the maiden I sent with her to tend to her needs."

Darrick cursed the delays he and his men had met with every step of their journey. "Continue," he ordered.

Rhys bowed his head. "May God forgive her. The serving girl did not stay as instructed. Fears of the old hermit hiding on the island were too much for her. She deserted your sister to fend for herself."

"Where's the servant now?" Darrick asked.

Rhys's gaze rose from his lap. He studied the men before giving them his answer. "She was reported missing at the same time as Lady Elizabeth. The DePierce mercenaries were waiting. Her arrest came as soon as she returned home."

Darrick searched the man's face for truth. "Damn it, man! How is this possible?"

"You must understand! The soldiers of Balforth are very efficient. The maid did not have a chance." Rhys's eyes shifted away. "Even now, I fear they are on their way to ferret out the safe keeping of the two women and end their lives."

Darrick leaned over, his face close enough to smell the pungent odor of wild onions on Rhys's breath. "Are your brains addled? You just said the other woman is no more."

A flash of impatience burned in Rhys's eyes before he hid them behind heavy lids. "Nay, 'tis true!"

"There is another?" Darrick asked.

The thin blanket bunched under Rhys's gnarled fingers. His voice continued to rise in agitation. "Aye, the stubborn wench. Too headstrong for her own good." He wiped the spittle from his mouth and motioned toward the door. "You tarry long enough. Leave tonight for the island. I pray you are not too late."

Nathan grabbed Darrick by the front of his gambeson. "You cannot mean to go there alone."

Darrick shrugged free. "I am capable of handling two women. 'Tis you who enters into Balforth's den of vipers. Don't draw attention until we station more men." He nodded towards the rumpled clergyman. "Watch him closely."

"Hear me, Rhys," Darrick called from the doorway. "If what you say is true, I owe you a debt of gratitude. To be paid upon my return. However, should you play me false, know that I'll be on your trail. And I will find you."

Barely acknowledging the threat, Rhys hid his eyes behind heavily hooded lids. "If you open your ears, I will instruct you on how to reach the island." His hand trembled as he pointed at Darrick, adding his own warning. "Do not harm the old woman, or 'tis I who shall find you." A bitter smile drifted to his lips. "One day, Sir Knight, one day, we will compare the pasts we share."

"We have no past, but we will surely have a brief, pain-riddled future if your information fails me."

Rhys thumped the cot with his gnarled fist. "No, Sir Knight! I dare advise you to keep in mind that size does not always measure the strength of your opponent."

Chapter 2

Sabine's eyes snapped open with a start. She meant to rest for only a second. Her muscles had stiffened during the time she sat on the hard-packed earth.

She glanced down, afraid of what she would not find. The baby was still there, cuddled in her lap. She sighed, slowly releasing her breath. "What am I to do with you?"

Gathering her scattered wits, she brushed her cheek against his cap of silky down. A foreboding shiver ran through her body. There was nothing she could have done to stop the attack, but still, she felt the weight of failing. With a determined shove, she pushed away the memories from the night before.

Sunrise created an odd glow through the small window. Dust motes danced in the amber rays of sunshine. Peering through swollen lids, Sabine concentrated on the particles floating in the filtered light. She listened for the birds, announcing the new day with their morning chorus. Her hand hesitated in midair. An uncomfortable silence settled on the cottage.

The birds were silent. Not a sound could be heard over the rumbling in the distance.

"God's blessed bones," she muttered, "another storm's about to break."

Hoping to clear her muddled head with the cool morning air, she inhaled as she wriggled her back up the door. Her nose stung at the first breath of the bitter cloud.

She lifted a corner of the leather hanging over the window. Mammoth flames engorged the sky. She had seen their like one other time. The vicious fire had claimed her home, Clearmorrow. "Holy Mother, DePierce's men intend to burn me out."

Her fears mounted. She dared not tarry. Soon the flames burning in the glen would rage over the island.

She swept Elizabeth's few belongings into the wadded blanket, adding them to her own meager pile, and tucked her dagger securely at her waist. The baby in one arm and the bundle draped over her shoulder, she stumbled across the room.

Sabine opened the door. Smoke rolled upward, coiling over the tops of the trees. The glowing inferno scorched the living with its dragon's breath.

Frantic bleating caught her attention, slowing her frenzied steps. With little time to spare, she ran to Matilda's goat shed behind the cottage. Grabbing the rope, she fumbled with the knot. Finally, it gave way, but not without costing her the precious time she had left.

Rapidly plotting her escape, she cut a path through the trees. She prayed those who set the fire had yet to discover her only means of flight. The little boat simply had to be where she left it, bobbing in the water.

Her lungs tightened from the smoke, forcing her to slow her pace. Aware of the valuable time she was losing, she counted out the seconds and then pushed on. Her steps unsure, she slid on the moss and dead leaves littering the ground.

Sabine glanced over her shoulder. Although the billowing black clouds seared her lungs, squeezing the fresh air out of her chest, the smoke temporarily hid her from the enemy. No one followed her trail. Yet, she could not trust that she was safe from harm. Her enemies would not be far behind. They expected her to surrender without a fight, as any meek and mild maiden ought. Sabine knew otherwise. These men would never request a ransom. Moreover, she was not the same maiden who ran in terror once before.

The smoke thinned as she neared the edge of the cliffs. Gulping in fresh air, she strained to fill her lungs. A cool breeze floated over her flushed face. She paused at a pile of boulders and felt along the wall of stone. With the bushes pushed out of the way, she found the fissure cut into the rock.

Sabine tied the goat's rope to a branch, then cradling the baby, she crawled through the opening. Once inside the cave, she placed the child on a pile of soft moss and pulled the blanket away from his face. Her spirits soared. Despite their jarring run through the grove of trees, the orphaned angel swung his tiny fists in the air and kicked out his feet.

"Who might your kinsmen be, my sweet love? I wonder if they are worthy of your bravery. No doubt, they are incapable of providing you protection." The baby wrinkled his face and began to cry. Grimacing, Sabine added, "How am I to feed you?"

Matilda's plaintive bleating roused Sabine from her thoughts. "Lord, love us. Of course." She caught the rope with one hand and gave a gentle tug, drawing the beast into the cave. "Darling," Sabine cooed through gritted teeth. "Come along now, or there'll be roast goat for dinner."

Matilda bleated once and ran through the opening of the cave. Sabine eyed the animal. A plan began to form. Her skill at milking the goat had improved since the first night on the island. When the clergyman Rhys had assured her she would find the required supplies, she hadn't stopped to think he intended her to fend for herself. It took many failed attempts, but Matilda had finally grown accustomed to her touch.

Her task completed, Sabine reached for the red-faced baby. To her dismay, the blanket was a sodden mess.

She dug through her bag until she found her favorite skirt. She purposefully ignored the stains. It would never be fit to wear once the baby had use of it anyway. In short time, the soft, buttery material was torn into several pieces. One rectangle successfully tucked around the infant.

Sabine rummaged through the bundle and found a small wooden bowl. She poured a meager amount of the goat's milk into the bowl and set it aside. After a moment of hesitation, she wrapped her blanket around the baby and held him in her lap. Armed with the corner of the thinning blanket, she dipped it into the milk. Careful not to lose a blessed drop, she touched the tip to the infant's lips.

Warm and dry, he looked up with his big dark eyes. He waved his arms in the air and gurgled with delight.

Sabine ignored the tug at her heart. Like it or not, until she found his family, the baby was hers to care for. She shook her head. "Sorry, little one, but I don't want the responsibility for another life. Not now. Not ever."

A lone tear fell from her cheek and landed on her hand. She watched as it dissolved the paste that disguised her age. The plan was to wait until 'twas safe for her brother Taron to come for her. However, many nights had passed well beyond the designated date. The fire was proof that she had waited too long. Her enemy was relentless, and she must leave the island before they found her. Or the baby.

Doubt gnawed at her newly discovered courage. What would she do if Taron were unable to come for her? Was he lying sick, or hurt? Or worse?

She flicked at the dried paste on her arm. "I won't think of such things. 'Tis not possible that DePierce could destroy all that I hold dear. I won't allow it. I'll find Taron and put things to right."

Smudging the trail of tears from her cheek, she looked down at the babe. Fed and dry, he was content once again. "I have to find your family.

I have no desire to keep you by my side any longer than I must. The sooner I deposit you in their care, the better."

Sabine reached for the bundle at her side and pulled out the usual lady's personal belongings: a brush, a comb, and a small dagger with jewels on the hilt.

"Well, my lad, your mother made an odd choice of traveling supplies." Frowning, she weighed the sparkling dagger in her hand. "The balance is wrong. How can such a small knife be so heavy?"

Her brother and men-at-arms carried swords that oft times held secret compartments in the hilt. She stared at the metal but could not see anything amiss. Laying the dagger down, she dug further into the bundle and found a silver mirror and a small bag of coins.

"Saints," she said. "Why would someone carry such senseless baggage? 'Tis a wonder she found the cottage at all."

Drawn to the dagger, she picked it up again. Its weak reflection bounced off the cave. She scratched Matilda's ears and held the knife out to the hairy beast. "What do you make of this? The hilt is in the shape of a swan."

The goat dutifully examined it with its lips.

"See?" Sabine pointed with a soot-smudged finger. "'Tis an emerald, where the eye should be." She rolled it repeatedly in her hands. Unable to discern a family crest, she sighed and packed the items away. "Once the fire is out, those fools will search for bodies. We'll try our luck and climb down the rocks leading to the cove."

The thought of the cliff made her head spin. Her stomach clutched and churned. The rocks had been slippery the night she arrived on the island. As long as she never looked down, she had managed to climb up the treacherous stairway. Afterward, when she had reached the top and could barely see the shore, she sank to her knees and could not move for hours. It took forever to force her legs to carry her away from the ledge.

"Matilda," she whispered. "How am I ever going to get down these rocks with you and a baby in tow?"

As if wary of Sabine's words, Matilda snorted in response.

After ensuring that the goat did not have a means of escape, Sabine offered a prayer under her breath. "Dear God, I need an angel sent from heaven." She glanced at the goat. "One with a very strong back."

* * * *

Sir Darrick of Lockwood pulled the oars through the body of water. Sweat streamed down his face despite the chill in the wind. His breath came in small bursts, leaving a trail of clouds in the cold morning air.

The sides of the wooden vessel squeezed against his body. He shifted his weight. The lip of the hull dropped dangerously close to the water. He had forgotten how much he despised boats. With a grimace, he drew closer to the shadows dancing on the pile of rocks. The bucking increased as the small craft neared the isolated island that lay straight ahead.

The wall of rock towered overhead. How did Elizabeth manage the cliffs? Prior to her disappearance, his cosseted little sister had faced nothing more dangerous than the decision to change the style of her hair. How great was her desperation? Was her marriage to Hugh so difficult?

Thunder, his large black hound, stood guard at the bow. His nose lifted to the scents floating by. As the rolling waves increased, he dropped from his perch and began a plaintive whine.

"Quiet. I know you would have preferred to stay warm and snug beside the hearth. However, your place is here."

The dog sniffed the air before hunkering down to the deck of the boat.

"Coward," Darrick muttered.

Thunder cocked his ears and let his muzzle drop to his paws.

Darrick strained to locate the jagged point through the thick mist. The little boat rocked and pitched in the churning water. He braced his legs, prepared for a rough landing.

"What place is this to send two women? Alone. Without one guard to protect them." He cursed the clergyman and added his name to the growing list of people he would take to task.

His thoughts darkened as they wandered to his family. He knew deep down, despite his father's doubts of lineage, the Lockwood blood ran through his veins. Whether any of them liked it or not, it remained Darrick's duty to protect.

He wagered his sister would certainly be in one of her moods. He hoped the hermit, said to live on the jutting island of rocks, would survive her viperous tongue. He could not fathom Elizabeth showing kindness to anyone, especially one under her station.

"I imagine our Elizabeth will have much to say when I find her."

Thunder raised his head, his muzzle quivering.

Darrick nodded. "I smell it too."

Overhead, smoke swirled from the point of the island. The air began to fill with its acrid odor. Flames licked at the sky.

Nearing the shore, Darrick jumped into the surging wave. Icy water lapped at his waist as he dragged the boat to the spit of land. He fixed the rope around a boulder jutting out from the sand.

Following Rhys's directions, he located the slit that served as a natural doorway. The stairway loomed before him. He crammed his head and shoulders into the narrow passageway. He could feel his throat begin to close off.

"Come, boy," he ordered through stiffening lips. "Nothing to stop us. Right?"

Darrick tested the first step and began the climb up the stairway. Behind him, Thunder's toenails clicked as they dug into the decaying moss that grew on the weathered stone.

The sound of someone singing a melody drifted through the passage. He shook his head and pushed on, certain it was only the wind blowing through the tunnel. That was all.

A stray beam of light glistened up ahead. He followed the beacon until he reached the top of the moss-covered steps. After motioning to the hound to stay put, Darrick pulled himself free of the opening.

Wary of what dwelled in the shadows, he moved silently across the hard-packed floor. A wiggling bundle caught his eye. He bent to have a better look and heard the rush of something coming from behind. Too late, he turned as his head struck the cave wall.

Darrick blinked at the bursting stars. His knees gave out, crumpling him to the floor. As his vision faded, he marveled at the sight. "Saint's bones! 'Tis...a baby?"

Behind him, Thunder growled, tearing after the assailant. Knowing the hound's protective nature, Darrick braced his body for impact. He groaned and swore he heard a goat's frantic bleat. Then all was silent. Save for the angel's voice...cursing.

Chapter 3

Without taking her eyes off the intruder, Sabine secured the cloak, making certain the woolen folds covered her face and hair. Her disguise as an old woman complete, she tightened her grip on the blade and readied for battle.

The dark hound stood guard. Its teeth bared, a growl erupted from deep within.

"Down," she ordered.

To her surprise, the dog hesitated then collapsed beside its master. It followed her every move as she edged toward the babe. Once satisfied the baby remained safe and out of harm's way, she turned her attention to the stranger. Scrubbing her mouth with the back of her hand, she gathered her courage and then rolled him over.

Shadows deepened his cheekbones. His jaw had a stubborn tilt to it. Heavily banded muscles led from his neck to his broad shoulders. She swallowed and peered close, looking for Balforth markings. Although he didn't carry any insignia to prove otherwise, she could not wait to ask him.

She grabbed a piece of cloth from her pack and tore it into several strips. The dog whined as she moved the man to his side and tied the cloth around his wrists. Next, she bound his legs together. Her shoulders burned as she strained against his weight. Exhausted from her efforts, she let his booted feet drop to the floor.

Once she was certain he could not escape from the bindings, she ran her hand down his chest, searching the folds of his woolen cloak for weapons. Her search stalled as cold metal caught her palm. She peered close. A brooch held his cloak together. An emerald eye winked back from a similar design she found in the lady's belongings. The similarities of the lady's dagger and the stranger's brooch were startling.

Sabine moved out of reach as he began to thrash against some unseen force. "Elizabeth," he cried, "where are you?"

Huddled in the shadows, Sabine rocked on her heels and waited until a deep sleep overtook him. Did he cause the lady to fall to her death? Or did he offer help? She and the babe had to leave their hiding place and do so with speed. Although she had not heard anyone outside their shelter, it would not be long before the Lord of Balforth's men found them. She had to discover where this stranger's allegiance lay.

Armed with memories from her days as the Lord of Clearmorrow's only daughter and eager student in the ways of healing, she gently touched his injured head. Her courage regained, she cradled the side of his face with the palm of her hand. A small amount of blood darkened his hair. She prodded the raised area. He would have quite a headache when he awoke. She felt the base of his neck. His heart beat rhythmically against her fingers.

Satisfied he would live, she rested her back against the damp rock wall. If the man lying on the ground did not travel alone, then his friends were sure to scour the island for him. And if he could find her, so could they.

She tested the knots binding his wrists and ankles. They would have to hold him. Until she knew her answers, she had a hungry mouth to feed.

* * * *

Darrick awoke to the sound of shuffling footsteps and the sweetest voice he'd ever heard. His angel had returned. The soothing tune poured over him as he retraced his last steps. His memories caught on the crone's shadow. If she was the hermit then perhaps Elizabeth was nearby.

Restless, he moved to rub his throbbing head and found strips of fabric bound his hands. The angel's song scattered into fragments as he struggled against the bonds.

"Release me," he roared and immediately regretted it. Gaining no immediate response, he lowered his voice, letting his words run over his tongue, his voice smooth. "Please. I mean you no harm." Certain he could coax his captor into submitting to his will, he continued. "I search for a young lady."

Silence. Darrick's frustration rose. *Where was that vile woman?* "Surely, you wouldn't allow a young innocent harmed."

Sensing his master's rage, Thunder barked. The baby began to cry. The noise echoed in the cave.

With great effort, Darrick lifted his aching head. It took only one look, but at least the great beast ceased its torture. Thunder flopped down and inched toward him.

Darrick worked up the energy to glare in the direction of the other torturous creature. Intent on cursing the noise, he recoiled at the sight of the old woman. Crusted strips of flesh fell from her sleeve as she patted the banshee's backside.

"What ails you, woman? Is the babe inflicted too?"

The hermit turned away, keeping her face hidden from his view. She retreated to the darkened corner, consoling the child with awkward pats on its back.

Her rasping voice was raw with anger. "We've endured this damp hole long enough. 'Tis high time you shake your lazy bones awake and explain your presence."

"We'll talk when you release me."

"Rest assured," she said, "before you gain release from the bindings, I will be satisfied as to your purpose here."

Met with his silence, the old woman began her interrogation. "Do you travel with the men that set this island ablaze?"

Darrick's eyes followed the rhythmic movement of her body. He could see that his tight-lipped response ate at her raw nerves.

Her voice trembled as it rose over the babe's wail. "Do you truly think I believe you felt the need for a pleasure trip across the water? Just happened to land your boat on these godforsaken shores?"

"If you are finished," Darrick said, "I will explain what I can."

The old woman stopped swaying and waited for his answers.

Darrick responded with measured authority. "You may address me as Sir Darrick of Lockwood." He ignored her snort of derision. "I have traveled to this deserted rock in search of someone."

"As you bellowed earlier. Are you alone, Sir Darrick of Lockwood?"

"I come only with that ugly brute lying over there," he said. The dog lifted his head as if to affirm the fact.

"Do you burn me from this island?"

"Are you daft, woman? I search for someone dear to me. Perhaps you have seen her. Sent here for safekeeping. Dear woman," he coaxed, "please release me so that I might find her and take leave of this desolate place. 'Tis nothing more that I want from you."

"Why should I trust what you say?"

"Because you must. I assure you. Had I truly wanted your life, the deed would have already been completed."

Darrick watched her gaze drift over his body, measuring his size against her own. He lifted his bound wrists and showed her the loosened knots. Her eyes widened when she saw he had already begun the task of shredding the bindings. He smiled, nodding, answering her spoken question. It was true. He could have rid himself of the binding with little effort.

His satisfaction diminished when she moved much quicker than one imagined of a crone. She knelt beside him, her face hidden by the cloak, her dagger held against his throat.

"If in truth, you come here to do harm, I will make you pay."

Darrick studied the lethal weapon held too close for comfort. "I swear on my father's grave, I'm not here to harm either of you. Now, untie me. Before I lose patience."

"Take caution, sir. I've no fear of slicing you open from ear to ear."

Darrick cooled his anger. It would not serve him well to have his throat slit by a deranged old woman. He stared at the space where he assumed were her eyes. "Have a care. 'Tis ill-advised to try your hand at outwitting a king's man."

The blade pressed sharply against his skin. Her hand shot out, flashing a sign for silence. Male voices drifted past the cave. Their steps were heavy as they broke through the brush.

Darrick felt the sting of the blade as it trembled at his throat. "You and I both know they may soon return with orders to search deeper," he said. "I've nothing more to offer you than my word that I mean you no harm."

The woman nodded but remained unconvinced.

"'Tis certain you've removed me from my weapons. I am defenseless against you. Moreover, if it soothes your nerves, keep the blade pointed to me at all times."

Slowly the sharp edge withdrew from his skin. Without a word, she began to cut away the bindings. Darrick could not help wondering why her resolve weakened so easily. Surely, the old woman had more sense than to trust his word. However, he was never one to look away from a gift. His irritation renewed in force when the dagger wavered over the reddened battle scars on his wrists.

"I would think the task is made easier if you watch what you are doing," he snapped. "I carry no desire for having a portion of my body sliced by your hand."

Gasping at his snide remark, she finished with an angry stroke of the knife.

As the blade set loose his hands, he swung around and grabbed her arm. "Do not...ever...tie me up again," he warned. Before releasing her arm, he snatched the dagger out of her grasp.

She grabbed at her cloak to keep her face behind the folds of the hood. "Please, I beseech you."

Exasperated, Darrick watched her curl her body over the child as if she was certain the sting of his fists were certain to follow. He sat back on his haunches. "Stand up, old one. I told you that I mean you no harm."

Behind him, he heard the foul animal move restlessly. Remembering the blow he received to his head, he held out his hand. "Under my honor as the king's knight, I vow that you and your child will not be harmed. Now, call off your beast."

Muffled laughter erupted. "'Tis only Matilda, Sir Knight. One very ferocious goat."

Darrick ignored her taunts and sawed at his bound ankles. Bested by a mere goat. He was thankful she could not see his disgrace. He would have to ensure that Nathan never discovered his embarrassment. The more he thought on it the more furious he became. With one stroke of the blade, his ankles were free.

He jumped to his feet and ducked when his head brushed the domed ceiling, narrowly missing the sharp points of rock that hung like evil, sharp teeth. He stretched the cramps from his legs and turned on the old woman.

"We must be going, Sir Darrick of Lockwood. I wager the soldiers are still looking for us."

He pried her hand from his arm, noting her slender fingers. "Of whose soldiers do you speak?"

"Sir Vincent DePierce. The Lord of Balforth."

Darrick stifled the flinch of disgust, but not quickly enough.

"By your reaction, I must assume that you are familiar with his reputation." She braced her wrinkled arms across her chest. "How well do you know DePierce?"

Bemused by her defensive stance, Darrick watched her closely. "I've met him only once. 'Twas enough to know he is not the man I would willingly join in battle. Not at any price."

* * * *

The stranger raked his fingers through his hair. Strength and confidence rested on his shoulders as if it were a tailored suit of armor. He wore it well. As if born to it. Much like her father and brother.

It had been almost a full year since Sabine's life had been left in turmoil. It started with her father's disappearance. Then the mercenary soldiers raided Castle Clearmorrow and its inhabitants. They were her responsibility and she had failed them all. The soldiers killed the castle folk, burning the village and fields, destroying everything in their path.

She had thought the worst was over when her brother Taron's garbled message instructed her to seek out DePierce's protection. But there, her troubles really began.

The giant knight was speaking again, interrupting her thoughts. "I search for a young maiden of nobility. Raven hair. Mist gray eyes."

Filled with an odd twinge of disappointment, Sabine forgot to whisper. "You must not love her well," she observed.

"I love her well enough."

Sabine recalled the despair on Elizabeth's face. She snorted in disbelief. "Not if you've managed to lose her."

"I was serving my king."

"I see. Of course."

"I fought against France. For King Henry. 'Twas my duty," he persisted.

"Duty? What of your duty to your love? Did you love her?" She shook her head. "What treatment, so terrifying, would cause her to run here?"

His head tilted to one side as a puzzled look crossed his face. "I never gave her reason to fear." He rubbed the back of his neck. "My father would not grant me entrance into the Lockwood keep that should have been mine by birthright. Please share with me, old woman, how I'm to care for someone when I'm not allowed near that person?"

"You must have found some way. Less than a year ago, 'tis what I calculate."

"Cease your riddles. What do you speak of?" he asked.

"Your Elizabeth, you fool! Was she your lover? Your wife?"

"Enough." Sir Darrick grabbed her. "Tell me where I can find Lady Elizabeth."

"I don't know." She broke free of his hold and snatched at her cloak, fighting to contain her identity. "If you aren't the one who her heart ached for, then tell me if it is you who seeks her death."

"If my sister was on this island," he whispered hoarsely, "I demand you tell me where she is now."

Sabine's heart pounded against her ribcage. "Sister?" Tears filled her eyes. She nodded towards the baby sleeping peacefully on the moss bed. "All that you have left of Elizabeth lies here, Sir Darrick. This is your nephew."

She saw the shadow of pain darken his eyes and she rushed to tell him what she knew. "Elizabeth arrived on my doorstep with very little. Even in the last stages of labor, she would not talk. Although she and the babe survived their ordeal, she wore her grief like a mantle of penance. 'Twas what worried me and caused me to follow her when she walked out of my cottage with the baby. It was beginning to storm. I could see her thoughts were unsteady."

"Continue—" His voice, filled with emotion that brooked no fallacies, broke "—with your tale."

She took a halting breath. "I followed her to the cliffs that stand not far from here. The storm was intensifying. I started to go after them."

"You let her go?"

"I've learned to listen to the sounds that don't belong," she said in her defense. "I waited long enough to believe it safe. I caught up with her straight away. Only to see your sister tuck her son under the juniper bush and walk to the edge of the cliffs. I thought I saw her turn back. Something...someone...moved out from the shadows."

"You did nothing to save her?"

Guilt racked her soul. Thoughts of the spinning heights taunted her. She shook her head. "I tried. Truly, I did. But..."

Her words were lost. She waited in silence for his angry response. Even though the hood continued to protect her face, she felt his penetrating gaze. Droplets, formed of her tears, fell to the floor. She could wait in silence no more.

"Your sister drew the murderer's attention from the child and directed it to herself," Sabine whispered. "Elizabeth sacrificed her life for her son." She spread her hands, pleading for his understanding. "I'm sorry that I could do nothing to save her. Afterward, I vowed to find the babe's kinsmen as soon as possible. Then the fires began.

"So, you see," she said. "My vow is fulfilled. I'll be leaving now that I'm not—"

Darrick placed his hand over her mouth, yanking her to his chest. The sound of footfall drew near. Muffled voices carried into the cave.

"Why must we continue our search?" the voice outside whined. "We found the woman we were ordered to bring back."

"You know his lordship. He would rather have someone else clean up his foul mistakes."

"Well, I'm gett'n tired of being in his service. 'Tis better coin to be made in France."

"Aye, but we best find the other woman b'fore we go. She may have seen something."

"Right you are. Should we fail, his lordship will send his soldiers after us too. Would hate to end up in that tower with the others."

"I heard 'twas another young maid that got away after he beat her. Course, just her, and the other one, s'all that ever lived to tell. 'Tis a waste, I'm say'n."

"He could at least toss 'em to us. Wouldn't mind a bit of creamy thighs o'wrappin around me middle."

"Aye, right you are. Let's find that wench. I've a hunger for a sweet tasting morsel before he uses that one up too."

* * * *

Darrick waited until they moved away from the opening of the hidden cave before motioning to the woman to gather all their belongings.

"'Tis time to leave."

The hope that his sister yet lived grew dim. He had seen the high cliffs. The rock formations slashing the air with their deadly edges. His blood boiled when he thought of the ill care his sister had received while under DePierce's protection.

Darrick's eyes dropped to the tiny infant cradled in the old women's arms. On his honor as both a Knight of the Swan and uncle, he would protect the child. As his sworn duty, he would ensure his nephew found his rightful place at Lockwood.

The crone began to gather their belongings. A strand of burnished gold hair slipped from the protection of her hood.

Darrick crooked an eyebrow. Under the guise of indifference, he watched her quickly hide the strands and then straighten her cloak. She tightened the leather thong that held the jeweled dagger at her trim waist.

He stayed her hand when she turned to pick up her pack and he tossed the bundle over his shoulder. His eyes widened when she plunked the wiggling babe into the crook of his arm. Her fingers shook as she smoothed the satiny fuzz on the baby's crown. Darrick did not know whether it was out of fear of him or the conversation they had overheard.

"You'll return with me," he ordered.

"No. I have a small boat that will take me where I need to go. Most assuredly, my path takes a direction other than yours. I'm weary of hiding and mustn't delay any longer."

"You'll find safety in my company."

Sabine shook her head. "I can think of no reason to travel with you."

"I realize there's naught that I can say on my behalf, but please, I implore you to consider the child. I've need of a matron to care for my nephew."

"For the baby." She smoothed her finger over the baby's rosebud pout. "Nonetheless, I cannot promise how long I will stay."

Darrick gave her thin shoulder a comforting squeeze. "Stay at least until I'm able to hire another woman."

His hand traveled across her back, hesitating for a brief moment. She was quite muscular for a hermit. She was definitely hiding more than her withered form. Before she left his company, he vowed, he would know her secrets.

"The goat must come with us. For your nephew," she demanded. "She won't be a burden to you."

Glancing at the goat, Darrick doubted it. His head and honor still throbbed from the damage the goat had wrought. After weighing the need of milk against his pride, he finally agreed. "Promise me that you'll keep the beast out of my reach."

She nodded and hurried to grab Matilda's rope. "Make haste. Get the baby to safety."

Concern caused Darrick's steps to falter. "The soldiers. I should be last."

"I'll follow with Matilda. She can be a bit stubborn."

He eyed the goat. "As you wish. I'll lead the way and prepare the boat."

With his nephew nestled close to his chest, Darrick crawled through the hole. Once down the stairway, he signaled to the woman that they had arrived safely.

* * * *

The stairway to the shore below loomed before her. Sabine felt the blood rush from her head. Its wake pounded in her ears. Her vision blurred. Bile rose in her throat. If she did not leave right then, her feet would never move again. Her fears would force her to remain on the island.

Her head spinning, Sabine gulped and steadied her nerve. She could not let DePierce win. "Come, Matilda. 'Tis time we took our leave."

After a few hesitant steps, the animal braced her little hooves and balked at the shadows stretching along the walls. Their weight shifted as Sabine dragged Matilda through the doorway. The heavy moss underfoot gave way. Before she knew what was happening, she and the goat were flying down the stairway.

At first tug, Matilda trailed behind. As their fall gathered momentum, the animal rolled past, hooves and gangly legs scratching for purchase.

Sabine's hand burned from the rope wrapped tightly around her fingers. She clawed at the wall and moss to slow their decent. Vegetation tore loose of its mooring. Green clumps soared over her head, striking Matilda's backside. Their tangled mass of limbs burst through the opening.

* * * *

Upon hearing a crashing noise coming from the crevice, Darrick decided it best to look in on the old woman. Like as not the damn goat had killed her. He turned to look on his nephew. The babe lay in the bottom of the boat. Dry and snug.

He ducked as chunks of rock sailed down the narrow stairway and out the opening. Two thrashing forms landed with a splash in the water pooling by the shore.

The goat was the first to rise and shake itself from head to toe. On trembling legs, it stumbled out of the pool and collapsed.

Darrick quickened his steps. He did not want to be left alone with the wild goat and a helpless infant. Her motionless body required a quick search for broken bones. That was when he first noticed her gown.

The hem crested a pair of thighs. Although it had been a long time since he had lain with a woman, he knew these limbs definitely did not belong to a crone. Her cloak had slipped off and hung at the entrance on a scrubby bush.

She lifted her head from the lapping water. Propped on her elbows, she gasped for air. Her long hair curled over her shoulders, hung down her back, making her look like a maiden of the sea. Darrick stopped in his tracks and waited, fearing he would spoil the moment. A surging wave washed over, revealing her fair maiden's figure. Satisfied that she would live, the corners of his mouth twitched as he enjoyed the view. He wondered if her visage was as beautiful as her backside. The answer to that mystery floundered at his feet.

* * * *

Sabine lay in the water trying to catch her breath. She pushed the damp hair out of her face and froze. Tiny rivulets of brown sludge trickled down her arm, joining the drops at the end of her elbow. Her disguise washed away with each lap of the water. Her breath caught. Panic began to build. So relieved that she survived the fall, she had forgotten to keep her identity a secret.

Now she would have to travel without the protection of her disguise. With a man she did not trust. Alone! Worse, he made her stomach behave disagreeably whenever he was near. All her experience with men beyond her father's land had caused her pain. How would she know if he could be trusted? Her brother and father had failed her. How could this man possibly succeed where they had not?

The boat. Perhaps it was still seaworthy. She had to find her little boat.

A warm tongue glided over her hands. Peeking between her fingers, she tried to dodge the hairy beast. Thunder's pink tongue flashed out, lapping at her face, mixing her tears with his slobber.

The sounds of splashing water moved forward. She flinched when Sir Darrick smoothed her hair, tucking it behind her ear. He lifted her from the water and carried her towards the boat. Oblivious to the danger of discovery, Thunder barked and splashed along beside them.

"Quiet, boy," the knight, commanded softly. "You'll create more damage than already caused by these two."

He cupped her chin with his fingers and tipped her face. Sabine imagined she felt his chest rise and fall in a rush. His eyes strayed to her mouth.

Seeing his intent to press his lips to hers, she struggled to pull away. "Fool!" she squealed. "Let me down at once. The soldiers will be here any minute."

Sir Darrick blinked. He released his hold, letting her slide slowly down his damp chest. His grip tightened when she brushed against his aroused manhood. A faint smile drifted across his lips. Sabine felt the heat rise to her cheeks. She glanced away.

"Your exit was not a quiet one. It makes me wonder how you stayed alive. Come. Let us get your cloak and shove off this pile of rocks. You can explain, while I row us back to the mainland."

"'Tis no need for explanation. I have changed my mind. You'll have to find another to tend your nephew." Shading her eyes with her hand, she looked over the shore. "I'm sure I can find my own transportation."

He led her toward the rocking boat. "You gave your word."

"But—"

"I'll not have your death on my conscience."

With one swift motion, he picked her up and held her much too close. As if an afterthought, he dropped her onto the bench in the boat.

Sabine blinked, at a loss for words.

"Here," he said, holding out his nephew. He barely allowed her time to adjust her sodden skirts and open her arms to receive the baby, before leaving to gather the remains of their little band of travelers.

Getting the yellow-toothed beast in the boat was no easy task. The goat's knobby legs kicked and thrust out at all angles. Eventually, Sir Darrick won the battle, and they were soon able to shove off from shore.

Waiting until the last minute, Thunder jumped in and shook the water from his coat. Darrick wiped the rivulets streaming down his face with his sleeve as if it were an everyday occurrence.

Sabine gripped the edge of the rocking boat. Afraid of tipping the crowded vessel, she sat in the exact spot where the beef-witted fool dumped her. She looked over their little group. *What madness has possessed me to agree to depend on this stranger?*

Chapter 4

The baby slept quietly, swaddled in the threadbare blanket and tucked in the crook of Sabine's arm. Behind her, Matilda huddled in the farthest point of the craft. Thunder stood at the prow, fearless in his stance even when the surging waves rolled the boat over the crest and down again.

Sabine tried not to glance at the man who sat too close. Despite her efforts, she could not tear her attention from the muscular planes of his shoulders as he strained against the oars.

Her body trembled. His brief touch nearly washed away the dark memories of the past. His manly scent, mingled with leather and the fresh smell of sea spray made her stomach quiver. Anxious to forget her body's betrayal, her thoughts returned to his belittling behavior. She swore he purposefully dropped her on the splinter of wood now sticking into her backside.

Sabine swatted at her hair, making one final attempt to tame the strands caught in the swirl of the sea-dampened breeze. The wet woolen cloak sagged around her and the infant in damp folds. She shivered and tried to ignore the musty scent and snapped the cloak closed. The over-powering smell assaulted her nose, causing her to fight the need to sneeze.

Her attention wandered back to Sir Darrick as he pulled the oars through the water. Sweat trickled down his temples, dripped from his jaw and into the neck of his tunic. She tore her gaze from the play of his muscles, glistening with perspiration.

Restless, she shifted on her seat and plucked at the damp linen gown clinging to her chest like a second skin. She glanced up, avoiding the view of his aroused manhood straining against his chausses. A wolfish grin lifted the corners of his mouth.

"Wicked man—" she muttered.

"'Tis rumored, I dare many things. Perhaps when we land..."

Sabine felt the heat rising in her cheeks. She yanked the smelly wool tighter. "I know not what you speak of. 'Tis obvious, the blow to your head has rattled your brains."

The fleeting smile vanished but his eyes gleamed in silence. It held a promise of things she would rather not know hanging between them.

"'Tis unnecessary for you to demonstrate..." Her gaze dropped down to his powerful limbs for the briefest second, but she knew he saw her gawking like some misguided maid. She swallowed the lump lodged in her throat. "...anything." The single word came out in a nervous, high-pitched squeak.

His gray eyes twinkled back at her. "You have me at a disadvantage, sweet lady."

"Ho! When have men such as you ever felt at a disadvantage? Why do men feel the need to remind us how much stronger or bigger they are?' She sniffed, before adding to her observation. "All men are made from the same cut of cloth and I sincerely doubt you are different from the rest."

Sir Darrick shook his head. "Don't say you've never spun a woman's web to keep the unsuspecting fools in your arms, pleading to do your will." He bent forward. "Now that I look closer, 'tis safe to say, you've never shared a kiss spun from the fires burning in a man's soul. You would then swear never were two men alike."

"Enough," she hissed. Her cheeks heated. The word sounded more like a sigh than an order.

* * * *

Darrick buried the smile tugging on his lips and observed the woman shift uncomfortably. She was trying, unsuccessfully, to avoid contact with his knees as they rocked and swayed with the motion of the current. His thighs rubbed against her slender legs when he stretched to make room for his feet. He swore he felt the heat radiating through the stinking cloak she kept wrapped around her body.

Grunting, he rowed harder and worked to regain his control. The puzzling woman kept too many secrets behind her fading disguise. Before their time together was through, he planned to have the truth to every one of them. Some secrets, he wagered, she did not even know she had.

"Why do you frown?" She looked over her shoulder. "Are the soldiers coming?"

"No, my thoughts are with a man I left on the mainland to find what he could about our mutual friend DePierce." He continued to pull the oars through the water and squinted into the young woman's face. "'Tis time to tell me your name, my mysterious woman, and why do you disguise yourself?

Her shoulders stiffened. Her glance flicked over him. "A moment ago, you did not care to know me while I was disguised as a wrinkled old woman."

"Surely, you cannot find fault with me for thinking of you as such. 'Twas no need to know your name then. Now, I require it. 'Tis all."

"Think you I disguise myself on a lark?"

"I see with my own eyes why you hide your beauty. But, I would still ask you of your name."

The woman leaned close and whispered, "Mayhap, I used magic to bewitch you. Perhaps I really am a wrinkled old hag and have cast a spell upon you."

Darrick snorted. "'Twas an artful disguise. Someday, you'll have to teach me your tricks of deception."

"And if you're wrong?"

"Then perhaps when I am very old, you will teach me the spell so that I might return to my youth."

She met his stare then tipped her head in surrender. "You'll not let go of this, will you?"

"I cannot," Darrick said.

"Very well then," she said. Puffs of warmed air blew from her lips. "You may call me Sabine."

"An unusual name to match an unusual woman. I thank you for entrusting me with it." Never missing a stroke of the oar against the water, Darrick bowed at his waist.

Satisfied with her answer, he glanced towards the island. No one appeared to follow them, but the skies were darkening from an approaching storm. Although it would help to hide them, it would make their approach to shore difficult. "From where do you come? Where are your kinsmen?"

Shadows passed over her eyes. He regretted causing her pain with his questions but he had to know what he dealt with. "Please continue the tale of your recent past," he urged.

He followed the way her slender neck stretched before she worked the words free. "I believe my father has met his death. And now, my brother Taron is missing. The last word I received from him was almost a year now passed." Her lashes lowered, shuttering her emotions and secrets behind them. "'Twas then that I received a message directing me to seek out DePierce."

"DePierce? How is your family connected to the lord of Balforth?"

Sabine avoided his gaze by keeping her attention on the baby in her arms. "I...don't know. My brother left in search of my father's murderer. Since that time, we had little contact until I received his last message. Now that I have had a taste of DePierce's hospitality, I vow to let my dear brother know that same brand of treatment."

She glanced up to see his shock registering from her hateful words. "Do not look at me as if I am vermin. My brother directed me to that den of depravity. Would he do so if he felt any affection towards me?"

"I don't condemn you for your feelings, but I urge you to listen."

"It was agreed that the clergyman Rhys would send Taron." Sabine sniffed back a tear. "But my brother never came."

The steady rhythm of the oars paused. "The longer I stay in these lands the more tangled the lies become. Your brother and Elizabeth are proof of this. I wager the men who burned you out and killed my sister take their orders from the one who holds their gold." Darrick returned to his rowing and measured his words carefully. "Do you recall if they spoke of people held in the dungeon? Those who are not allowed visitors? Rhys also spoke of this—"

"You know Rhys?"

"The clergy? We've met." He did not have the heart to tell her that when it came to that crow-eyed man there was something that did not sit well with him. "Sabine, I mean to uncover who is held there or if they hide by choice."

"Are you implying that my brother hides behind Balforth's walls?"

Darrick stopped rowing and folded his hands over hers. "I'm saying I don't trust easily. There are always leaks in a fortress and we will find that weakest point."

He smoothed the pad of his thumb over her knuckles. "Despite the fact that you believe I didn't protect my sister as I should have, I do love her dearly. She was spoiled, but she never caused anyone harm, nor did she know how to defend herself. If the stories are true and her husband, Hugh, is already dead a year, then I must learn what forced her to run in her delicate condition. At whose neck do I place my blade? To understand this I must discover the identity of my nephew's father."

"You cannot seek revenge alone."

Darrick drew his thumb across her knuckles in a swirling pattern. "You and I must search out the truth. Stay with me, Sabine."

"But what can so few do against such odds?" she asked.

Hope in finding answers to his mission began to rise. He stared at their hands, fingers interlocked, bound together. The warmth of their bond heated his blood. "We'll go to Balforth and find our answers there."

"No." Sabine yanked on her hand at his suggestion. "I won't go back. I'll go anywhere else. Anywhere you choose. But not to Balforth!"

"We must—"

Lightning creased the clouds. Soon after, thunder shook the air. The darkened skies threatened to break open at any moment.

Sabine's face was pale. Her lips were pressed into a thin line. Fearing she might tip the little boat in her agitated state, he gently released her hand. "We'll think of something."

He tightened his grip on the oars and let the sentence hang between them. Rowing away from the storm and their enemies, he raced toward the safety offered by the land. He would be relieved to get out of the cramped, rocking boat. He needed to put space between himself and the puzzling woman.

They had formed a delicate truce. Nevertheless, to find the answers he needed, he had no other choice. They would travel to Balforth.

* * * *

The weight of the clouds refused to be held at bay any longer. The black skies opened up. Rain began to pour down as Sir Darrick jumped from the boat and pulled it to shore.

"Welcome to England's western shores," he muttered.

Sabine stumbled after the man, his strong back moving between the trees. He had opted to carry their bundles and lead Matilda, instead of carrying the baby. Despite the miserable conditions, she smiled at the hesitation he had shown toward his nephew. The baby had been quiet as they crossed the water. She had fed and changed him while Sir Darrick observed her every move.

While he watched, she felt as if they had shared a past. She knew that was foolish thinking. If she were to voice that idea, he would consider her a crazed woman. The heat from his eyes made her blood flush. Her nipples pebbled. She wondered if he felt the fire arc between them. Had he noticed anything beyond the stink of her woolen cloak?

The thought of their tight seating arrangement in the boat, his knees bumping against hers, made her thoughts go fuzzy. It was all she could do to hide the urge to reach out and lay her hand upon his arm. She had to speak with him. Make certain he understood she would never return to Balforth with him.

The baby squirmed and began to cry. Soothing him the best she could, Sabine covered his head with the folds of her cloak to keeping the rain from striking his tiny face. The heat from his small body radiated against her skin. If they did not find shelter soon his chances of survival were dim. "Hush, baby," she cooed.

Sir Darrick stopped. His frown cut deep creases between his brows.

"I know we must be quiet," Sabine said. "But the baby. I fear he may be taking ill."

He placed his palm along the infant's face. His frown deepened. "We haven't far to go. I stored my things with one of the fishermen at the bottom of the knoll. They'll let us stay in their barn for a while. Once there, we can help the little one."

"You are drier than I." An uncontrolled shiver ran through her body. "If you carried him inside your cloak you could keep him dry."

Sir Darrick nodded and tied Matilda to the nearest sapling. He lifted the edge of his cloak over their heads to take them all in. "Quickly now."

His warmth washed over Sabine as they huddled together to make the transfer. Her cheeks flamed. Water streamed down his black hair and along his bare neck. Tendrils of steam rose from the muscled planes outlined by his tunic.

When she lifted the woolen cloak, the chilled air bore deep into her flesh. Torn from the shelter, the infant's cries renewed with vigor. Sabine shielded the baby's face from the driving rain, and placed him in his uncle's arms.

She opened her mouth to voice her gratitude, but the words stuck in her throat as he abruptly turned, motioning for her to follow.

The driving rain made it hard to see the buildings hidden amongst the wooded glen. The occasional strike of lightning illuminated the path that went on forever. Sabine's foot caught on a tree root as she blindly stumbled through the dark. The wind and rain ripped at her cloak, releasing her hair to be grabbed and torn.

She trudged through the muck. Each step sucked at her worn slippers. Every step located all the bruises from her fall down the stairs. Exhaustion seeped into every muscle and joint.

Her fingers ached from gripping Matilda's rope. The palm of her hands stung from the rope burns she received earlier. Her leg throbbed where she had struck it against the passage wall. She was unsure which was worse, her aching body, or her injured pride. Her face flamed with embarrassment from the memory of her fall. *What must that arrogant knight think of me? Disguised as an old crone. Then I end up flopping like a landed fish.*

The trip would have been less hazardous had Matilda not traveled with them. She should have left her behind to roast. Sighing, she shrugged her stiffening shoulders. What else could she do? The baby needed the old goat.

Her pace quickened as she listed the healing herbs she had grabbed before running from the cottage. The small amount of medicinals she carried would have to go to the baby. If any remained, then she would see to her own wounds.

Her stomach growled, gnawing somewhere next to her backbone, reminding her that it had been almost a day since she last ate. She ignored the hunger and trudged on. It was hard to remember that only three nights ago she had helped deliver a baby.

The wind whipped the branches, making it harder to keep up with Sir Darrick. She squinted, searching for the knight's broad shoulders moving through the trees. Spying the shape of a building off in the distance, she hastened her steps.

Sir Darrick stood with his big hairy beast at his side. His typical frown remained pasted on his face. "If we are to travel together, you'll need to pick up your pace."

"Not another word," Sabine snapped. "I could have fallen to my death on that hill."

She picked at the sodden mess clinging to her legs. Her cloak and gown were beyond repair. The dirty linen, weighted with mud, wrapped around her feet. Untangling her legs, she looked down and realized the squishy feeling oozing between her toes was due to the lack of a slipper on one foot. There was no telling where she had lost it.

Amusement glittered in his gaze as he pressed his lips together.

Sabine attempted to contain her temper. She really did. Nonetheless, these last days of her life had proved to be too much. Ignited, her temper finally boiled over. "You have no chivalry at all."

She pushed her way through the doorway. The year of isolation and fear was nothing to the despair she felt at that moment. Tears seemed to form out of nowhere.

* * * *

Darrick grudgingly acknowledged he may have behaved abominably and turned to make repairs.

She gripped the doorframe as if it was the only thing to keep her from falling. He raised her chin with his forefinger and thumb.

Her eyes sparkled with unshed tears. One escaped and ran down her cheek. Forgetting his vow sworn only moments earlier, his thumb trailed down the moist path. Very carefully, he smoothed the tear away. His hands strayed to her shoulders as she leaned into him.

A sigh escaped from her parted lips. The soft breath tickled the hair on the back of his hand. His pulse quickened when she licked her parted lips and a soft moan caressed his cheek.

Eyes wide, she drew away from him. Her face paled under the specks of drying mud. Her arms dropped to her sides. A protective wall rose. A drawbridge had been raised against him.

He stepped back, bowing with a mocking flourish. "Once again, I must apologize."

"Please." Staying his arm with the light touch of her fingers, she gave a hesitant smile. "I don't know what came over me. 'Tis inexcusable."

She dusted some of the flakes off his sleeve. Quickly withdrawing her fingers from his arm, she looked around. "Your nephew—"

"He sleeps. But I worry 'tis a fevered sleep. I've a small amount of medicinals, but my knowledge stops with the injuries of soldiers. I fear I know not what to do for such a wee one as he."

"I've a few herbs of my own. Mayhap, if we dilute the mixture it should be safe to give to him." She glanced at the sleeping child. "Would you think it wrong, if we were to give your nephew a name? I know, I have no right—"

"No one has ever had a champion as you. Shall we name him Chance?"

She wrinkled her nose. "An unusual name."

"He'll need every chance in this world to defeat those who threaten to steal his birthright."

"So he will." She smoothed Chance's brow. "We must break the fever tonight."

Sabine untied the blanket and sifted through the items in her bundle. Once she found all that she needed, she laid out the herbs.

"I believe we have escaped DePierce's soldiers. I'll look on the animals and let the fisherman know we are here," Darrick said. "Although, with the entrance you made, I think all who inhabit the coast would know."

"Churlish villain," she muttered.

Darrick dodged the wet rag that flew towards his head. He shut the door before she found something of sterner substance to launch.

* * * *

Sabine paced the floor. She prayed her calculations were correct. Chance was so tiny. If she did not prepare the herbs properly, then 'twas certain he would die.

After stoking the fire in the brazier, she pulled Chance's little bed under the crude tent of blankets. The herbs simmered in the pot of water. Healing steam wrapped around their heads.

Sabine tried to ignore the heat and sang as she walked the floor with Chance. *Lord, but the room feels as though it's on fire.*

Sweat trickled between her breasts. Her wet hair stuck to her scalp. The weight of her gown grew with each step. Grime irritated a path against her skin.

Praying Sir Darrick would take his time walking the perimeter, she pulled her gown over her head. Without the press of the sodden gown, the threadbare chemise whispered against her skin. The caress of the warm air was glorious. She touched her shoulder, locating the place where his finger grazed her skin. How long had it been since someone had offered her comfort?

His face was beautiful when he smiled. It softened the hard edges. If only he smiled more. She shook her head. They were running from people that had killed before, who would not hesitate to kill again. There was no time for sweet memories of any kind.

She continued to pace the tented room with Chance. His crying had ceased. He did not labor to bring air into his lungs. She pressed a kiss against his forehead. Relief washed over her. His fever was breaking. She laid the baby on his makeshift bed and tucked the blankets around him. They would stay in the steam tent until the morning sun peeked through the clouds.

Sabine sighed and arched her back. With nothing clean to wear, the prospect of donning filthy clothes was uninviting. Perhaps tomorrow she would find a way to wash her gown and locate her missing slipper. After wrapping a blanket around her body, she sat down on the pile of tattered sails and laid her head on her bare arms. Concern nibbled at her consciousness as she drifted into an exhausted sleep.

Her knight had been gone for a very long time.

Chapter 5

Darrick's steps faltered as he peered into the shadows. He cringed when he saw his best blanket hanging from the rafters. Sabine had turned it into a steam tent. One end clung to the beam. The other end dragged along the dirt floor. It billowed from the breeze let in through the open door.

He looked in on his sleeping nephew. The babe's brow no longer burned his hand. His breath was no longer labored.

Darrick stoked the fire under the pot and dropped the bundle of herbs Sabine left beside it. Left alone with his thoughts, he admired the way she fought to keep Chance alive. Despite her troubles, her spirit remained strong and undefeated.

His conscience bit at him, reminding him of his vow. He had promised Rhys that he would protect her. It should have been a simple task. After all, the knight's code included saving women from trouble, even if it was a particularly stubborn, beautiful woman. God's blessed bones! 'Twas an easy promise. Of course, that was when he thought of her as a haggard old woman. This sweet vision made his promise difficult to keep.

Searching for the object of his thoughts, he found her curled up deep within a pile of old sails and fish netting. Try as he did, he was unable to turn away. The thin chemise clung to her form, outlining every hill and valley. Even the dried mud did little to hide her from his over imaginative mind.

He focused on her face instead of the feminine temptations nestled below, and noted the tranquility that surrounded her when she slept. Her temper had vanished. Left in its stormy path was a stubborn chin and a pert little nose. Her cheeks were rosy from the heat of the room. Golden strands of hair and bits of dried mud still caked her brow.

His gaze traveled down her slender neck and shoulders. Bruises marred the delicate skin. He moved closer for a better look at her injuries. His attention caught on the smeared mud clinging to various parts of her body. As she lay on her side, he viewed her trim waist and rounded hip. Her limbs peeked out from under the hem. *How had she survived on that island?*

A soft moan escaped Sabine's lips, leaving him to wonder if she could read his mind. He turned his back and began to pace the floor. Sucking in a few breaths, he steadied his pulse and returned to his perusal of the damage done to her flesh.

His attention traveled to where his honor had stopped him earlier. He swore at her foolishness. He needed her to care for his nephew. She knew the danger if she chose to let the wounds go. Guilt racked his soul. He had failed her. He commanded an army of calloused men with ease but this single woman brought his weakness to the forefront. She may not believe it, he vowed, but he would not let her down again.

For now, he would have to remain disciplined and see to her care. Shoving his hands behind his back, he gripped them together. If only his body would listen.

Darrick turned toward the snuffling sound as the baby wiggled in his bed. He smoothed the light fuzz on the child's small head. His warrior's hand covered Chance's thin pate. He owed the boy a debt of gratitude for his timely interruption. He had saved his uncle from an embarrassing lack of control.

Darrick left the shed and returned within minutes. He hauled in a massive brass tub and his own medicinals. His men may have ribbed him for dragging the brass monstrosity wherever he went, but once he found one that would accommodate his body, he was not about to leave it behind. While he waited for the water to heat over the fire, the vision of Sabine submerged in the steaming bath floated before him.

He shook himself from the distraction and continued to prepare the bath. Perhaps Nathan was right and he needed to spend more time with the women who graciously followed King Henry's army. Then his imagination would not run amok with the form of a sleeping lady. After rummaging through Sabine's meager belongings, he soon discovered the reason she had not seen fit to care for her wounds.

Fearing their noisy entrance would be met with reprisal from DePierce's minions, he had escaped to the fisherman's cottage, ensuring they had not been followed. No soldiers could be found. In his haste to secure the grounds, he neglected to give her the herbs and healing oils he carried in one of the chests. She used her medicinals for Chance and did not reserve any for herself.

From a small packet, Darrick withdrew the herbs he kept for injuries and pain. Thanks to the king's apothecary, the packet consisted of lettuce, gall from a castrated boar, briony, opium, and henbane. He mixed up a portion he hoped was equal to Sabine's size. The hemlock juice was kept separate. Too much and the dose would easily cause death. The sooner she was restored to health, the sooner they would be on their way to Balforth. His concern mounted when he sat down beside her and she did not stir. Her head and neck braced, he pressed the vial to her mouth, letting the wine and herbs slip past her lips. He watched as her breath came and went in a steady pattern. Certain his calculations were accurate and he had not given her too much of the medicinal liquid, he returned to his other duties.

While Sabine slept, he carried in the chests his men stored in one of the out buildings. He laid out the matching silver brush and comb he had purchased for his mother and one of the soft woolen gowns for his sister. He had hoped they would receive his gifts. They were the only women that he had ever felt worthy of his time.

Although rumors of his mother's many lovers were spread throughout the nobles, he had never seen proof of their validity. Unfortunately, his father thought otherwise. Their last meeting before his death was cold and dismissive. Embittered from his wife's betrayal, his father's heart was hardened against him. His father's message spoke clearly. He questioned his only son's paternal lineage.

Darrick's thoughts turned to his sister. He would not grieve for Elizabeth; not yet. The enormous responsibility of keeping Chance alive weighed heavy on his shoulders. He could not give up that easily.

The mercenaries' conversation they had overheard gnawed at the back of Darrick's mind. The answers to many of his questions kept leading him back to Balforth. Two people, Elizabeth, and Sabine's brother Taron, had disappeared without a trace. Each one, perhaps ending in death. Both connected in some way to DePierce and Balforth Castle. Even the fair Sabine was connected.

She knew more than she told. He prayed her secrecy did not jeopardize one more life. Wearily, he rubbed the back of his neck. Whatever secrets she held regarding Balforth terrified her. He could not leave that piece of knowledge alone. Nor could he postpone touching her.

The heat emanating from the fire demanded he strip from his padded tunic. With the fire burning brightly in the brazier, he used the flames to light his way as he moved towards Sabine.

"'Tis a simple daily task," he muttered. "If the mistress of any good household can do this, then surely, so can I. Come Sabine," he whispered as he bent to retrieve her. "Let us wash and tend your wounds."

When he lifted her in his arms, she began to struggle and fight. Her knees and fingers poked, scratching at her tormentor. Her enemy, in the pain induced dreams, taunted, and teased, causing her to cry out.

Darrick struggled to hold onto her flailing body. "Stop, Sabine, I mean you no harm."

His worries mounted as she pushed against his chest.

"So many bodies. Please," she begged, "you cannot do this! I, Lady Sabine of Clearmorrow, demand you let them go."

Darrick stroked her hair. "You're safe," he crooned. "You're safe."

The sound of her heavy breathing filled the little room. Just as he thought her terrorizing memories were over, her fight began anew. She pulled at her wrists as if tied together. Sobbing, she moaned, "Get away! Must escape…"

"Wake up, my lady," he whispered. "You are safe. I would never harm you."

Quieted by his soothing hands, she laid her cheek against his shoulder. Her tears fell down her face and nestled in the curly mat of hair on his chest. She slipped into a deep sleep, beyond his voice. No matter how he tried, he could not rouse her.

Fearing she would damage herself further, he decided to join her in the tub. Holding her carefully in his arms, he wrestled with one boot and then the other. After kicking free and tossing them to the side, he chose the better part of valor to keep his chausses on. The last thing he needed was to terrorize her even more with his disobedient body.

Slowly, he lowered into the massive tub. Sabine gasped when the heated water lapped at her legs. Whispering, he let sweet reassuring words roll off his tongue. Smiling, she relaxed, only to flinch when her back met his chest.

Pressing her close, he nestled her bottom between his legs and concentrated on keeping his hands busy by washing her hair. Using the rose-scented soap he found in her pack, he made a sudsy lather and gently scrubbed at her scalp. He threaded his fingers through her burnished-gold tresses, freeing the relentless bits of sticks and clumps of mud that clung to the strands of silk. He washed her shoulders and slender neck. Pieces of dirt slowly disappeared.

Darrick's hands trembled as he tucked a bath sheet over the transparent chemise. With every movement, steaming water lapped at the rise of each breast. His knuckles accidentally brushed their curves. Carefully lifting her arm, he slowly soaped each fingertip. Bending her arm at the elbow, he ran the smooth wedge of soap over the tender skin.

Water lapped at the sodden material laid over Sabine's chest. It wavered, and then sank, wrapping around her form. The cloth he used for cleaning hung in his hand, forgotten. His breath caught in his throat as he struggled for air. The task had not been as simple as he hoped.

Darrick lifted her waist-length hair and found his concentration spiraling out of control as her hair curled around his shoulders.

"Damn you for weaving me into your spell," he sputtered.

Sabine sighed. In the land of blissful dreams, she drifted.

Darrick methodically lifted her leg out of the water, resting it on his knee. The grit and mud cleaned away, he could now tend her injuries. The cut left for last, he gently probed at the gash and decided that stitching was not required.

He felt her penetrating gaze boring into the top of his head. She was looking up at him, watching his every move with those dark bottomless pools. Bracing for a fight, he spoke quietly to soothe her fears. "I mean you no harm. Your wounds needed cleaning."

"Hmm." Her eyes, glazed with medication, worked to focus. Fingers, warmed and wet from her bath, pressed against his mouth. "'Tis a wonderful dream."

She stroked his lips as she spoke, tracing the edges with her nail. Darrick could take no more. Turning his head, he nipped at the inside of her flesh.

"What," she hissed, jerking her fingers away. Bewildered, blinking once, her mind worked furiously to clear the confusing mist. Her cheeks flamed.

He cleared his throat, struggling to regain his balance. "You should have told me you were wounded. I could have helped you." He shifted uncomfortably under her gaze. "I have only your back to wash and…your…"

"Go away," she said, swatting weakly at his hand. "I've no need of your help."

"I always finish what I start."

"But…"

"Lean forward. I promise not to peek."

Gripping the material wrapped around her chest, Sabine clung to the bath sheet as if her virtue depended upon it. Her shoulders jerked forward, revealing another bruise. Soaping his hands, he skimmed over her back. Enjoying the dips and curves, he carefully smoothed the muscles under her bruises. Although he did not want the sweet torment to stop anytime soon, he could see Sabine flinch every time his hand drew near. Tucking the sheet tightly under her arm, he put her off his lap and stood up.

Toweling off, he walked over to look in on his sleeping nephew and turned in time to see Sabine rising out of the tub. The sheet offered little modesty. She was the Goddess Venus, rising from the sea.

Knowing the hunger in his eyes would scare her, he was careful to speak over his shoulder. "Wrap yourself and lie down on the fur so that I may work on your injuries."

"Don't care to," she mumbled.

"You will."

He shoved the smelly jar under her nose. "The unguent will soothe your fevered skin."

"Don't want to."

He ignored her petulance and continued, "Then we'll work on the cuts and bruises."

"You're a stubborn man." She swayed by the makeshift bed "I want only to get warm again and sleep. Sweet, blessed sleep."

Darrick placed a fur over her shoulders and directed her down to the pile of furs. "Lie down. We'll rest until daylight."

"DePierce…"

"I'll take the watch. No one will be allowed to enter."

Chapter 6

Darrick held his nephew while Sabine slept. And in that time, he grew to care for his sister's son. He nuzzled the babe, the fresh scent of new beginnings. He would protect him with his life.

"Stop!" Sabine shouted, tossing in her sleep. *What did the Lady Sabine of Clearmorrow fear even when in deep sleep?*

He paced back to her side, touched her skin. No fever. But demons haunted her dreams. What chased her from the peaceful rest she should have had by now?

The sound of horses' hooves stopped at the door. Extinguishing the lamp, Darrick crouched by Sabine's bed and laid Chance in his makeshift cradle.

The door swung open, allowing the heat they had worked so hard to build to escape from the room. The chilled air swirled, causing Chance to waken and cry.

The intruder formed a shadow that filled the doorway. A four footed entity rushed through, knocking the trespasser to its knees. A bellow erupted from the thrashing body. As it began to rise on its haunches, another furred beast knocked it to its belly. The beast caught the cape with its teeth and began tugging at the fabric.

Darrick grinned and whistled for Thunder to return to his side. The hound struggled to rise and ran over.

"If you and that ugly beast are done wrestling, you may get up," Darrick said. "Unless, of course, you are too old and stiff to move."

The familiar figure lay in the shadows, sucking in great gasps of air. "Do you forget how well I know you? I wager, not only do you have that whoreson dog to guard you, but you also have your trusted dagger in your fist. What I did not expect was a beast from hell and a screeching banshee to catch me off guard."

Darrick shifted to his side and nestled Chance a little closer. "No, since you and I parted ways, I found more to protect than my backside."

"Rightfully so," Nathan said. He pulled himself from the floor and stood. "You're right not to light the lamp. I have found many frightened vassals on these lands. They fear more than their own shadow. DePierce's arm grows longer every day, but his strength weakens by the constant wielding of force he must show."

"Shut the door, will you?"

Darrick rose and set about lighting a lantern as Nathan turned his attention to the door. He knew when Nathan spied the young woman lying on a pile of sails and old netting. Darrick turned. Surprise registered on Nathan's usually unflappable face.

"What have you here?" Taking a cautious step towards the woman, Nathan was greeted by the clatter of hooves racing towards him.

"Matilda! Hold," Darrick called out.

The mangy goat stopped, and planted her feet in front of the prone woman.

Nathan's eyes widened at the sight of the baby. "Looks like you have been busy. Are there any more surprises?"

Darrick chuckled. "Unlike you, my friend, I do not work that fast. Nonetheless, I do have some useful information. How did you fare? What did you discover at Balforth?"

Nathan motioned to the woman. "Can she be trusted? I have some bits of information. Information, perhaps, only you, will understand."

"Trust her," Darrick considered for a moment, before he spoke. "'Tis a fragile commodity at the moment. Be wary of her. I do not know how 'tis possible, but I believe she trusts me even less. For now, she sleeps. How long?" he shrugged. "Who can tell? We must speak quickly and carefully. She fits in this mire of vipers. Why? I have yet to unravel it all. Perhaps you have heard of her." He bowed toward the woman. "I introduce, Lady Sabine of Clearmorrow. She is unaware I know her full name. Sabine is all she would reveal. I learned of the rest in the midst of her delirium."

Darrick stifled a wide yawn with the back of his hand. "She is not very trusting of others, for good reason I imagine. Terrified to return to Balforth. She is the old woman Rhys spoke of."

Speaking softly, he motioned towards the baby bundled by his side, "And this is my nephew."

"And Elizabeth?"

Unable to meet his friend's gaze, Darrick continued, "If I am to believe her story, Elizabeth was murdered."

"Elizabeth? Dead?"

Darrick lifted his head, staring icily at his friend. "Mark my words; I will see her killers roasted on a spit. Their heads; impaled on a pike for all to see."

"I pray 'tis not true." Nathan said.

Darrick nodded, knowing no more need be said. His jaw cracked with impatience. "Tell me of the old man Rhys. Does he live?"

"'Twas a miraculous recovery. He awaits our return from this cursed land." Nathan peered at the baby. "If Hugh was killed in battle, then who is the father?"

"I hoped the information you have would bring light to that very same question."

Nathan leaned forward. His hand on Darrick's shoulder, he said, "As I walked through the local marketplace, I noticed someone we know from our childhood. One of the villagers from your family manor. When I finally convinced young Brendan that I meant him no harm, I discovered your brother-in-law Hugh sold a number of Lockwood serfs to DePierce. Moved to Balforth, they work the lands he has been gathering through every foul means possible. A handful of the elderly were left at Lockwood."

"The old ones we spoke with earlier? You talked with them again?"

"Aye. They said the boys were taken from their families to work the fields. The young maidens have simply disappeared. Rumors are, he uses them, and then they are no more. Darrick, young Brendan had been working in Balforth for less than a fortnight. That could very well mean that our messenger was a ruse and our dear Lord Hugh is alive."

Darrick paced the cramped room. His exhausted mind tried to work out the twisted puzzle. If Hugh lives and is not the child's father, then his nephew could still be in danger. Their time limited, they could not afford to tarry. He had to get them all to safety.

"And the dungeon? Did you discover who is being held there?"

Nathan shook his head. "I hate to report that I was unable to unearth that bit of information."

Darrick rubbed his forehead. The puzzle was a jumble of string all tied in one giant knot. Once he found the end, he could unravel the threads, one by one. Truth to be told, he was uncertain what he would find at the end, and if he would like the outcome.

"What is our first move, Darrick?"

"Discover who killed my sister."

"And what shall we do with them?"

Chapter 7

Sabine awoke to the sound of raised voices. Lying still, hardly breathing, she focused on their conversation and searched the room.

Sir Darrick spoke to the man with the fiery hair. She was sure his shoulders were two ax handles wide. His hands, the size of hams that hung in the smokehouse, gently cradled the baby while he rocked back and forth, and listened intently to whatever Sir Darrick had to say.

Sabine tried to move her legs ever so slightly but the weight of the pelt imprisoned her limbs, pressing them into the pallet. Lifting the fur off her body, she peeked under the covering. Confusion mounted; she could not recall how her clothing had disappeared. Nor how the bandage around her thigh came to be there without her knowledge.

Her head ached and her discomfort rose as she heard the men talking. She wished they would finally agree on whatever they argued about and leave her in peace. She debated whether to stay where she was, nestled under the soft fur someone had tucked around her and forget her vow against DePierce, or let the men know she was ready to forge ahead. Closing her eyes, she tried to ignore them and pretend to sleep, but thoughts kept dancing in her head. Who was the stranger? Had she been betrayed yet again?

While Sabine struggled with indecision, Chance began to fuss. Wrapping the fur around her chest, she planned how she would quietly slide off the makeshift bed and slip over to the baby. Perhaps she and the baby would best escape the wrath of DePierce on their own. They would fare just fine without the help of the overbearing man and his too large friend.

Silence echoed over the room. The men had stopped talking and were watching her. Prepared for whatever battle they might throw her way, she straightened her shoulders and glared.

The man with the fiery flowing mane smiled like one of the fools who came to Clearmorrow to entertain her father and brother with their antics. His mouth stretched into a generous grin. He smothered the smirk, hiding his ill-concealed humor behind long tapered fingers.

Sabine raised her chin in defiance and rose from the bed. The fur slipped, baring her shoulders for all to see. Her chin wobbled, threatening to drop under their scrutiny. She took a step and her feet entangled themselves in the folds of the fur. She dared not risk casting a glance at Sir Darrick's frowning countenance.

"I believe you have somewhere to go," he growled at Nathan. "As you see for yourself, the lady is rested and will soon be ready to ride."

"So I see. However—"

"Get the men ready. 'Tis time we took our leave of this place. We ride within the hour."

"What has changed your mind? I thought you wanted to stay until your patients were stronger. Although, after seeing the distraction you have, I can understand your hesitancy in moving from this cozy nest."

"Beware, Nathan," he warned.

Nathan waggled his brows. "Although, if I were you, I would take the time required to explore all the secrets that she carries."

"Leave us," Darrick ordered.

Nathan shrugged innocently. "As you wish, my friend. As you wish."

Sabine watched the man he called Nathan duck his head as he left with a broad grin plastered to his face. From where she stood, she could see the anger glittering in Sir Darrick's eyes. As his hand shot out, she flinched, prepared for the blow that would strike her to the ground.

"For the love of God, I meant only to steady you. I did not want you to fall and expose yourself any more than you already have," he growled. "I realize 'tis an easy thing for you to find young Nathan to your liking. Most women do. However, he does not need your distraction. Too many lives depend on him."

"Why would I want that man's attentions?" Sabine wrapped the heavy fur tightly around her shoulders and lifted her chin imperiously. "If you do not mind, I prefer privacy. I have a baby to care for. I am sure he is wet and hungry. Probably be too much to hope for, but have you thought to check on him? Or feed him?"

She spun on her bare heel. The fur slipped from her grasp. Her heart thudded as she turned.

Darrick stood unmoving, staring at the fur pooled at his feet. An unfamiliar heat curled in her belly.

He bent down, very slowly, as if enjoying every inch of the view. He held the fur aloft. "I believe this is yours."

"If you are done looking your fill, I would appreciate the fur," she snapped.

Dangling the rich fur from his fingers, he held it out of reach. "Not at all, Milady, but I believe 'tis a problem if we waited for my fill. 'Tis a most hungering view."

Sabine eyed the offending man, knowing she would have to bend over even more if she ever wished to snatch the desired prize. "You really are a fool." Grabbing the fur, she whipped it around her shoulders. "Oh, leave me be."

Darrick blinked and shook his head. "I cannot do as you wish. While we speak, my men are gathering to join us in our search for truth. The answers will be found. Like it or no, it matters not to me. We leave within the hour. Be prepared to ride to Balforth Castle."

"Wrong," she ground out. Lord, but her jaw ached from grinding her teeth because of this man. "I travel by myself. You and your men will be caught before you reach the border of DePierce's land. I already told you that I would not go back to his castle. I meant it then and I mean it now. I will not lose the very life that I have worked so hard to hold onto."

Covering the space between them in two steps, Darrick grabbed hold of Sabine's arms. Pulling her close to his chest, he said, "You would put your desires before a helpless infant? Then, 'tis you, who is no different from DePierce. I had hoped that you were unlike all the other women I've had the misfortune of knowing."

Sabine struggled to pull free from Darrick's grasp. "Release me at once. I never made you any promises."

"You promised to stay until I find a woman for my nephew. Do you deny your selfishness? 'Tis a shame your word cannot be trusted," he sneered. "I pity you."

Running a finger down her cheek, he tapped her chin once to gain her attention. "Listen carefully," he ordered. "You travel with me. How else will I ensure you will not betray me to DePierce?" He thrust her away and ground out another command. "Dress and be ready to travel by the time I return."

Sabine stumbled, grabbing his arm before she fell. "Please, try to understand, I cannot do what you ask, lest I become snared in his traps again."

Darrick stared deep into her eyes. Sabine squirmed as he searched for the answers, the truth to the secrets that she held.

Desperate to stall the trip that loomed ahead, Sabine thought quickly as she made her last excuses in vain. "What of the baby? He needs feeding and his nappies changed. And…and my clothes," she stuttered, nodding her head. "My clothes. They are unfit to wear. How do you expect me to travel in mud-soaked clothes? And I have no slippers, no shoes to cover my feet."

Trailing his fingers down her face, he smiled bitterly. "Had you noticed, instead of making doe-eyes at my large friend, you would have seen there is a clean dress and cloak laid at the foot of your mat. The shoes may be a tight fit, but I am sure you will make do."

Holding his hand up for silence, he continued, "Before you disparage the integrity of my manhood or my many useful qualities any further, know I am a capable uncle. One who takes great joy in caring for my nephew. He was fed and changed before you awoke."

Struggling to compose herself, she sputtered, "I do not know what to say…" Her hand danced across the fur pelt, smoothing the velvety surface. "I suppose I should thank you, I…"

"I do not want your appreciation. I did it for the baby and for my men. You would have been an obstacle in the way of my plans. Even with all my planning, you still delay our ride. You are proof in what I have always believed to be true: women should not be allowed to follow camp. They make my men weak and slow. Their minds are occupied with the fairer sex, thinking about passion-filled days and nights, and their brief bit of pleasure brings nothing but disaster. It gets them slaughtered."

He brushed his fingers across the crest of her breasts. "Although," he hesitated, his stance wavering, "perhaps some rules are meant to be broken."

Waves of heat flushed her cheeks. The warmth of his touch, the heat of his gaze, lured her. It offered the false promise of hope and passion for one another. The room spun in dizzying circles. Leaning against his chest, she steadied herself, trying to hold on to the fragments of her dignity. She fought the betrayal of her body as she felt drawn towards his bitter smile.

Struggling to regain her senses, she recalled his cutting words and stared into his eyes. What she saw confused her. His gaze was cold as ice. His smile bitter from something eating at him from within. Shaking free, she was relieved to know that she was not the source of his despair. His pain was not her problem.

She lowered her head and spoke through gritted teeth, "You misunderstand me. I do not offer an apology."

His chiseled jaw tightened as he prepared to argue. Before he could speak, she rushed to explain. "Do you not see? DePierce has people stationed everywhere. No one is to be trusted. Learn from my mistake. Those that I trusted are either dead or serve him."

Sabine grabbed the front of his gambeson and drew in his rigid form. In her efforts to gain his attention to her warnings, the fur fell away. The pelt caught between them before it landed on the floor.

Darrick pried her fingers away and turned towards the door. "As I stated before, we leave when I am finished assigning duties. Bundle Chance up in the clean blankets I have provided." Ticking off her chores in stiff military fashion, he prepared to leave the fisherman's crowded shed. The whisper in his voice, the only sign that his control battled against desire. "Beside the babe's bed is the bag of goat's milk. Put the extra in the flask. Rest assured, as long as you do not tarry there will be enough time to clothe yourself properly."

Their icy stares cut into each other like a knife. His cloak swirled as he turned to leave. He stopped at the door, adding, "When I return I expect you to be ready to ride."

Sabine turned to find something else to hurl at the door. She stopped before she tossed it against the wall, unable to break what was not hers. Marching across the dirt floor, she fumed when she thought of what that huge oaf had ordered.

"Be ready, he says. What a hateful man. He thinks he cannot trust me. Me! I saved his nephew. Under whose power does he think he commands?"

Chapter 8

Sabine jumped at the pounding coming through the door. Her nerves were already frayed, and her heart thumped in her ears. "Go, away," she shouted.

"Sabine," Darrick bellowed in return. "We go now."

Being of practical mind, she had prepared for travel while storming around the little room. Sabine tore open the door and stomped out with the baby.

She tossed an order over her shoulder. "The baby's rags are there by the door. If you would be so kind," she added with an acidic smile, "please bring them to me."

The other big oaf was already seated on his mount. Sabine had to tilt her head back to see Sir Darrick sitting astride his horse. Her traitorous eyes traveled along his booted calf, noticing how the soft supple leather strained against his great calves. His muscular thighs tightened as he kept the horse still. Admiring the curve of his hip as he sat astride the saddle, her stomach flipped, going all tingly inside. Her eyes traveled up to his broad shoulders. A slight movement drew her gaze to his visage. His steel eyes gleamed back. Dear Lord, she was caught. Searching frantically, she looked around for anything to look at instead of the arrogant man sitting on the horse.

Heat traveled up her face. "Well," she bristled, "if you are ready, then let us ride to our destruction."

The black wing above his eye lifted in response. Silently, he motioned Nathan to pick Sabine up and deposit her on his saddle.

Two ham-sized hands wrapped around her waist. Without a word, he plunked her down in front of Sir Darrick.

"Next time, you could just give me my own horse to ride," she complained.

"No," Darrick grunted. "You've already shown yourself to be a distraction to my…men. Besides, 'tis easier to watch over you if you share my mount."

It appeared she had no choice where the surly knight was concerned. She gave in, for the time being. Seated in front of Sir Darrick, she kept her back stiffened.

He adjusted his arms, pulling her close. Sabine gasped at the sudden contact.

Turning to Nathan, he barked. "Do the men ride in the direction in which we spoke?"

"Aye."

"Wait." She grabbed Darrick's forearms. "What of Matilda? We need her for the baby."

"The goat is bundled in a cart with one of our men," Nathan said. "They'll not travel far behind."

Nathan turned to walk away. He paused as if coming to a decision and returned. "Excuse my lack of manners, my lady. I go by the name, Sir Nathan Staves. Should you have any other requirements please do not hesitate to call on my honor and sword to aid you."

Accepting the game he played, Sabine tipped her head towards her new acquaintance, "My thanks to you." She smiled sweetly, letting her words drip off her tongue like honey. "I shall hold your offer dear."

Hearing Sir Darrick snort at her pretty words, she decided it would not sit well if she tried to push his patience further. Nevertheless, unable to contain the imp inside her head, she smiled as innocently as possible and added, "Perhaps, when this old warhorse tires I will share your mount."

She pinched herself to keep from laughing. The stunned look on Sir Nathan's face and Sir Darrick's stiffened reaction was almost too much for her to contain her mirth. Hearing his breath hiss between his teeth as he steadied the horse, she realized she might have pushed her luck a bit far. Ducking her head, she kept busy with the baby, ignoring the friction between the knights.

Darrick motioned his head with a silent jerk. With a snap of his reins, they began to move out.

Concerned, Sabine noticed that only Sir Nathan accompanied them. The men Darrick promised would protect them were nowhere to be seen. Worry that DePierce would catch up with them at any moment gnawed at her insides, making her restless in the saddle.

Looking down at the moving ground, she noticed the knight's sword glistening in the setting sun. It rode at the base of Sir Darrick's hip, nestled in the jeweled scabbard belted at his narrow waist. The hilt of the sword was in the shape of a wing. She had recently seen something similar in design, but she could not quite put her finger on where. 'Twas like an itch that could not be reached.

She twisted to see Sir Darrick and cringed. He had shuttered all expression from his face. 'Twas as if carved from stone. She was tempted to hold a hand up to his nose to make sure he was still breathing. After looking to see if Nathan still rode nearby, she found comfort in knowing there was another sword arm available to protect them. A sigh escaped and her muscles grew lax.

The sway of the destrier's stride rocked her back and forth until her eyes grew heavy. Her head bobbed with each step they took toward the unknown.

* * * *

Sabine awoke with a start. Jerking up, she caught Darrick under his chin. His teeth clacked together. She feared she made him bite his tongue in the process.

"Quiet," he murmured.

Afraid to move and rub her head where it throbbed from hitting his chin, she whispered, "Where is Chance?"

Placing his hand over her mouth, he added near her ear. "You were sleeping. Nathan protects the babe. My men scout ahead. Others double back behind us. We'll have an answer either way."

The horses stood still, stopped in a thicket of trees. The sun had set. There were shadows all around. Sabine was unable to tell who was friend or foe.

"Sit still," he hissed. "Word has come. Torches draw near. We are uncertain where they came from."

Sabine gasped as shadows appeared from behind the rocks. The trees began to grow men as they swung out of the branches overhead. Swinging from the treetops, hanging from their feet with spider-like grace they dropped towards the ground.

Shouting for Nathan to follow, he kneed his mount and pushed through the trees. Branches caught at Sabine's hair, tearing at her dress and cloak. Darrick leaned over, shielding her body with his own. He wrapped his arm around her waist as the horse tore through the trees.

Arrows flew past, striking the branches, taking the leaves off as they whistled through the air. Darrick cut the horse in a sharp turn. The marauders moved in to surround Nathan's horse.

Sabine pushed the hair from her face. She searched Nathan's arms. "The baby?"

Darrick wheeled their steed around. Did he really intend to ride into the fray?

"Stay low," he ordered.

Sabine nodded and clung to the horse as they raced towards the attackers. Yelling his battle cry, he wielded his great sword, arching it overhead. It swung in great circles. The air sang with a high-pitched whine.

An arrow from above whistled through the air. It tore through the thin leaves, slowing in its deadly trail. Darrick jerked, and then dropped against her back. He bent over Sabine, pressing her into the horse's neck. "Keep down," he whispered.

Their attackers turned and stared at the apparition as it charged through the trees, mindless of all else but its target. They froze as the thundering horse charged and a black demon jumped out from the brush. Its teeth gnashed and bit, hungry for their blood. *Darrick's hound, Thunder.*

Matilda followed close behind, butting her head into their unsuspecting backs. Overpowered and distracted by the demons from hell, the attackers retreated to the protection of the shadows of the trees.

Doubled over by his weight, the air squeezing out of her lungs, she prayed for patience while she waited for him to get off. Hoof-beats pounded the ground as they drew towards their mount. Impatient to know that Sir Nathan and Chance were alive and riding beside them, she raised her head as Darrick lowered his face to speak to her.

"Do not move, I beg you." His harsh breath came in shallow pulls." We need to wait…just a moment."

Sabine turned as she heard a horse ride close. "Sir Nathan. 'Tis a relief to know you are still alive." She tried to push up from the horse. "Chance?"

"Not particularly happy with the ride, my lady, but he fairs well. Can you make it to camp?" Nathan asked.

"I'll be fine," Darrick said. His breath came in pants. "But once we get there you will have some work to do."

"So I see. My lady, are you able to ride?"

"From what direction did our attackers come?" Darrick hissed through clenched teeth.

Sabine struggled with the growing weight of the huge man leaning on top of her. "Sir Darrick. You are crushing me."

"He hears you not," Nathan said. The tone in his voice held concern. "An arrow impales his side.

"He is hurt?" she squeaked. "How can that be? He never spoke of it. What are we to do? I told him 'tis not safe to travel."

"Calm yourself. We will have to make our way to safety. There is a cottage not far from here. If you are not afraid of what we may find, we can go there."

"I fear DePierce more. He is the devil himself. We must keep Chance away from him."

"The babe is safe. First, we must take care of Darrick. Then we will decide what to do. For now, to keep him from falling, we are going to have to tie his hands around your waist and his legs around the horse. You will have to ride in front to steady him. Do you know how to ride as a man?"

"This I can do. Let us be on our way."

* * * *

Sabine sighed under the weight of the knight's limp body. Her shoulders, bruised from the fall, burned from straining with the reins. *Lord, but he must weigh at least twenty stone.*

Sir Nathan had said there was a cottage not far from where they were. She prayed that he was correct.

Nathan brought their mounts to stop in the shadows. He searched the trees and bushes before motioning her to proceed.

Chapter 9

Fighting to regain consciousness, Darrick's head rested in a cloud of rose and heather. Smiling, he recalled his mother smelled almost as sweet. He wondered, after all the time that had passed, if her fragrance remained the same. Poking and jabbing at the shadows, something nagged at the dark corners of his mind. He drew the wonderful scent in, filling his lungs. This, he discovered, was unwise as the pain shot through his ribs. Groaning, he fought the darkness that warred within.

Memories crept in. The invisible enemy was busily opening doors that many years before he had locked securely behind him. Happy times floated by; kisses on his cheeks and the occasional hugs from his mother. He and Elizabeth shared laughter over a prank played on the servants. The proud look of his father, his firm hand pressed on his shoulder.

And there were times of torment. Pain erupted; the squire's fists, pounding on him as he strove to deliver more pain than he received. Cold looks of hatred from his sister, whispers of his mother's infidelities, and the names of her lovers, danced through his mind. The fierce Lord of Lockwood watched from the blackened corners of his mind, shaking his head in shame. With tears running down his face, he turned his back on his only son and walked away holding Darrick's mother and sister at his side.

His body tensed, Darrick threw his arms out, pleading with them to stop. Fighting the internal ghosts, he wrestled for his life.

* * * *

Sir Darrick's health was rapidly diminishing. His breathing was labored and shallow. Sweat streamed down his face. Sabine wondered what, beyond the arrow protruding from his side, attacked his body with such vicious force. They could not wait any longer. The knight must be moved into the cottage and allowed to rest.

Locating the wispy trail of smoke coming from the chimney, Nathan silently watched the cottage for signs of life. Saying nothing to Sabine, he dismounted and moved toward the cottage. His broadsword drawn, he slammed the weathered door open.

"No one is here. Judging by the pot of stew bubbling over the little fire, the owner of the cottage will soon return. Our host's reception may not be a welcome one."

Sabine rode her mount up to the door. Her mouth was set in a thin grim line as she sat astride the weary horse. "Whether our party is considered welcome or not, we will be staying the night."

Nathan shrugged and prepared to help them dismount. He untied Darrick's wrists from her waist. "You'll have to steady him. I'll pull him down after I have untied his legs from the horse. Are you ready my lady?"

"Yes, let us make haste." Sabine was losing her grip on the horse. "Careful, he is quite ill. He lost consciousness on the ride in."

Nathan grunted. "Never fear, he is a strong man."

Sighing as Nathan helped the heavy burden slide off her back, she gingerly dismounted the old nag, her legs trembling from fatigue. Rubbing the small of her back, she gave little thought to where the owners of the cottage hid themselves. Despite Nathan's bold claim, Sir Darrick would not last if the arrow remained in his side. The injured knight needed a place to lie down and she needed to see to his wound.

Nathan carefully lowered his friend to the cot, mindful of the protruding arrow. Darrick groaned as they placed him on the unforgiving surface.

Rising, Nathan turned to Sabine. "Are you able to give me a hand with this, my lady? 'Tis possible the arrow is not a death shot. See here? Blood does not bubble from his mouth or the wound. But we must get the arrow out very soon."

Sabine gulped the nausea back down and nodded.

"I'll break off the end of the shaft then push it through to the other side," he said.

"Can you not simply cut it out?"

"No. The head of the arrow is barbed. If we pull it back through, it will tear the flesh, lodging deeper into his ribs. Judging by the length of the shaft that is exposed, 'tis a shot that near went clean through."

Sabine looked doubtfully at the bleeding wound. "And you have experienced this procedure before?"

"Not I, personally." His gaze lifted to match hers. "Our other plan would be to let it stay where it is. Let Darrick rest. Then move him to where our men are camped."

Sabine shook her head. "He has already slipped into a sweat. Have you noted his labored breathing?" She sniffed the air. There was a rank odor coming from the wound. If only she had her father's books at hand. Or dear Nandra's healing knowledge. "This is not a shot from a simple bow. I fear a poison coats the head of the arrow."

Nathan's brows beetled as he released the word under his breath. "Poison?"

"I'll do what I can," she said.

Juggling the baby in her arms, Sabine looked around the little cottage. The small cot in the corner was barely able to contain Darrick's large body, his long legs draped over the end. The only light, other than the meager fire in the fireplace, came from the dimly lit oil lamp. It sat on a short wooden table along with all sorts of clutter. The walls, covered with shelves, held various jars and vials. Hopeful, Sabine lifted the bottles and sniffed at them. She recognized some of the scents as essential oils extracted from herbs. Dried flowers and weeds hung from the ceiling. Some of the dried stems were the herbs she used while living at Clearmorrow Castle.

A heavy black cauldron hung over the weakening fire. Warm steam rose lazily from the simmering pot. She leaned over to check the contents. Her stomach growled at the familiar smell of bubbling stew. "At least we will have supper for tonight."

Nathan looked up from Darrick's bedside. "Right now, his wound needs tending. I must go out and find a safe place to hide the horses until we discover our host. Like it or not, you'll be called upon to help."

Sabine bristled. "Have I yet to show myself unworthy of the task?"

Nathan grabbed her free hand. "'Tis not that you've been unworthy, but more the case that you have not earned my trust or my friend's. He would ask the same as I, how do you suppose DePierce knew where to send his men? Perhaps he has help in places we are not yet aware. What say you, my lady? Do you know of these allies?"

Sabine struggled from his grasp; she felt as if his fingers wrapped around her throat instead of merely her wrist. "I have done nothing to deserve this treatment. Nor have I anything to say to your accusations."

"You leave too many questions unanswered, wench."

Unable to pull away and afraid her grasp on the baby would slip, she forced herself to stop struggling. She unleashed her words in a rush. "Again, you, and your friend, insult me. 'Tis Sir Darrick I will forgive, because he cannot defend his thoughts right now. You, I cannot. If I am a spy for

DePierce, please tell me how I came to be abandoned on the island. How did I come to be in possession of Elizabeth's baby? Sir Darrick chose me to travel with him. I, too, was a target today. If I am a great threat to this little caravan, why did your friend choose to protect me? I told Sir Darrick they would be after us and he felt he had enough men to protect us. You were in the lead, Sir Nathan," she stated bluntly. "Perhaps you are the traitor."

"Traitor is a deadly name to give a man."

Sabine chose to ignore his warning. "You were in charge of deploying the men. Where are they now? Moreover, how did you know of this place? I believe, you too, have a lot of questions to answer."

Nathan let his hand fall away from Sabine's wrist. Running his fingers through his auburn hair, he turned towards the door. "I will not say how I knew of this place. I find my information in many ways. 'Tis what I do. As for the men, a few coins can change a man's mind. You brought up questions that I will have to discover the answers to."

Sabine sighed and grabbed at his sleeve. "Let it be, Sir Nathan. At this moment, I am more concerned with getting the arrow extracted and finding a poultice to draw the poison. 'Tis plenty of time to figure things out while he heals. Please understand that I would give my life to protect this baby. I will do all that I can to help Sir Darrick. DePierce is my sole enemy. He has stolen everything from me."

She glanced down at Darrick. His breathing had become rapid and shallow. A sheen of sweat covered his pale skin, dampening his dark hair. "Will you place our friend's life in my care, or will you let him die by doing nothing?"

"Aye," Nathan said. "I have no choice but to trust you. For now."

Sabine gazed up at the bear-sized man and gave a weak smile. "'Tis all I ask. Tie up the horses if you must. I will search for the herbs we need. There appears to be quite a selection here."

Nathan gave her an incredulous look. "You have knowledge of healing potions?"

"I learned from the best healer known to live on Clearmorrow lands." Sabine held up her hand to stop any other comments. "Healing, not witchery. Although, until I encountered your friend's family, I have had little practice of late." Shooing him with a flutter of her hand, she added, "I urge you to make haste. We dare not tarry."

"Bar the door behind me. The owners of the cottage cannot be far from home." Nathan slowly opened the wooden slats and slipped out.

Sabine shut the door firmly behind him and picked up the half-empty bag of goat's milk. How much longer would they have to wait for Matilda's return? She fed the baby before she gathered the needed herbs from the rafters. She didn't know if they would help Darrick, but she would do her best.

She did not really lie to Sir Nathan, she just happened to stretch the truth a bit. She had read the books her father kept in his laboratory, and Nandra had shown her a few methods of healing, but there had never been much time to put any of it into practice. She just hoped and prayed she could remember most of what she'd learned.

His stomach full, Chance fell asleep by the time she gathered all the supplies she would need. Finding a basket, she laid him gently inside the woven shell.

Sabine crept towards the man lying on the cot. She scrubbed her hands down her skirt. The arrow protruded grotesquely from his side. The blood seeped through the hole in his tunic. Feeling the thread-thin heartbeat under his jerkin, she was relieved to find that he held onto his life. Gently, she tried to pull the tunic over his wide shoulders but it would not move past the arrow's shaft. After pondering her limited choices, she shrugged. The man could yell at her later...provided he lived...if he did not approve of her reasons for destroying his clothing.

Taking the dagger that hung from her waist, she sliced the tunic open, gently peeling it back. After deciding it was beyond repair, she cut it into smaller strips. Once boiled, it could be used as bandages.

Now bared, Sir Darrick's broad back was marred with many scars, some old, and some new. Muscles rippled down to his chausses. Sabine slowly looked over her patient, measuring his strength to hers. She would definitely have to wait for Sir Nathan's return. She would need his help should Sir Darrick awaken and struggle against her.

Trying to recall her studies with her father, she remembered their discussions regarding his theory that battle wounds became black from the dirty water and tools used by the surgeon. Unable to locate fresh water in the cottage, she found a clean piece of cloth and poured wine over the wound. Expecting him to be past feeling anything, she was caught off-guard as his massive arm swung around to deflect the pain-inflicting apparition. She held her small dagger over his chest

"Hold, wench," Nathan bellowed. "What do you think you are doing? Do you dare to take his life while I am away?"

"For the love of Mary, when will you see I mean no harm to you or Sir Darrick? I'm cutting away what's left of his tunic." She nodded over her shoulder. "We'll have to tie his arms and legs down before we can work on his injury. Although his strength weakens, he is too strong for me."

Staring at Darrick's long tapered fingers, she forgot Nathan stood beside her. Just looking at his huge hands made her warm all over. Her body tingled in intimate places she thought best left undiscovered. Her breasts pushed against the soft material of her dress, aching for his...

Nathan cleared his throat, bringing her out of her musing. "If you are ready."

He moved Darrick's heavy leg over. "We'll have to tie them at the knee. His legs hang over too far to tie them at the ankle." Taking his friend's arm, he gently moved it to the head of the cot.

Wiping Sir Darrick's brow, Sabine turned to get the herbs she had gathered earlier from the shelves and rafters. Nathan leaned all of his weight on top of his friend to keep him from thrashing about while she poured the potion down Darrick's throat.

"We must do it now, Sir Nathan, or the herbs I gave him will wear off. I will press the shaft of the arrow down and try to pass it through. If luck and God's will are on our side, then it shall miss his lungs, and not catch on any ribs."

"Then let us pray God is with us, and be done with it."

Sabine examined the broken shaft. Nathan had already rid it of its feathers. Shivering, she noted it might as well have been a log instead of the arrow's narrow shaft from an archer's bow. Cursing the archer that set sail the deadly missile, she offered a prayer and began the arduous job of pushing it through Darrick's satiny flesh.

The shaft quivered in her hand. Startled, she released her hold. Glancing over, she could see Sir Nathan, concentrating on holding Sir Darrick down. Sweat already dripped off his grim face.

Her heart went out to Sir Darrick. The mountainous man was helpless, depending on her skill to keep him alive. She wondered how he could be so quiet. Memories of his gentle care flooded back. His long lashes covered his steel gray eyes. His raven black bangs were sweat soaked and lay over his forehead. The desire to stroke his brow overrode her consuming fear. Pushing back his hair, she felt the heat of his body radiate through her fingertips. She gasped from the fire raging in his body. Time was working against them.

Bending over, she whispered, "All right, Sir Darrick, we will be doing our part, your friend and I, but you must hold on and come back to us when we are finished."

Nathan cleared his throat. "Excuse me, my lady, 'tis time we start. Do you know what to do?"

"Just…gathering wits." Swallowing the knot that had formed in her throat, she wrapped her fingers around the arrow's shaft and pressed down.

Darrick's body jerked. He yelled as if under attack.

With sweat dripping down her face, she renewed the pressure.

Sir Nathan held on to Darrick's shoulders and growled impatiently for Sabine to hurry up and get the damn thing out. Her whole weight dropped onto the arrow as she gave one final shove. The arrow broke through the skin. Sabine fell on top of Sir Darrick. Resting her head, she pressed her ear against his back to listen for a heartbeat. Looking up at Sir Nathan, she nodded. He was still alive. For now.

"Make haste, Nathan. A dagger is needed to pry the head out the rest of the way and then, I pray, one more push should do it."

Both hands busy, Nathan motioned with his head. "Over there, 'tis on the table."

Sabine ran for the dagger while Nathan continued to keep his friend from moving. Gasping, she turned the dagger in her hand. Jewels encrusted the handle. The shape of a swan's head gazed up at her, winking with its emerald eye. It was the same emblem and styling as the dagger in Elizabeth's pouch. Upon hearing Darrick begin to groan and Nathan cursing at her to hasten, she quickly turned and laid the sharp edge to the wound.

As the blade of the dagger cut through, the arrowhead finally protruded. Darrick yelled once and then he went limp.

Sabine triumphantly held the prize she sought, the deadly missile dripping his blood onto her hand. She threw what was left of the arrow across the room towards the fireplace.

Nathan caught it before it landed in the flames. "'Tis needed. Perhaps it will tell the story of our attack and what poison might have been used." He patted her shoulder. "Go wash up and tend to his wounds. I will see to the baby. Thank God, he slept through this."

Sabine washed the blood from Darrick's wounds and packed them with the healing herbs. When she was done, she noted her depleted supplies of herbs. Soon as she was able, she would have to leave the cottage and search for more. Sitting beside her patient, she worried he would not survive the attack. They had retrieved the arrow, but they still had to fight the poison and watch for signs of infection.

They rolled Darrick to his back. Sabine kept a wary watch for his flailing limps. "Sir Nathan, what of the owners of this cottage? Do you think they will return soon?"

"'Tis certain. I'll scout around when I go out to look after our mounts. I cannot help wondering what happened to Thunder and your crazed goat. They should have returned by now."

"Will they be able to find us?"

"Aye, if Thunder has any say in the matter. He has managed to stay by Darrick's side through many a battle. Will probably be your pet goat that he'll have to convince to go with him."

Sabine sniffed at the insult directed towards Matilda. "She is not that bad."

"Hah!" he snorted. "Darrick told me about the cave and your tumble."

"I think more than necessary has been said."

Chuckling and shaking his head, Nathan laid the sleeping baby down on his pallet. "I'll discover what delays our furry friends. Remember to keep the dagger by your side." Hooking the stool with his foot, he dragged it over. "Brace the door with this. If any surprises should come visiting, yell out. I'll not be far."

After bracing the stool against the door as ordered, Sabine gathered the things she needed to care for Darrick.

Taking a closer look at his battered body, she gasped at the number of scars tracking his chest and rock hard stomach. A deep furrow ran across his stomach. Layers of muscles rippled with each breath. She wiped at his chest, enjoying the feel of his hair tickling her fingers, springing up at her touch. His waist narrowed, nipping in at the waistband of his bloodied chausses. Her hands followed the delicious trail as her eyes dropped past his flat stomach, dipping down to his lower regions. Curious, she let her fingertips slide down the path of coiled hair. Feeling quite daring since her giant was sleeping, she decided to bathe him thoroughly; to gain the full benefit of a healing rest, of course, her conscience added.

She tugged off his chausses, uncovering his muscular limbs. Admiring the strength of his legs, Sabine wondered how many hours on horseback it took to build such strength, and how many battles did it take to gather the numerous scars? Her brother and father may have worked side-by-side with the stonemasons and villagers to build the manor house. However, they would never succeed in gaining Darrick's stature. His was that of a warrior.

When she was a little girl, her old nurse, Nandra, used to fill her head with stories of giant warriors. They were super humans in height and strength. They fought battles for silly fair maidens who were always helpless and could not think for themselves. And the best part, Nandra always told of a special love where only the blessed of souls would find their one true love. The mighty warrior would fight for his ladylove and take her away to a very special place. She remembered standing at the top of the castle, waiting for her protector to rescue her from the tower. Time and time again, she was called away from her perch with promises of another day to watch for her love. Sadly, her warrior never came.

Instead, she watched her mother wither from loneliness and then a terror that caused her to plunge from the parapet. Her father, his head stuck in his leather-bound tombs, had wandered off into the forest to a clandestine meeting. He was never seen again. Her brother, Taron, went to fight for King Henry. Upon his return from the king's court, he left immediately in search of their father. Now, he too, was lost.

Even Nandra had disappeared. Always a loner, she went off by herself. By now, Nandra was no doubt with her very own warrior. Perhaps, she had finally found the one she was always waiting for.

Dark memories of her last days at Clearmorrow crept in, as they were wont to do when her defenses were down. Aye, one by one, her kinsmen dropped out of sight. Their disappearance left her to care for Clearmorrow and the people living inside its walls. When the raiders attacked the castle, only a handful of her household yet remained. Their payment for loyalty had been torture and death. The lucky ones perished the moment they fell. Those who were captured were taken to Balforth and cast into the dungeon. There, DePierce kept those who served his needs, either for pleasure or for his constant search for strength and power. There could be no doubt that he would continue his raids until King Henry put a stop to it. If only the king and his men would return from France.

Sabine swore under her breath, cursing DePierce and despising her stupidity. To think she actually rode to that monster's castle for help. The moment she crossed his threshold, she became DePierce's prisoner. She could not leave her room unless escorted by one of his minions. If not for Rhys orchestrating her escape, she would never have been able to break free from Balforth. It was still a mystery to her as to why Rhys was willing to help.

Lost in thought, Sabine caressed Darrick's muscular thigh with the palm of her hand. The pad of her fingers followed the sloping ridges of his body. Enthralled with the contours of her patient, she failed to hear the door creak open, tensing only when she heard the shuffling footsteps draw near.

Her hand crept towards the knife laying on the edge of the cot. She caught hold of the cool metal.

"You do not belong here." A hand wrapped around Sabine's shoulder.

She turned with a start at the sound of the graveled voice. "Nandra! 'Tis been so long."

"You still live? How can this be? I was told you died in the raid. How did you manage to hide for so long?"

Sabine was confused. Why was Nandra angry to see her? Sabine's senses humming, a wariness of her childhood friend crept along her skin. Telling herself it was exhaustion and not Nandra that caused this feeling, she decided to ignore the warning.

"Tell me, child," Nandra questioned, "who lies in my bed?"

"A knight. One who shall help us defeat DePierce."

"Humph," Nandra snorted. "Looks more dead than alive. Are you so foolish to think one man can defeat someone as powerful as DePierce?"

"I vowed to repay DePierce." Reaching out to touch the back of Nandra's hand, she held the gnarled fingers in her hands, pressing them to her cheek. "Now I have you by my side to help."

The old woman snorted and withdrew her fingers from Sabine's grasp.

Squaring her shoulders, Sabine studied the haggard old woman that stood before her. Once beautiful, she was now marred by a hard edge glittering in her eyes.

"Nandra? I, too, thought you died the night they raided our keep. I did not see you during the attack, nor when I fled to Balforth. I heard that his men torched your cottage. Where have you been?"

"Foolish child. I hid in the forest just like the rest who were unprotected by your family. Why do you ask?"

The humming grew louder in Sabine's ears. "'Tis just that you disappeared so quickly."

"I learned to save my skin long before you took a breath. 'Tis of no consequence." The old woman bristled. "Seek help for your man, instead of wasting time on me."

Sufficiently chastised, Sabine knew her questions would have to wait. Darrick could not. "I've done all I know to do. The wound bled freely after I removed the arrow. Then I slowed the blood flow with a tree moss poultice. Nevertheless, I cannot help worrying 'tis not enough."

The old woman's watery glance slid towards her and then bounced away. "Why is that, child?" her reedy voice crooned. "Surely, you did all that is necessary. Is there perhaps something," the old woman whispered, "more you wish to tell me?"

Nandra, whom Sabine remembered as truthful, was unable to look her in the face.

"I fear there was poison on the tip of the arrow which struck him. He slips deeper into an unnatural sleep. There must be an antidote, but I cannot recall what it is. Perhaps you know of one."

The old woman's skin stretched tightly over her cheekbones, looking as if she were made of stone. Unmoving, Nandra weighed her answer.

Sabine could not understand her hesitation to help. "Please," she pleaded.

The old woman's eyes filled with hatred, her skin drew even tighter, masking her face with tension. "I ask you this, child. Who is the man that lies here? Did you foolishly spurn DePierce's offer, for this man?"

"DePierce has never held a love for me. He wants only the land that Clearmorrow offers. Please try to remember that this is the man who will deliver DePierce's defeat."

Sabine looked over at the man lying motionless on the cot. The bandages wrapped around the upper half of his body were stained red with his blood. His chest barely rose with each rasping breath. Sweat ran in streams down his face. She feared the precious time of healing was running out.

"It will be over soon enough. Tell me, girl, is there an army waiting to lay siege to DePierce's castle?" Grabbing her shoulders, the old woman's bony fingers dug into Sabine skin. "How many men does he have?"

Sabine began to fear her old friend had lost her mind. "It matters not. You must show me which elixir I can use for an antidote against the poison. I already used some of the herbs but they have not helped to counteract it. I beg you, Nandra." She placed her palm against the leathery cheek. "Try to remember."

Nandra loosened her grip, letting her hands drop to her side in defeat. "So you have made your decision. To him, you have attached your alliance." She turned away and shuffled slowly to the door. Her hand on the latch, she spoke over her shoulder. "As always, you are determined to have your way in this. Just like your mother, you are. So be it, then you will gain the exact help you justly deserve."

Sabine took a step towards her.

"No need to follow," Nandra said "Tend to your fallen knight and I will be back to fix this little matter." She hobbled out into the dark, leaving Sabine to wait and worry.

Chewing on her lip, Sabine wondered why Nathan had not returned. He had been gone for quite some time. She was certain that the concern for his friend had been real. Doubts began to form. Was he the traitor who betrayed their position to the mercenary soldiers? She rubbed her temples. Nothing in her life made sense anymore.

Nandra was taking an eternity, poor thing. She prayed the woman remembered what she went out to fetch. She would have to trust that the dosage would be correct. Darrick depended on her.

Bending over Chance, she looked to see that he was safe and sleeping soundly. She tucked the blanket tightly around the baby's limbs to keep him warm. Relief had poured through Sabine's veins when Nandra failed to notice the baby.

Unease settled over her soul. She could not ignore the shiver that ran down her back. This was not the same woman from her childhood. It had been almost a year. Could people change as much, in so short a time? Had Nandra always behaved this way and she never realized it until now? Maybe that was the reason her father was always so terse when he discovered she went alone to visit with Nandra at her cottage in the forest.

Darrick thrashed his limbs against the leather bonds holding him down. Sabine rushed to his side and struggled to keep him from breaking opens his stitches.

"Hold, Darrick. Help is coming," she cried. "Please be still."

His lids fluttered open. "As you wish." His voice, hoarse with pain, broke. "How can I disappoint you again?"

"So, he still lives, does he? 'Tis hemlock that ails him." A scratchy voice cackled somewhere from behind.

Gently lifting Darrick's head from her lap Sabine struggled to control her impatience. They could wait no longer. She stood and attempted to take away the vial clutched in Nandra's claw-like fingers.

"Is this what you really want?" Nandra chuckled under her breath, mumbling unintelligible gibberish. She jerked her head to face Sabine, catching her in a cold fish-eyed stare. Slowly her fingers uncurled and the vial dropped.

Sabine dove and caught it before it hit the floor. Her hands shook as she shoved her hair from her face. "Tell me at once how to prepare the antidote."

Nandra's lips peeled back in a grin. "'Tis a foolish child that follows stupid ways. Your choice is made. Heed my instructions. To break the poison's hold you must give him all. Do not dilute it. 'Twould break the strength of the mixture. You understand me, girl?"

Sabine took the vial, barely daring to turn her back. She cradled it close to her chest. Apprehension began to gnaw at her flesh, leaving a trail of chills. She knelt beside Darrick while keeping one eye on the elderly woman. Sabine tensed as Nandra shuffled toward the baby.

The muscles in Nandra's jaw tightened and jerked in a ticking motion. Her fingers trailed across each item held in Elizabeth's pouch that lay upon the little table. She picked up the swan brooch and clutched it in her bony claw. Her watery eyes widened, gleaming with something akin to wicked-joy.

"Whose babe is this? Yours?" she crooned.

Sabine shook her head as she unstopped the vial. "No, the little one is Darrick's nephew. That is why I know he will help me rid our land of DePierce. 'Tis his enemy, as well as ours. Do you remember DePierce's nephew? Hugh? We believe it was Hugh and DePierce who ordered the murder of Darrick's sister."

Sabine sniffed warily at the bottle she held in her hand. *Foxglove?* Recognizing the noxious odor, she knew it was an herb that was best given in small amounts. Too much and it would be just as deadly as hemlock. Was her friend mistaken? Sabine gave Darrick two drops. She would increase the dose if needed.

Nandra's tittering in the corner caught her attention.

"There is a child? Lady Elizabeth's baby. Won't our old friend be surprised?" Nandra winked slyly. "Tell me girl, would you know who is responsible for your young knight's death?"

Sabine froze. Fearing the worst, she placed her palm on Darrick's chest. "Death? He cannot die. I won't allow it."

"There, there, my girl, no need to fear. All will be well. All will be well once again," she crooned. "Come with me, my sweeting. I've a lovely place waiting just for you."

Chapter 10

The blow to Sabine's head jerked her to one side. Stars shattered into a million pieces as her knees buckled underneath. Pitching forward, she grasped the blanket covering Darrick. It ripped as she fell to the floor. A log lying by the fireplace dropped beside her. Slipping into the gray folds of the mist, she peered up at the old crone standing over her.

"You still live? No matter. Go, child, 'tis but a short step to the other side."

Nandra yanked Sabine's head back. Sour breath from rotting teeth blew in her face.

"'Tis so much blood," Nandra exclaimed. She fluttered bloodstained fingers in front of Sabine's blurring eyes. "You look so like your mother as she bled to her death."

Sabine felt the hot trail of tears run down her cheek. She could not fight the dark mist any longer. It wrapped its cold tentacles around her head and squeezed. Helpless, unable to move, she watched the crazy old woman walk away.

The door swung open. Sabine struggled to see beyond the murky shadows as Nandra's shadow exited the cottage; leaving them to die.

* * * *

Darrick's teeth clicked against each other as another chill ran through his body. *Cold.* The room was dark. The fire in the hearth had burned down to ashes. *Why won't my limbs move? Where is Sabine?*

He pulled in a breath, testing his ribs. Fire ripped through his chest. Damn, but his head pounded. The tiny hairs on the back of his neck tingled, warning him to lie still and listen to his surroundings. He tensed as someone entered the cottage. Two muffled voices moved towards him.

"Well, Spurge. What say you? Did ol' Nandra speak the truth?"

"Aye, Gregor, Looks t' me like she's dead. What with all that blood coming outta her head and all."

Darrick watched though narrowed slits as the two voices began to take shape. Despite the protruding bulge hindering him at the waist, the leader of the two leaned over. Motioning to the man to move closer, he stepped over the oddly shaped lump lying on the floor.

Spurge shuffled over to peer at the deepening halo of blood. "Might not be dead yet. But she won't last long. 'Sides if the old woman played any mischief on her, she'll not be moving from here, no how."

The fat leader scratched at his scruffy beard. "Aye, but it makes me wonder. If Nandra is so powerful, why'd she have to go and break her head?"

"Don't know. All that alchemy gives me the shivers. Not right to go fooling with the way of life. 'Tis devil's work, is what that is."

"What about the one lying over there on the cot? He dead too?"

Spurge shrugged. "Appears so."

"Well," Gregor growled, "is he dead or not?"

Spurge tugged on his ear. "Um… well, I did go over by the man. Course, I did. 'Tis right you are. I went right over by him whilst you were a look'n at the other one. Didn't you see me?"

Squinting, at the fidgeting Spurge, Gregor grunted and cast another look around. "I'm sure you missed something."

"Do you see any signs of a baby?" Spurge whispered. "I was for certain I saw something in that red-headed giant's arms when he was riding in."

Gregor rolled his eyes to the ceiling. "Do you see any babies around here? Our orders are to get rid of them two. Dispose of them real good. And that old hag did just that. As for that giant outside, Nandra says he would be a good one to test those new elixirs she's been working on. We'll take him to Balforth. They'll know what to do."

Gregor scratched at his beard. "Hope his high and mightiness will be satisfied. He was in rare form when that other one got away."

Skirting the cot, treading carefully around the body on the floor, the skinny Spurge joined Gregor's side. Bending closer, Spurge looked at the woman.

Darrick prayed they would soon depart. The dark halo surrounding Sabine's head had spread.

"That woman in the tower? We got her back, didn't we?" Rubbing at his crotch, Spurge whined, "Here now, why'd you s'pose old Nandra had to kill this one before we got to her? We could've had some fun ourselves. Looks familiar, don't she? Almost like that other one in the dungeon."

Gregor batted away the stick Spurge was about to use to lift her skirts. "Don't touch her. What if death jumps from her to us? I've heard tell of it happening. Nandra would know the spell."

"Aye, she'd cast it too." Spurge scuttled towards the door. Shaking his head, he looked at Gregor. "I say they're both dead. What say you? Should we burn the cottage down around them?"

"No, too much trouble to light the damn thing. Let the wild animals take care of the bodies, like old Nandra said."

Darrick listened to the men depart. He sucked in a breath of air, testing what his injured ribs would allow.

He lifted his head to look for Sabine. If what he had overheard was correct, then she was left for dead. He prayed that the men were as careless as they appeared.

His muscles trembled. The blood he had lost had left him weak. His ribs ached where he had taken the arrow. He examined the bandages, lacking the strength it took to care for his wound. Satisfying his curiosity, he left the bandages where they were. He would have to change the dressing but his low reserve of strength was needed elsewhere.

After dragging his weakened body to Sabine, he placed his hand upon her chest. Her heart beat, ever so lightly. Her breath stirred his cheek. His hands shook as he brushed back the bloodied hair and stroked her face. She lay on the floor, wrapped in silence. A log, stained with her blood, lay beside her.

Sabine still clutched a vial of elixir in her hand. It was almost completely full. He removed the stopper. The plant's scent filled his nose. He recognized it instantly. Foxglove. Remnants of the double-edged brew still coated his lips. A little helped those in pain, but too much caused death. He would count himself lucky if all he got this eve would be a powerful headache, and a violent stomach upset. He was thankful she knew not to give him any more than she did.

He gathered his strength and rose. Herbs from the rafters. He pulled them down, sniffing, and identifying each one. Eggs. He had to find at least one good egg. The egg white would be used as a healing agent.

He recalled the angel with the golden tresses. She had cried while she cared for him, her tears washing away the tormenting, pain-filled memories. Soothing hands had pushed the hair away from his face. A cool cloth had slowly wiped at his sweat-soaked body. She had helped to save his life. And now she had been harmed because of him and his family. He would not let death gain another life today.

If it were not for his fear that she would take off on her own, he would have already taken her to the convent where his mother was exiled. He knew Sabine was a stubborn wench and would demand her own revenge. But at what cost? They had already lost so much.

By death's hand, Elizabeth had been taken. The babe, Chance, was a helpless pawn. He could not understand where the child had disappeared to while he was unconscious. The men had mentioned a babe. 'Twas obvious from their conversation, they did not find one in the cottage. If this were true, then where was the child?

And now, Nathan was DePierce's prisoner. Darrick could not fathom why they should take him. Ransoming Nathan would bring little coin.

He stroked Sabine's head as he ran through the plans he would have to make as soon as they recovered from their wounds. She had yet to awaken from the deep sleep. His hand sagged from the weight. The constant removal of the damp cloth draped over her head had sapped his strength.

This quest appeared doomed from the beginning. Why did he allow his men to be sent to Rhys? He should have listened to Sabine. She knew there were dangers in the woods and he thought he was too great a knight to allow anyone to harm them. These lands, at one time, had been his to roam without fear. Now that DePierce was here, they were overrun with his mercenaries.

"I'm sorry love," he whispered. "Hold on till I am strong enough to help you."

He placed his hand upon Sabine's chest. The light flutter of her heart, the soft whisper of air reassured him that she yet lived. The weight of his arms and legs were too much to move. He closed his eyes. *Just for a moment.*

He shivered. *Fool that I am. I should have braced the cottage door.*

Chapter 11

White-hot stars exploded, shooting across the black curtain that draped around Sabine's head. Nausea dipped and swirled, tossing her about in its wake.

Short, hot blasts of air blew across her face. She turned her head from the fetid stench that bore its way into her consciousness. The shooting pain intensified. Groaning, she swatted at the offensive odor that continued to poke and prod her brain. Her reward for the rash movement was more pain slicing her forehead in full force. Groaning again, she prayed for death to come quickly.

Instead of relief, she was left to wonder if perhaps death was already upon her. The stench, so bad, mayhap it was the rotting bodies of hell. If so, she added a prayer that Nandra would soon be joining her.

A sob escaped, as she recalled the last seconds before she was knocked unconscious. At last, she now knew how her mother had died. She could not fathom why Nandra would do such a thing. The old woman's eyes haunted her memory. They were crazed with hate, and something else Sabine could not understand.

She had just given a few drops of the elixir to the knight right before she was attacked. Dare she hope he yet lived despite the old woman's attempt? He had already lost so much blood. With the poisoning of his body, 'twas too much for any mortal man to survive. Like his nephew, their alliance had not been an easy one. Her lips quivered. Had death taken them away?

Perhaps death wrapped her senses in its putrid odor. She shut her eyes; fearing the white pain, fearing what she might see. Another sob slipped from her lips as a tear ran down her cheek.

The rancid air returned, this time in short panting breaths. Something wet and leathery lapped the tears from her face. She screamed as she fought past the engulfing pain. Past the fear of those that lay dead around her. Past the beast that was trying to eat her alive.

'Twas hard for her to accept defeat. Thoughts of Darrick and Chance brought a renewed desire to live. *Fight! Do not give into the darkness.*

"Sabine," Darrick called to her, pulling her from the thick mire. "'Tis Thunder that awakens you."

She looked up to see her knight. His long black hair fell past his shoulders and brushed her breast. Dark circles ringed his steel gray eyes. A frown forced a 'V' to form between his brows.

She trailed a fingertip lightly around his lips, tracing the outer edges. They were hot to the touch, satin against her fingertip. Tantalized by the contradiction between the smooth texture of his mouth and the coarse plane of his jaw, she brushed the back of her knuckles against his visage. His jaw was rough from the dark growth of whiskers. His beard, visible against the ashen color of his skin. She tickled her fingers back and forth enjoying the feel of the contours of his face and mouth, reassuring herself that he was still alive.

Darrick groaned against her palm. A sigh of pleasure escaped. He shifted his weight and leaned forward so that their lips barely touched. Closing her eyes, she waited, preparing for his kiss.

The sound of toenails scratching on the packed earthen floor came from behind them. A great hairy mound of stench threw itself on top, covering them with tongue and fur. Pain returned threefold. Sabine grabbed her head with both hands and Darrick rolled to protect the wound on his side.

"Make him stop," she whispered. "He will wake the babe."

Darrick suddenly stopped wrestling with the hound. Sabine watched the play of anger creep across his stern visage. Like the tides that rush in at the shore, it bore across his face. When it washed away, his expression remained shuttered behind a stony fortress.

* * * *

Darrick turned his back on the maiden who had held his careless attention. How could he forget what had taken place? No matter the fears she carried of Balforth, he would broach the subject with her. He vowed to get Nathan and his nephew back alive. If necessary, he would force her to speak of her secrets.

In the meantime, how would he tell her of the missing child? She had formed a bond with the babe. It would not bode well for them when she discovered the truth.

"Where have you been, boy? Whose stench of blood do you carry?" Slowly running his fingers through the hound's matted fur he gently kneaded Thunder's skin and muscles. One of the hound's ears was torn. It hung in a lopsided angle throwing off the balance of the beast's large head. The blood-splattered wound above his ear would give him a permanently quizzical look. On his right flank, he carried another wound that could have come from a blade. The dog had given his all trying to protect his master. Darrick was relieved the dog survived the battle. He would need Thunder to lead them to Nathan and the babe.

Prodding the hair surrounding the wound, Darrick noticed the matted fur around the hound's mouth. He hoped that whomever he bit carried an even larger hole in their hide. Should they ever encounter their attackers, both Darrick and the beast would know.

Sabine lay still. Her chest rose with each shallow breath. Her movements agonizingly slow. Darrick watched for signs of the throbbing in her head to ease up. He was thankful her brain did not seem to have any permanent damage. Many men had lost their wits when struck so heavily.

He needed to see if it were too late to stitch the wound on her head. Her eyes were squeezed shut. Darrick could see she was waiting in silence, listening to the empty sound of the little cottage. After a few moments, he knew she would realize that he had yet to respond to any of her questions.

"Darrick," she pleaded. "Tell me, please, I beg you. Where is Chance? Why do I not hear him? Is he…? Is he all right?" she whispered.

Knowing that whatever he told her would not spare her heartache, he spoke plainly, his voice raw. "Gone."

"What do you mean?" Sabine struggled to sit up.

Darrick waited as she pushed her golden mane of hair away from her face. He could see the clouds drift over her eyes while she fought the dizziness. Dark circles ringed her sherry-colored eyes. The side of her face was swollen and discolored. He had been able to wash off most of the blood, but it still mingled with the hair flowing past her waist.

Drawing her into his chest, he gently cradled her until he felt her strength return. He passed his hands over his eyes, his voice hoarse with exhaustion. "I don't know, love. Can you tell me what you remember?" he asked.

Sabine laid her head upon his chest. He could feel the rhythm of her heartbeat matching his own. She relaxed as he slid his fingers through her hair.

After a time, she said, "Nathan and I tended your wounds. Here, in this cottage. The tip of the arrow had been dipped in something foul."

His hand stilled. "Poison?"

She nodded. "Nathan left to feed the horses and I have not seen him since that time. Sweet Mary," she lifted her head. "Do you think he would have taken Chance?" Confusion drifted across her face. "But, why would he do such an evil thing?"

"No, Nathan would never betray us. Nor would he abandon us. But, I heard those two men, Spurge and Gregor, speak of an old woman. Who is she to you?"

"DePierce's men?"

"Yes, but you hedge from my question. I did not see the old woman. They spoke of her being a witch and that Nathan is bound for one of DePierce's hidey-holes. They also mentioned a maid, getting away from the castle with something very important. DePierce wants her back and what she has stolen, returned. However, they did not find the babe. The babe was already spirited away."

Darrick's voice broke as he whispered. "That woman has the babe. I would stake my life and sword on it. Again, love, I ask you. Who is she to you? Why would she take my nephew?"

"It makes so little sense. I knew her from my childhood. Nandra was my friend." Sabine covered her face. "I thought her dead. I have not heard from her since the night Clearmorrow was attacked. She disappeared before the battle even began. 'Twas as if she knew ahead of time that they were coming to raze the castle to the ground. The men who attacked my home knew where we were the weakest. We were betrayed." She looked up, her gaze matching his. "How did Nathan know to find this cottage in the midst of the forest?

Darrick tensed. Did she suggest that his most trusted friend had betrayed them? He shoved aside the question. "Mayhap one of the scouts mentioned it. We'll ask him once we find him." He forked his fingers through her tresses. "Tell me more of Nandra."

Sabine took a shuddering breath. "She arrived soon after Nathan left to tend the horses. Even though she brought healing unguents, her odd behavior made me doubt her sanity. She must have realized that I questioned her instructions. She struck me from behind." Sabine dropped her head into her hands. "Dear lord, you're right. She has Chance. But why?"

"It does not matter why. We will track them down. Then take care of Sir Vincent DePierce."

"And Nathan?"

Darrick sighed. "Yes, and Nathan. He'll be found and allowed time to explain his disappearance."

Her voice muffled, Sabine mumbled into his chest. "We must be wary. She has killed before."

Darrick stopped playing with her hair. His movements stalled by this revelation. How much danger were they in? Attempting to remain unfazed, he kept his voice calm. "Who?"

Sabine swiped at the moisture on her cheek. "She described how my mother died. How she watched her bleed until her life slipped away."

Darrick wrapped his arm around her shoulders and held her until she no longer trembled with quaking sobs

Chapter 12

Darrick's brow furrowed as he concentrated on repairing the tear in Thunder's skin. The hound sat obediently, his brown eyes following his master's for his next order. With each stitch, the needle and thread moved slowly through the air, dancing with precision.

Sabine watched him from where she propped her back against the wall. "You've done this before."

Darrick nodded, knotting the last stitch. "He's had a great deal of practice getting his flesh pulled together. The dog has more lives than a cat. Survived my care before. And so will you."

Her head snapped up as she regarded him with wariness. "What exactly do you think to do to me, Sir Darrick?"

"So, 'tis back to 'Sir Darrick,' is it?" He ran his hands up and down the beast's back, ruffling the fur as he spoke. His gaze slid over her. "What happened to calling me by my given name?"

Sabine shifted her gaze to his face. Her countenance warned him to keep his distance. "You've yet to tell me what you want from me."

"In due time."

The smooth rhythmic play of his hands against the dog's fur soothed his desire to pull her into his arms. Thunder rested his head on Darrick's lap, using his thigh for a pillow.

A small groan slipped past her tightened lips. Somehow, it drew the dog's attention. Lumbering to her side, Thunder sat down, and pressed his body into her side. His great head dipped over her shoulder, planting his muzzle near her ear.

Sabine growled at the malodorous animal. "You smell worse than the latrine channel at Balforth."

The disheartened dog moved to the safety of the corner by the fireplace. Thumping his tail on the dusty floor, he waited for her invitation to return to her side.

Darrick rose and touched her stiffened shoulders. "Your head must ache terribly. Do you wish me to help you with it?"

She turned and propped her cheek on her folded arms and offered silence for an answer.

Peering from above, he did his best not to notice a portion of her skirt, trapped under a well-turned hip, had drawn the material taut against her round bottom. Although the sight was a pleasant one to behold, her silent disregard for his simple question was maddening.

Breasts filled his vision, straining against the thin fabric of her gown. The valley formed between her breasts begged his lips to slide along the crevice. A curtain of honey-colored tresses draped over her shoulder.

He touched the silken strands. With each stroke of his fingers, the scent of roses and heather enfolded him, wrapping around his being. He was lost completely when her lips parted with a faint sigh.

His mind wandered in a field of wildflowers. They offered an oasis where he would willingly lay his weary head and rest, losing himself in their lustrous beauty.

He could see that she was peeking between her lashes; pretending to sleep. Darrick drew back from the enchantment and let her hair fall through his fingers. "Come Sabine."

"Go away. Don't require your help," she mumbled into her arm.

"I believe otherwise."

Tucking one arm around her shoulders and one under her rounded bottom, he lifted her with ease. He placed her on the stool that stood by the fire. The flames danced across her cheeks, illuminating her ashen face. Despite his earlier efforts to wash the stain of dried blood, it stuck to her temple.

Her every curve spoke defiance; her back, ramrod stiff; her slender arms, folded across her chest. She clenched her jaw. Her lush lips thinned with irritation. "What, no putrid swill for me to drink?"

He held her gaze. Although her vexation was apparent, he would not relent. "We'll have to make do with what little we have."

As Sabine opened her mouth to complain, Darrick silenced her with a look that refused an argument. "There'll be no more talk of this. We haven't the time to argue."

He pulled his thoughts together. If not for the meddlesome delays, he would be well on his way, battling those who attempted to conquer his lands and family. He knew how he would normally handle the attack if it were he and his men-at-arms. It would be a simple matter of laying siege to the castle and wait them out. Time was precious. With every delay, Nathan became entangled deeper into DePierce's dark plot. But his friend must wait.

Darrick needed to find his nephew before the trail grew too cold. Once he found Chance, he must get him to safety. Perhaps he should heed his conscience and dispatch Sabine and the babe to the convent. Some would say he was being too cautious. 'Twas only a woman and child. The hazards of war. He certainly did not hold a tender spot in his heart for the maiden. Yet, he could not ignore the fact that she and his nephew were the last connection he had to Elizabeth.

Darrick brushed Sabine's hair from her cheek. Tilting her chin, he looked into her defiant eyes. No, he would not let her leave his side until he liberated Nathan from the tower dungeon. He would find a way to force her to tell him what she remembered of Balforth.

He hastened to complete the task of bandaging the cut at her temple. He buried his concern behind a mask of indifference and focused on pulling the needle through the delicate skin. The neat little stitches would knit the folds together as they healed. She would have a scar but 'twas better than the alternative of death.

"Breath, Sabine. Inhale. Then exhale."

"Easy enough for you to say," she snapped. "'Tis my flesh that is getting stuck. Not yours."

Darrick lifted an eyebrow. "Really? If memory serves me, I believe I, too, carry a few fresh stitches added to my collection."

After neatly tying off the thread that held her flesh together, he gently cleaned away the blood that trailed down her face. Using the egg he had found in a basket, he sealed the edges of the wound with the white. The route for infection would then be cut off. The simple procedure had helped many of his men injured in combat. He prayed this too would work for Sabine.

Finished, he lifted her chin with the back of his knuckles and examined his work. "I didn't thank you properly for patching up my wound. Did I?"

"Unnecessary," she ground out through clenched teeth.

"Oh, but my lady, I do disagree." He replied with a tone that forbade any further argument, "Upon my honor as a knight, the code does say one must be chivalrous towards as dainty and chaste a lady as yourself."

Tickling her nape with the brush of his words, he whispered. "I fear you must accept it. I am avowed to show my gratitude for your care."

He nuzzled the lobe of her ear and nibbled on the tender flesh. He felt her flesh ripple with excitement as his teeth brushed her neck. His lips traveled further, slowly devouring her collarbone. With each delicate site, he decided to camp for a while, enjoy the sweet nectar of her body.

Sabine's rigid back began to thaw. Her arms lifted and draped around his neck. She melted into his chest. Devouring his lips, she traced his every move with her mouth. She pressed toward him, wanting more. A sigh rippled in her throat.

The tempo of arousal shifted as she moved in. He strained against his chausses, his body urging him to find release. "If it pleasures you—" Her answer came as she cupped the back of his head and arched her back.

He methodically traveled further to the rise of her breasts. Lifting each globe in his hands, he teased the succulent buds bringing them to arousal. He brushed his thumb across her nipples as they stood up proudly, pressing against the bodice of her gown. Releasing the ribbon that held the bodice together, he pushed the fabric off her shoulders.

Increasing the advances of his campaign, he drew each aroused bud to his lips. His tongue danced around her silken flesh, promising more to come. Each time he circled, he brought his mouth a little closer. He could not lift his gaze from the glorious vision. Each one, tipped with a budding rose, waiting to be plucked. They beckoned his lips to come and feast once more. Devouring the treat, he retraced his path up past her slender neck, following the cords straining for his touch.

Finding his way to her mouth, he renewed his assault. His tongue danced around her lips in light circles. Each time he brought his dance closer, capturing, and gently tugging, whispering his deep appreciation. Lost in their kiss, they propelled down a path that neither could readily turn away from.

With Sabine cradled in his arms, he gripped her delectable bottom. The notion that he would be the first to delve into her innermost secrets aroused him further. Not one for attachments, he never ventured towards the thought of deflowering a virgin. He could not ignore the longing; it was imperative he experience her exquisite charms.

Moving towards the cot, they became entangled in the gown pooling at her waist. Stopping to gain their balance, not a word was required as they simmered under each other's heated gaze. Darrick let Sabine slide slowly from his arms, holding her close as her body grazed his chest. Gliding down his aroused flesh, she brushed against his need that threatened to escape his hose. Desire rose, shutting out all other thought from his mind.

Thunder rose with a low growl. The white of the hound's teeth glaring, his lopsided, bandaged head stood out in the reflection from the fire.

Darrick pressed his fingers to Sabine's lips, quieting her inevitable questions. He listened for the sounds that alarmed his trusted friend. Cursing his lack of self-control, he blew out the lamp's flame. Dashing water on the fire in the hearth, he pulled her with him.

Turning sharply to brace his back against the door, the sudden movement brought renewed pain. He had forgotten about his wound while he nibbled on her delectable morsels. Darrick cursed his behavior. He meant to melt the icy wall she had erected, to punish her for her defiance. But her response in his arms had proven too much for him to maintain his disciple.

Although honed from years of battle, his soldier's senses were dulled by his preoccupation with her many charms. He should have heard the movements out in the brush long before the dog had time to sound the alarm.

Here was his proof: Women were a dangerous distraction. They turned a man's brain to jelly. Pure and simple, women should remain by the hearth, far away from their men.

* * * *

Sabine shivered from the cold that seemed to seep through every stitch of clothing. Darrick's body no longer heated hers with a consuming passion. Their fire that flamed bright had died as quickly and efficiently as the flames in the hearth, doused with freezing cold reality. All that remained were soggy embers.

Huddled by the wall, she folded her arms across her chest. She had been prepared to freely give herself to someone she barely knew. Let alone trusted. All that she knew of him would not even fill a bird's nest.

Her hand brushed over her sensitive breasts. Shamed at what he must think of her wantonness engulfed her thoughts. She had been selfish, thinking only of her pleasure and not of his nephew. If not for Darrick's glorious kisses and his maddening tongue, they would have rid themselves of this wretched place. Just thinking of his sizzling caress brought images of what might have been. He awakened dangerous feelings in her body that she could not explain. There would be trouble if she were to allow those unfamiliar feelings to continue.

A rustling outside tore Sabine from her thoughts. Leaves crackled, rubbing together as someone attempted to slip up on the cottage. Footsteps drew toward the front of the cottage, clumsily crushing the vegetation underfoot.

Thunder charged the door. He pitched forward, his haunches braced should something try to break through the door.

Darrick stroked Sabine's arm, and whispered, "Stay where you are. I'll let you know when it is clear for you to move."

She gestured her protest but was cut short by the glare from his steely eyes.

"Find a weapon," he commanded, as he slipped into the darkened corner, adding as an afterthought, "Do not light any fires while I am gone."

Sabine rolled her eyes toward the heavens asking for patience with the man. Had she not survived on her own before he dropped into her life?

"Of course not. I'm not a fool," she muttered to the empty room.

As soon as the words were spoken, she wished them back. He had indeed promised to care for her. And her head no longer thumped in cadence with her heart. She tested her love-swollen lips with the tip of her tongue to see if she could taste him. Sabine wrinkled her brow. How could she have let him leave the cottage? Perhaps she was a fool after all.

Chapter 13

After growing accustomed to the pitch-black room, Sabine moved around the cottage gathering their few belongings. She touched Chance's blanket and imagined it wrapped around his tiny body. She stuffed it in her pack.

Turning towards the table, she felt along the floor where she had fallen. Her fingers skimmed across the rough plank boards that ran under the bed, searching for the dagger she had dropped. Her hand bumped against an iron ring attached to the floor. A trapdoor? Could it lead outside the cottage?

Thunder stayed by her side while she continued to look for the knife she had taken from Elizabeth's pouch. It was not really stealing, she argued. She had need of it and Elizabeth did not.

Carefully, she slid out from under the cot. On hands and knees, she crawled towards her pack. Feeling along the floorboards, she found the pouch. Inside, the cool, smooth metal of the mirror assured her that it was safe. The blurry reflection swirled in her hand, reflecting her uncertainty. Perhaps when they got to safety she would confess her sins and tell Darrick about the silver mirror. Its hidden secret. Her secret. But not yet.

She scrambled across the floor and dug her fingers into Thunder's coat. "Find Darrick. Bring him back."

The hound raced out the door.

Sabine's heart threatened to break through her chest. Something thumped against the wall. How many varmints surrounded the cottage? Her stomach overpowered her fear and growled. She crawled to the cupboards.

Half way to the hearth, she remembered the pot of stew hanging over the fire when she and Nathan first arrived. Left unattended, it had congealed into a thick paste and was a bit burnt; nevertheless, it would keep starvation at bay.

Sabine could not help but wonder what kept Darrick and Thunder. She moved toward the trap door.

Shoving the bed over, she slipped down the little hole and dropped her bundle of belongings down into the dank cavity. It was darker than she expected. Feeling in the pocket of her skirt, she felt the candlesticks she had placed there earlier. Afraid to light the wick too soon, she waited, holding the trap door open.

Seconds turned into minutes and still Thunder did not return with Darrick. Sabine tugged the neck of her gown. Sweat trickled down her back. She was about to climb out of the hole when a commotion came from the corner of the room.

Thunder slipped through the opening of the window, followed by his master.

"Sabine," Darrick called, his voice strained with urgency. "Where are you? DePierce's men are not sparing the horses and ride at full speed towards the cottage."

She motioned toward the shaft in the floor, and then realized his sight was limited by the lack of light.

"Sabine? They carry torches. The roof will be on fire in no time at all. Come on, love. Answer me. Where are you?"

Sabine popped her head out of the hole in the floor. "Down here. 'Tis another way out."

Darrick turned toward her voice. "What have we got here, lass? Have you an idea where it leads?"

"No, but it holds promise of leading away from this dreadful place. You said so yourself, that soon the roof will be on fire."

Darrick warily eyed the little hole. "I cannot fathom how my shoulders will fit."

Sabine watched the great man who knelt beside her. Even in the shadows of the room, she could see the perspiration trail down his pale face. His hands, clenched in fists, rested at his hips.

"How do you know 'tis better than this?" he asked.

She touched his hand. "Darrick, we must take that chance. You said they come to burn the cottage. They do not want survivors or any trace of our being here."

Getting no response from him, she grabbed his wrist and tugged. "'Tis all right," she reassured. "You will fit wonderfully in here. I remember Nandra used to have a tunnel like this under her cottage in the woods near Clearmorrow. As a child, I played in it. I promise you, 'twas quite safe."

The sound of horses charging towards the cottage was like a storm brewing overhead. The flames flickered against the little window as the band of men drew closer. They would have to be well through the tunnel if they were to escape the damages of the smoke.

She tugged on him again. "We'll put Thunder through first. With that miraculous nose of his, he will lead us to the other end."

His lips stretched into a snarl. "I hate the thought of dying without putting up a fight." He motioned her to give him room. "I'll join you just as soon as I gather our things."

"I already have them."

His brows rose in appreciation. "Busy wench. Well then, move over."

Sabine climbed down the ladder. Picking up the bundle, she moved over to the side of the tunnel.

Thunder's hind legs pawed franticly at the tunnel walls. Once he reached the floor, she soothed the beast's fur. "Easy, boy. Think of all the wonderful smells you can follow down here."

Darrick dropped beside them and shut the trap door. With their only light removed, everything went dark.

Sabine took the candle she had stuffed in the pocket of her gown. She pulled out a flint.

Darrick stilled her hand. "We don't know if there is fresh air down here. As you pointed out before, we'll follow Thunder's lead. He has a keen sense of survival. If there is a way, he will find it."

They began their journey through the tunnel. Darrick held the scruff of Thunder's neck, following wherever he led. They paused as a tiny breeze fluttered past their faces.

"Do you feel it?" Sabine asked. "Do you feel the air? The opening must be close by. Now may we light use candle to light our path?"

Darrick waited for the breeze. At his side, Thunder sniffed about on the floor, interested in pushing on, and not positioning for a fight. "'Tis safe. Light the wick."

The flame sputtered and then illuminated the surrounding walls. Darrick rested his back against the damp rock. Shoulders hunched, he tucked his head down to keep from scraping the roof of the tunnel. His tight smiled returned. "Obviously this rabbit-hole was made for a person of smaller stature."

He ran his fingers down her cheek and pressed his palm against her neck. "Can you make it a little farther?"

Sighing, she leaned against his hands drawing strength and energy from his presence. She traced his mouth and brow with dirt-smudged fingers. "I'm rested and ready to leave this place."

He pushed himself off against the wall and captured her fingers. "Your wish is my desire, my lady." He kissed the back of her hand. "Thunder," he called. "Lead on."

Darrick cursed as the scent of smoke swirled past their heads. "I fear they've torched the cottage. There's no turning back now. I pray we find the way out before the tunnel fills with smoke."

Running at a trot, they followed the dog until he stopped at the end of the tunnel. Pacing the floor, Thunder whined and scratched at the wall.

"A dead end," Sabine cried. "We should have stayed and taken our escape as you wanted."

Darrick placed his hands on her shoulders and gave a reassuring squeeze. "We're not finished yet. Give me a moment."

Sabine released the heavy bundle and watched Darrick run his hands along the wall of earth. She followed the patterns that he drew on the dusty stone.

The stench of smoke began to wrap its tentacles around their heads. Foul air surrounded them, filling their lungs.

"We're almost there. I believe I found the entrance. Just a bit covered up is all."

Darrick began to dig. She pressed towards him, determined to help. Taking the dagger from her waist, she held it out. "Here, use this. See if it will help dig us out of here."

He winced as another cough tore through his injured ribs. He dug around the rock, hidden under the dirt. With the blade of the knife, he found the crease in the wall. One more cut of the blade and the light filtered through the crack.

"If we give one big push we should be able to leave this place."

"Wait!" Sabine squealed, grabbing Darrick's shoulder. "Nandra had a lever that triggered the door to open, but if forced, it would bring the ceiling crashing down on top of the intruder. Feel along the wall. In the corner should be a wedge of rock. You'll find a trigger to open the door."

Following Sabine's directions, Darrick found the lever. It was nestled beside the wedge of rocks, just as she had warned. Flipping the iron peg back, the door opened slightly.

Smoke swirled as they shoved against the door. Darrick held them all in check, refusing to allow anyone to rush out to the fresh air. Crawling through the narrow doorway, he hid behind the bushes that wrapped around the entrance. With a silent gesture, he motioned Sabine to join him behind the brush.

Crawling out of the tunnel, Sabine sucked in all the fresh air she could gather into her lungs. He crawled over to give her a hand to pull the door shut. They glanced at each other and shared a moment of relief.

"We made it, love. A sorry sight, but we are still breathing. We will have to travel a little further. I know you are hungry but I don't want to wait around for someone to remember the tunnel." He pointed to the flickering light of the torches as the men searched through the trees. "Let's go. They are moving about us."

"How do we know which way to go? We may never find Chance and Nathan if Thunder cannot find their scent."

"Do you have something that belongs to Chance in that bundle of yours?"

Darrick took the blanket Sabine immediately produced and held it under Thunder's nose. Without a sound, Darrick motioned him to follow the scent.

"He won't allow us to cross paths with the band of men. We'll travel towards Chance's location first. Nathan would not want it any other way."

Hungry and exhausted, they traveled only a short distance before they could journey no farther. Darrick found a shelf of rock that sheltered them from the night air and gave them a wall to protect their backs.

Daylight seeped out of the sky. Sabine's stomach growled as she sat beside him. Darrick rubbed his side. Shadows emphasized the weary bruising under his eyes. Pushing up from the old tree stump, he bent over and rested his hands on his knees.

"Where do you think you are going?" Sabine hissed. "You must rest."

He rubbed the back of his neck. Fatigue made his shoulders droop. "We need food to sustain us."

Warmth washed over her as she looked up at the bedraggled knight who towered over her. Even covered in dirt he was still her protector.

"What would you say if I told you we already have our food for the night?"

She pulled out the clay pot and lifted the lid. The scent of stew rolled out, wafting up to greet their hungered senses. "'Tis cold and pasty but looks to be a filling mixture." She answered the questioning look he gave her as he lifted his raven eyebrows. "I found it simmering over the hearth in the cottage."

Darrick warily eyed the cold congealed stew. He gave a sample to Thunder, allowing him to taste it before they did. "The dog has keener senses and will leave it alone if 'tis unfit to eat."

Together, they watched the sample disappear. Thunder sat, wagging his tail, waiting for another morsel.

Darrick handed the pot back to Sabine. "My friend here says 'tis safe to eat. However, we'll rest on the side of caution and watch him for a time.

You truly are a wonder. Do you have any more tricks up your sleeve? Some ale or wine perhaps to wash it down?"

Sabine shook her head. "I didn't have the time." She bit her lip, peering through the dark at the dog lying down at her feet. "Will Thunder be all right? Do you really think she poisoned it?"

Hearing his name, the hound lifted his head from his paws and thumped his tail on the ground. Wriggling closer on all fours, he scratched his way towards her feet. Finally, close enough to be within reach, he rolled over on his back to have his belly scratched. His pink tongue lolled out in something oddly resembling a grin and waited patiently for his new mistress to pay attention to him.

"We won't be safe for the night where we are. But we dare not travel in the dark without a mount." Darrick shook his head. "Or the ability to light a torch. The soldiers would see it from a great distance. I have to find us shelter."

He rose again and this time, Sabine did not question his orders. His gaze searched the growing shadows. He paused and then without explanation, he left her side.

She hid along the rocky wall. The longer she waited for his return, the more her fear grew. Her palms sweated. Her heart stuttered with every sound. How long could she wait for his return? Sabine tensed.

A shadow came toward her, stealing her breath. Was it DePierce? Fear froze her mind. The scream locked in her throat.

Darrick stepped out of the shadows. "We must move."

"Saints." Sabine hugged her legs, resting her forehead on her knees.

"Make haste, my lady. The soldiers are nearby."

Chapter 14

Stumbling, Sabine caught an overhanging branch with a free hand and held on. "I cannot go on. This is madness. 'Tis too steep. We shall surely die from our fall."

"Death will only come if you don't move your feet and continue to provide your backside as a target for the bowman."

The distance to the ground made her insides tilt off balance. "Leave me. Save yourself and the others."

"Sabine, don't be so foolish. Let go. The bush will not hold your weight much longer. See here," he pointed, "the roots have begun to pull away from the earth."

"I cannot," she whispered.

Darrick climbed back down. Prying her fingers from the slim branch, he wrapped his strong fingers around her wrist, tugging her towards the rocky ledge. Squeezing her hand, he looked at her bruised face and smiled, hoping to reassure her.

"I won't allow you to die."

Together, they reached the ledge that loomed overhead. Shrubbery covered the entrance to a cave-like formation. Behind the bushes, the crevice yawned deeper into the ground. It gradually widened, drawing them into the cave's mouth.

"We'll rest for the night and break camp when day breaks." Lifting his head, he sniffed the air. "Do you smell it?"

He led the way deeper into the cave. Following the scent of damp rock, they neared the edge of a pool. The floor was smooth. The rough edges rubbed smooth by many years of water lapping at the white stone. Moisture gathered and dripped from the ceiling, pooling in deep pockets dug into the stone. Locating a dry spot in which to rest, Darrick laid his cloak upon the floor and motioned her to sit. "Rest."

He settled his back against the cave wall. Sabine sighed and snuggled closer. The warmth drew them, pulling them into a swirl of misty thoughts.

* * * *

Sabine fought the dream but could not escape its web. Perspiration slid down her nose. Her head throbbed.

She had returned to her home and hid in her great bed with the pillow over her head. Unable to ignore the sounds, she peeked out from the edge of her blanket. She called out for her father and mother. No one came. She started to call for Taron's help, and stopped. Her brother had disappeared. She could not remember why. Perhaps off fighting for the king?

She had wriggled off her high bed. Stumbling when she hit the floor, she wondered at the size of her hands and feet.

She was a little girl again, alone, and afraid.

The window in her bedchamber opened out to the bailey. She stood on tiptoe to reach the ledge and looked out.

Although night had come to Clearmorrow, the skies were alight with dancing flames licking at the sky. Women were screaming, running with their children in their arms. Those who fell were left behind to fend for themselves.

A dragon grabbed at them, its roar ripped through the air. The home she had known all her life was torn asunder with each swipe of its claws. With every swing, it knocked down the heavy stones of the great wall that had always protected her.

The villagers were at her bedroom door, pounding, pleading for her to come and soothe the dragon's ire. "Make peace with it, my lady. You have but to give it what it desires. Send it away."

Sabine ran to bar the door. Could they not understand she was just a little girl? Pressing her forehead against the door, she cried, "There is naught that I can do."

No matter how she tried to ignore them, the pounding and wailing continued. Running to the small archers' window, she peeked from behind the opened shutter. The beast stood amongst the destruction.

The old woman was there. Nandra stood beside the dragon. Sabine called out to her friend, but the woman began changing until she became the dragon's twin.

Sabine raced towards the solar. She would find safety there. The dragons followed close behind. There was no hiding from the beasts.

She slammed the doors shut. Her father's bow hung over the fireplace in the great hall. She took it down. The weight of the bow knocked her back. Bracing her feet against the wooden frame, she grabbed the line strung across the ends. With trembling fingers, she stretched the strings and nocked the arrow.

She swung open the shutter. The dragons' fiery breath scorched her face. Surrounded by the pair, she could not decide which direction to aim. Freezing with indecision, she shut her eyes and prayed for help.

Her eyes snapped open in time to see a giant swan flying overhead. Its wingspan, so vast, the dragon's flames were extinguished. The giant swan landed upon the balcony and motioned Sabine to climb upon its back, promising to carry her up into the clouds.

Sitting astride the great swan, she dug her fingers under the soft down hidden beneath its feathers. Looking from high above her castle, she knew the dragons were still alive. 'Twas then that she vowed she would never give them what they wanted. One day, she would return and fight the dragons.

Much to her surprise the great swan turned to look at her with startling gray eyes and spoke. "You will fight. But the next time you will not be alone. I promise."

Tears streamed down her cheeks, Sabine buried her face in the soft feathers as the winds wove through her hair.

Chapter 15

Darrick knelt beside the sleeping Sabine. Despite all that she had been through, she still retained her beauty. He held a piece of crispy meat under her nose to awaken her.

"Hungry? Thunder is willing to share. He found a warren of rabbits. Took him a while to convince them to give up their lives, but he can be very persuasive."

Sabine sat up and rested her back against the cave wall. She dodged his look, choosing to examine the charred meat he shoved in her face. She snagged the hunk of meat and stuffed it in her mouth.

"My lady has an appetite today?"

Keeping her eyes averted, she daintily licked her lips. Speaking past the wad of meat, she mumbled. "'Tis Delicious! But are you certain 'twas safe to leave? What if something had happened?"

Darrick's gray eyes snapping, he answered coldly. "Thunder and I are capable of discerning when to hunt."

"What of your injury?" she persisted. "You might have fallen and reopened your wound."

"I assure you, it doesn't slow me down a whit. I've ridden nonstop, day and night, with worse injuries than this."

"'Tis not safe. You said so yourself."

"I also know when the need outweighs the danger," he snapped back.

"Oh? Of course, that is why we ran our horses into the ambush. 'Twas guaranteed safe then too."

It irritated him to no end that she continued to question his abilities. He was a highly skilled knight of the realm. At the prime age of fourteen, he was already advanced in the art of armed combat and subterfuge. Rode by his king as a Knight of the Swan. He'd led his battalion of men into battles ever since he could remember. What could this troublesome woman possibly teach him that he did not already know? Her questions rubbed at his raw nerves.

"How, indeed." His glacier stare held hers. "You knew what would happen when we rode out. I have to ask myself how that foreknowledge came to pass."

Darrick scooped up the blade beside Sabine. He tossed it in the air. Blunt-end-over-pointed-end, the jeweled knife flipped. The jewels glittered under the light of the torch. The hilt of the blade landed heavily in his hand.

He stood by the torch. His fingers danced over the gilded edges. An emerald stone, representing the green eye of a swan, winked back. He flipped it again.

Peering closer, his breath blew out in a whisper. "How is it possible that I missed it?"

His mind raced back. His concentration had been distracted by Sabine's tantalizing charms. At the time, he did not notice the familiarity of the blade he lifted from the bundle she had been carting around ever since he found her. Prepared for another sleepless night, his only thought was set on escaping the confines of the cave.

A sense of urgency sent his blood racing. His glanced toward Sabine. She nervously chewed on her bottom lip. Her liquid brown eyes watched the blade twirling and reflecting in the light of the fire.

Darrick hissed as he let out the breath he had been holding. His nostrils flared. Turning on her, he held out the blade. "Where did you get this?"

Sabine edged away from the threatening dagger. She nervously tucked the folds of her skirt around her legs, refusing to look at him, or the blade.

His mood disintegrated until his clenched jaw felt like it would shatter. He was determined to have all the answers from her. Her denial would not be allowed. After all, did not the bards sing of his cold determination when the battle lines were drawn? Even his men knew not to cross his direct orders. This woman cowering before him would learn to answer to his mandates.

Silence echoed in the cavern. Darrick scowled, unflinching, waiting for Sabine to finally find her voice. She surprised him when she leaped up, and stood toe to toe.

Her hands balled into fists. Teetering on tiptoes, she leaned in with a defiant stare. "Your sister was carrying a pack with her. That dagger was in her pack."

Bemused, he watched the maiden turn into a fighting shrew. He lifted a suspicious brow. Why did she overreact to his question? In fact, she did look as if she was caught thieving a pastry from cook's bakery. Inhaling her womanly scent, he knew they were standing dangerously close. The sweet perfume was wrapping its tentacles around his senses. Shaking his head to clear it from distracting thoughts, he forced his jaw to unclench. He exhaled and kept his voice to a cool ripple. "'Tis a simple question. Perhaps you misunderstood. If so, accept my apology. However, you will explain, again, how you came to have this in your possession."

Sabine snorted. Stalling, she fiddled with the dirty gown.

Darrick watched her agitation mount. She was behaving like a mad woman. One moment indignant and raging at him and the next, she got all nervous and twitchy. He narrowed his gaze. She stood in front of him, her little nose almost pressed to his chest. He wagered she was dreaming about revenge and sticking the blade in his back.

Wondering what she would do next, he relaxed, comforted by the knowledge that he was the one that held the jeweled dagger. He vowed to allow her only one more moment to her thoughts, and then he would have his answers.

She brushed at the tears streaking down her cheeks. "What importance could the dagger possibly have?"

"Ah, your questions have returned. Why is it that you can never give a simple answer?" Seeing she did not plan to respond, Darrick smiled thinly and sighed, weighing his answer. "'Tis special. It was in my father's possession. A talisman he kept with him at all times. Hidden in his boot." Fear of how it came into his sister's pack constricted his chest. "Only those he knew well or those that felt the sting of his blade had knowledge of this dagger. Perhaps my sister was responsible for his death."

"No! Darrick, you're wrong. Elizabeth would not hurt your father."

"What proof do you have? People can be pushed to do things they would never dream of themselves."

"I have no proof, but I know she did not carry the coldness in her heart to kill. She gave her life to distract her murderer from harming Chance. 'Tis not an act of a killer."

Deep in thought, he stroked his chin. 'Twas not often that he was told he was wrong. It did not sit well this time, either.

"When I received word of my father's death, it came on the whispers of an ambush of mercenaries. Elizabeth's disappearance set other questions to flight. Yet now all I find of my father or my sister is a knife that connects them in some way. My sister would have been with the ones who killed my father."

"'Tis usually more than one snake in the nest," Sabine murmured.

Darrick handled the sharpened dagger, watching the metal blade flash against the firelight. The stone in the swan's eye winked back, daring him to understand the secret that it held.

"What is it about the dagger that mystifies?" Sabine stood beside him. "The first time I held the blade, I felt it too."

"The weight is wrong." He frowned at the jeweled hilt. "'Tis been a long time since I have seen it. I was a child the last time my father allowed me to touch his precious blade. There was a special secret about the handle but I cannot recall it at the moment."

He sat down and ran his hands over the gilt handle. He barely noticed when Sabine sat down beside him. His fingers danced along the edge and around the blade. A slow smile lifted the corners of his mouth. "I remember now. There is a hidden compartment. Father used it to carry missives for the king."

He slid his fingers over the handle; this time feeling carefully for any irregularities. He noticed one tiny stone. It was raised a bit more than the others. Pressing on the side of the swan's head, the emerald eye clicked and a miniature lever on the handle flipped up. The hilt opened, revealing its secrets.

A rolled up piece of fabric peeked out of the handle. It was wrapped around something hard and lumpy. Holding his breath, he unrolled the last bit of cloth, revealing a man's ring. He touched the ring, tracing the design that resembled a swan's head.

Sabine gasped. "It cannot be!"

Startled, Darrick turned to Sabine. Even in the poor lighting, he could see she was disturbed by its presence. "What is it?"

"My brother, Taron…" She whispered, reaching out to touch the glittering ring. "'Tis my brother's ring. I am certain."

"When did you last hear from your brother?"

"I don't recall, 'twas so long ago." She shook her finger under his nose. "You are wrong, Sir Darrick. My brother would never cause your family harm. He's counted among King Henry's favorites. King Henry himself gifted my brother with that ring."

Drilling her finger into his chest, she added to her brother's defense. "Taron's only fault is that he was never home to protect our lands. He could never deny our king anything. He may always be away on business for his wretched friend, but he loves Clearmorrow. I am certain of it. Do not dare to think of harming him. He is the only family I have left."

In her agitation, her hand banged into his and the fabric fluttered to the ground. On the backside was a faded scrawled message.

Darrick knelt and slowly lifted the material from the floor. In her rush to see, Sabine narrowly missed bumping into his head.

"If you could be patient, I will discover what it says. Sit over there," he commanded, pointing to the cloak. As a second thought, he added with a growl. "If you please."

Sabine folded her arms. "I'm not about to move from this spot. If Taron is involved in some way, I want to know what has happened."

The woman was too stubborn by far. He feared that one day it would land her into more trouble than she had ever known. A chill spilled down his spine. "So be it. Deal with whatever gruesome details that might be written in the missive." Moving the torn bit of fabric in the light, he noted, "The fabric comes from a lawn shirt."

Once white, the material had faded to a dirty gray and sprinkled with brown. Perhaps dried blood, splattered from a wound. Scratched out in brown was a smudged message that he read silently. *'Many lives at stake. Stop DePierce. Protect the bearer of this message as if one of your own. Sir Taron of Clearmorrow.'*

He folded the note and tucked it inside his belt. *How can I protect her? Would she recognize the stains for what they are?*

Sabine held her hand out for the missive and waited in silence.

His better judgment warred with her determined gaze. Knowing she would not be deterred from reading the note herself, he laid it in her hand.

Her fingers trembled as she spread out the bit of fabric and traced the line of each letter.

"Dear Lord, 'tis as I feared. Those bits of brown stain could have very easily come from Taron's broken body."

When she looked up, her horror tore at Darrick's soul.

"Are we too late to help anyone?" Grief-stricken, she shook her head. "'Tis my fault. I waited too long."

He smoothed her tousled hair from her face.

"No, this only means we are certain of our enemy. Your brother must have been at Balforth Castle with my sister. He may yet live and we will not stop until we know for sure. But we must first find my nephew." He tilted her face to look at him. The anguish he felt reflected in her eyes. "You said you had all of my sister's possessions with you. I would have you show them to me now."

Sabine fetched the few remaining things she had managed to carry. She knelt with the bundle and carefully untied the string. First, she withdrew a small bag of coins, then a silver hairbrush. Her hand dropped hesitantly over the silver mirror.

Darrick stared at the odd collection of items Elizabeth chose to carry. He willed them to tell the tale of his sister's last days. The danger of delivering the baby at Balforth must have been very great. She packed as if knowing she would have to travel fast. Did she know she carried a note in the handle? Did she understand the significance that both her brother and father possessed the same symbol as Sir Taron?

Could Taron be his nephew's father? Although unconsecrated by the church and born out of wedlock, the thought of young Chance fathered by anyone other than Hugh was much easier to stomach. The idea of someone as vile as Hugh or Vincent DePierce touching his sister filled him with rage.

Darrick ran his hands over the growth of beard. How did Sabine fit into this? Why did DePierce want her dead? What did she know that she had yet to reveal? His thoughts came to a halt; she did it to him again. Every time he questioned her fear of returning to Balforth, she managed to distract him. Perhaps now was the best time as any to pry the truth from her.

Frantic barking echoed in the cave, interrupting his plans.

Sabine wrestled with Thunder, trying to make the dog let go of the blanket. Every time she tore it away and stuffed it back in her bundle, he pulled it out and ran to the tunnel that led from the back of the cave. The hair on Thunder's back stood on end. His legs quivered with excitement. Trotting over, he dropped the blanket at Darrick's feet and waited for him to follow. When Darrick did not move, Thunder lay down and groaned.

Her eyes wide with fear, she whispered out of the corner of her mouth. "Is it the stew?" She blinked twice, anxiously chewing her lips. "Do you think it was tainted?"

Darrick shook his head. "No."

"Well then," pushing the hair from her face, she squared her shoulders, "you cannot allow him to tear up the baby's blanket. Kindly find the foolish hound something else to play with."

He waved her quiet. "He's found the scent. Pack up your things," he ordered. "We've not a moment to lose."

Thunder waited, eyes glittering, his haunches quivered with anticipation.

Chapter 16

Sabine jogged to keep up with the knight and his hound. They followed a narrow passageway she would never have found had she been searching on her own. They made an abrupt turn to the right and she ran into Darrick.

Sabine snatched her hands from the small of his back. He might have well been a chunk of ice. His questions hung between them. Her nerves were coiled. She would rather he would begin and be done with it.

She had intended to tell him about the letter hidden in the back of the mirror, and the unspeakable crimes she had seen DePierce commit. Her body trembled whenever she let the past drift in. It haunted her dreams when she slept and haunted her thoughts during the day. The memories were too fresh…too real.

The night she had appeared at his gate, begging for help, DePierce was overjoyed. His mouth had twisted in a soulless smile. In his excitement, he informed her that he had been expecting her and her chamber was already prepared for her stay. He knew what had happened at Clearmorrow before she could retell her harrowing experience. He had known before the attack had taken place.

Set on attaining what he wished, he was willing to punish her family in the process. Situated comfortably in a significant position of society, his lineage called for respect, none of which he could personally lay claim to.

DePierce's muddled honor placed her into a narrow room in the tower instead of the dungeon with the other survivors from Clearmorrow. Typically cold and drafty, the chamber was barren of all furnishings, save for the hard cot. There was not one single thin blanket to warm her limbs. Not one chunk of wood left for the fireplace. She would have been overjoyed to find even a threadbare tapestry to cover herself, but that too had been nonexistent. She found little comfort that first night. But, unlike the village girls he had taken from their homes, her plight was vastly different.

With Rhys's help, she was able to escape through the latrine hole before DePierce's henchmen could do their worst. She never would comprehend why Rhys had been willing to risk his life for her.

Her departure from Balforth may have put the others in jeopardy. The blood on Taron's shirt was a stark reminder of the duty entrusted to her. She was to protect her home. She had failed her family and people.

Guilt weighed heavily on her heart as she stumbled through the cave. Panic began to build. Would they ever find the exit? Moisture streamed down her face and traveled through the valley of her breasts. She let her gaze bore into Darrick's broad shoulders.

Shoving the dark thoughts back into the corner of her mind, she reviewed her plan once they found Chance. "How long do you think we have been crawling through this tunnel?"

Darrick answered her with freezing silence and moved on. Without missing a step, he motioned her to speed up.

She was weary and sore from the blow to her head. Struggling to keep up she wondered how he was able to go on without rest. Her head pounding, she pushed on, determined not to hold him back. She prayed they would find the baby at the end of the underground passage.

"Surely your side must ache from the exertion so soon after your injury."

His silence echoed against the pale white rock. Only the faint sounds of their breathing could be heard.

"We have to come to the end soon." A hint of cool air brushed against her sweat-dampened cheek.

He stared up at the rocky ledge. The burrow narrowed to a steep crawlspace before it opened up to the hole in the earthen wall.

A gentle breeze ruffled Thunder's thick black fur. Sensing their newfound freedom, the dog quickly scrambled up the stony ledge, showing them the way out.

Darrick pulled himself up the stone ledge. He gripped the rough boulders with one arm and held out his hand.

Looking up, Sabine's head spun dizzily. As much as she wanted out of the tunnel, her fear of letting her feet leave the solid secure surface of the ground almost took over. Shifting her gaze, she focused on the strength of Darrick's outstretched hand. His simple gesture to help her broke through fear's hold. Forcing her arm up, Sabine grasped his hand and began her climb to freedom.

Silently, they moved as one, to the top of the shelf of rocks, their feet clinging to the narrow ledge. Their fingers still entwined, they rested against the stone and let the cool, fresh air rush past.

Darrick tucked a few stray wisps of hair behind her ear. Tilting her chin, he looked deep into her eyes, pouring into her soul. Sabine swore he searched for the truth wrapped around her heart, for the secrets that she would keep to herself. Her frustration rising, she opened her mouth to complain, to tell him to search somewhere else. His finger sailed across her lips for silence. His mouth pressed to hers in a kiss, spreading warmth throughout her limbs.

His cold silence seemed to be forgotten for the time being. She almost hoped he had forgotten his questions, but she knew better. Three times the fool, she knew Sir Darrick, Knight of King Henry's realm, did not forget. Lives depended on him to keep a clear head.

Darrick lifted his mouth, and gazed around the cave. "How did that old woman climb up the face of the wall?"

Released from his embrace, Sabine's mind was a jumble. She could not imagine how she had allowed it to happen. He had immediately dismissed the stolen kiss, acting as if it never occurred. Of course, she had welcomed the distraction. It kept her from thinking about her feet standing where they did not belong. And that was the only reason, she decided, that she accepted his kiss.

Now that the brief distraction was no more, she noticed the cramped space in which they stood. She shook her head, fearing her feet would remain frozen to the ledge forever. Sabine closed her eyes, refusing to see how far off the ground they stood. Her knees quivered, threatening to collapse. Yet, he did not seem to notice anything amiss. How was this possible?

"Thunder is never wrong," he went on. "He would not lead us here without reason." Darrick's steel-gray eyes hooked on his prey. "Look," he pointed. "Over in the corner. 'Tis a coiled rope wedged in that needle-shaped crevice. Someone has traveled this way before."

A knotted rope, not far from their heads, hung from a wedge of rock. After testing its strength, he was satisfied it would hold his weight. He grasped the rope with one hand and braced his feet, pulling his body up to a wider ledge. Making a basket-swing with the rope, he dropped it down. "Put Thunder in the basket and I'll use the rock and rope as a pulley."

Sabine watched as the dog and the basket moved away, high over her head. Left alone, darkness moved in. Her resolve for bravery scattered in the tunnel's abyss. There was something she was to do, yet she could not quite grasp what it might be.

"Sabine," a voice called out, breaking through the fog in her mind. "'Tis your time." The blessed thick rope lowered. Blinking rapidly, she tried to focus on where to put her hands.

"Sit in the basket as you would a swing. I'll pull you up."

Fumbling with the knots, she sat down gingerly and held on for dear life. Focusing overhead, she watched the daylight break through the pitch black of the tunnel. When she reached the wide ledge, she tumbled out of the ropes and fell prostrate on the flat stone.

Darrick helped her to her feet and wiped the smudges of dirt from her cheek. "We're almost there."

He shoved through the ivy-covered entrance. Squeezing her fingers, he motioned Sabine to move quietly as they pushed their way out of the shrub-covered opening.

"Clearmorrow." She covered her mouth with dirt-smudged fingers and whispered, "I never knew this tunnel existed."

Judging from the growth over the mouth of the cave, the safety of her people had been in jeopardy for quite some time.

"Perhaps Nandra has returned with the baby."

The sun was setting behind what was left of the castle walls. A burned-out shell of its former self stood in front of them. Blackened timbers lay in abandoned heaps. Burned beyond recognition, where the great walls to the castle once stood, was now a pile of rubble. The tops of the buildings were spires of charred roofs. Slate shingles had fallen; allowing the weather to destroy what little remained.

"I never imagined it would be this bad."

She searched for something to lean on and her hand caught only air. She stumbled backwards. "This was my home." Under her breath, she added, "and I am responsible for its destruction."

* * * *

Darrick sat on a log with Sabine nestled in his lap. She had finally stopped pacing. Her sobs had ceased, except for the occasional hiccups that shook her body.

His warrior's mind took in the surrounding land. He was stunned by the lack of planning her father and brother had given to the protection of the castle. It was a prime spot of land and perhaps, at one time, the half-timber walls had been sufficient, but surely, by now, they would have known to fortify the walls with stone.

The main keep stood high upon a grassy knoll. High enough to see if anyone came by water. Their towers were positioned to look out over the water to the southern Welsh lands. The other towers would have overlooked the valley on either side. Aye, the location was a prime bit of land but one needed more than that to keep it safe. Was this the reason for DePierce to defy his king and take what was not his? For strength and power over others?

At first glance, it was obvious that there were many weaknesses in the protection of the land. His fists clenched. How long had this castle languished in careless hands. Hands of those who were away on the king's business, too busy to see about the protection of their loved ones. It amazed him that anyone survived.

Darrick shook his head. Why did DePierce lay fire to Clearmorrow? 'Twas smarter to leave the keep occupied by men-at-arms, protecting what they took. A siege always did less damage than fire. Why have the villagers destroyed? He could have had them working for him.

If DePierce was so eager for this land holding, why leave it unguarded? Darrick knew that if this castle were his to protect, his men would be camped out and rebuilding the outer wall, this time with stone. He would replace the half-timber keep with a strong wall of stone and rounded watchtowers fortifying every corner.

Sabine's hand trembled in his. He squeezed her fingers gently to reassure her. They moved to search the grounds. With a whispered word, Thunder walked cautiously by their side.

They carefully made their way towards the burned skeleton of the tower. The threat that they were not alone made the hair on the back of Darrick's neck stand on end. Sabine shivered, whether from the chill in the air or the painful memories, he did not know.

Shadows danced with the wind that blew on top of the craggy hill, flickering across the tumbled walls. Laughter pierced the cool night air. It echoed against the scarred stone that once was the great hall's fireplace.

Hand in hand, they rushed towards the eerie sound. With Darrick pulling her behind him, Sabine ran to keep up with his long strides. They stopped, keeping to the shadows.

Pressing their backs against the outer wall of what was left of the great hall, they watched with alarm.

Sabine clutched his arm and pointed.

Firelight danced across Nandra's face as she held the crying baby aloft.

"We'll show them, won't we my little one? Soon we'll have what is ours. Yes, we will. Yes, we will," she crooned, as she danced around the floor. Her tattered dress swayed as it dragged across the cold stone. Her gray hair had long since lost its pins and now hung at her waist.

Sabine slipped her hand out of his and lurched out into the center of the room. Worried that he would startle Nandra, causing more damage to the situation, he watched in horror, cursing Sabine's impulsive nature. Fear for Sabine and the tiny babe froze him in his tracks. Thunder bristled and struggled against his hold. Darrick hated to do it, but he knew he must wait it out and see what response Sabine would get from the old woman.

Nandra stopped crooning to the wailing baby, and stared at Sabine who had suddenly appeared in the fire-scarred room. Still swaying and dancing, Nandra peered closely. Her eyes widened, her lids pulled back in fear.

"Why are you here, Lady Mary?" she cried.

Sabine froze. Why did Nandra call her by her mother's name? She swallowed the questions in her jumbled mind and fell in with her ruse. "Yes, Nandra," Sabine stuttered. "'Tis I."

"I want what William promised me. And I intend to get it. Taking care of my own, I am."

"Mayhap I can help," Sabine offered.

"You know as well as I that men cannot be trusted with your heart. Not even family."

"'Tis your heart that needs repair." Sabine took another step closer.

Nandra shook her fist. "Do not come any closer, Lady Mary. I sent you away before. I will send you away again."

The old woman was backing away from her. Sabine could not allow the space between them to grow and took a hesitant step closer, following the crone. Holding out her hand, she commanded, "No, Nandra, not this time. Hold where you stand. You admit you took my life. You must repay what you have taken. Hand me the babe."

Nandra looked around wildly, backing towards the fire. "They'll be furious with me when they find out, won't they?"

"Please," Sabine pleaded. "Hand over the baby. He means nothing to you."

"No! You denied my child's birthright. This one here will bring me what is mine. It was promised."

Darrick slipped up from behind the deranged woman and waited for the right moment. He hoped Sabine had seen his movements in the shadows and was prepared to catch the babe should Nandra decide to let go.

She shuffled toward Darrick. She was in reach. He wrapped his arms around her middle as she lunged towards the fire with the baby. In the struggle, Chance fell from her grasp.

Sabine dived for the child and landed underneath to break his fall. She sucked in a shuddering breath.

Struggling against the deranged woman, Darrick could hear Thunder barking from the shadows. Fighting to get a clear line of vision, he prayed that Sabine would roll out of the way. He stumbled towards the hearth. His back to the old woman, he turned when Sabine called out his name. Thunder broke free of the shadows.

Nandra's silver hair spun in a cloud as her head slammed into the ledge of the hearth. The hound followed, sliding into the wall with a yelp. The old woman lay crumpled at his feet.

* * * *

Sabine knelt beside the old woman she had once called friend. Her hands shook as she rolled the motionless body over. Nandra had hit her head sharply against the hearth. Expecting to find the woman knocked witless, she found her frail body crumpled and lifeless.

She knew she should be relieved, knowing that the woman could not harm them any longer, but she was unable to find it in her heart. Someone or something had pushed Nandra to the point of madness. With her passing, she may never know the truth. Looking up, she found Darrick standing close beside her.

He knelt down. "Go on, Sabine, take care of Chance. I'll do what needs to be done and will join you in a moment."

Grateful for his help, Sabine nodded and turned towards the baby.

* * * *

Darrick watched Sabine move gracefully around the burned out shelter. Coming up from behind, he laid his hands on her shoulders, gently kneading her tired muscles. She leaned into his touch.

"How does Thunder fare?" she asked.

"He is fine. What of you and the baby?"

"I'm fine. Surprisingly, he was well cared for except for being a tad hungry. I pray we find Matilda. She probably ran away the first chance she saw."

Sabine rested her back against his chest, drawing his palm to her cheek. Holding her close, he thought of the danger she had put herself in. Struggling to control the fear he had felt when he saw her confront Nandra, he pressed her near his heart.

"Never do that to me again," he growled.

"What?" she whispered.

He felt her tense at his simple warning. Turning her to face him, he pulled her to his lips, hoping to silence the enraged words threatening to spill out. Her mouth relaxed, her lips parted for his kisses. Delving deeply, he explored her sweetness. The velvet caress of her response caught at his heart.

The heat of her body pressed into his as her hands traveled over his shoulders. He sucked in a breath as her hands ran over his back.

Backing away from his embrace, she tugged at his hand. "Come with me. I have much to show you." She raised the wings of her brows, giving him a coquettish wink. "I think you'll be pleased."

Darrick grimaced as desire ran through his veins. Pulsing with excitement, he hungered for her body. "Stay," he growled.

Choosing to ignore his warning, Sabine whirled around to fetch the baby. She swished her skirts around his booted feet.

Chance gurgled sweetly in his sleep, warmed by the heat from the fire. Stirring from his dreams, he waved his tiny fists and kicked at his blankets.

With the baby tucked snug in her arms, she motioned to Darrick to follow. She led them along the tumbled down buildings.

Thunder ran ahead, acting as if he knew exactly the direction she would travel. Every little bit, he turned around, making certain they were following. His eyes, glittering in the night, were all they were able to see of him.

* * * *

Sabine followed the path she knew by heart. Her thoughts traveled to the past as she led the way through the dark. A long time ago, she had been mistress of this keep. One day she would have her family living there again. For now, they had need of supplies to keep them alive and she knew where these treasures were.

Thankful it was too dark to see the total destruction of her home; she prayed everything would be as she'd left it. With little light to guide her, she almost ran into a portion of wall that should not have been lying across their path.

She led them further from the main tower and down the path, leading to what resembled the outer curtain wall. Even in the dark, she could see it would require repair and fortification to protect the good people who would one day live there again. Picking their way around the rubble, the path grew precarious as their footing slipped from the loose stones under foot.

"Sabine, love? 'Tis unsafe." Stopping their progress, he gently touched her elbow. "Whatever you search for will wait until morning. You can show me in the light of day."

Looking up into his weary face, she knew she must press on. The chill night was seeping past the worn fabric of her gown and into her bones. Although he was a strong man, there was no telling how the cold would affect his wounds. Moreover, the baby's health was in question; Chance would not last another night out in the damp.

"We must find it. Then you'll see."

Thunder barked ahead of them. They turned in time to see the moonlight flash across his black pelt. He stood with feet planted, his tail waving like a banner in the night.

Hearing the faint bleating of a goat, Sabine rushed over and found what she dared to hope. Matilda stood, a disgruntled beast, staring back at them. The animal was fiery mad at having been tied up and aching to be milked. Digging her little hooves in the ground, the goat tugged against the restraint.

"Poor thing, I think she wonders what took us so long," Sabine said.

"She doesn't appear to appreciate the care she has received, does she?"

"Has the patience of someone else I know," Sabine muttered under her breath.

"What a miracle to find the goat after all this time," he said. "'Tis another wonder that you knew where to look, isn't it. I don't like surprises. Once we locate a place to rest, you'll enlighten me with all of your knowledge."

Sabine remained silent, unable to meet his gaze. Her head bent, she continued to struggle with Matilda while she cradled the baby in her arms.

Darrick's hand brushed impatiently at her fingers and moved her over. Whipping out the dagger, he cut the moldering rope with one slash of the blade. The dagger's jeweled eye winked back, mocking them with the inability to find the answers to their questions.

Sabine spun around and motioned him to follow. Her shadow flitted under the haze of the moon. Unaccustomed to following someone else's directions, he growled at the goat to keep up.

Chapter 17

Sabine was the first to reach the heap of loose rubble. The others trailed not far behind. Unwilling to wait, she began shoving at the rocks. The scraping of stone against stone echoed across the still night. The shadows shifted and the moon bounced off the ragged surface.

Darrick strode up from behind. "For the love of God, can't this wait till morn?"

"If you're unwilling to offer your help, then kindly stay out of my way."

Sabine continued to work over the charred ruins. Trying to juggle the babe in one arm, she shoved at the rock, barely driving it back.

"I've no desire to stand here all night." Darrick wrapped his hands around her waist and lifted her into the air, depositing her gently out of his way.

Laying his shoulder into the stone, he rolled it over as bits of rubble crunched under his boots. Pushing and shoving, he removed the last remaining pieces of the crumbled wall.

The wind whistled past the opening buried beneath the wreckage. Matilda skittered away from the grinding growl of the tomb hidden below. Her hooves danced along the earth. Thunder stiffened in his stance, prepared to do battle with whatever crossed their path.

Darrick peered into the blackened hole. "'Tis another dirt-encrusted tunnel."

She leaned over and whispered in his ear. "I knew you would be surprised."

His steely eyes narrowed, his nostrils flared. "Surely, you jest."

"If you'll but listen."

"Told you, I do not like surprises," he growled.

"But 'tis the answer to our problem."

"I am not a creature of the earth." His lips tightened, white lines creased at the corners of his piercing gray eyes.

"Nor, am I."

"Besides, I am certain my shoulders will not fit."

Exasperated with his stubborn nature, Sabine nodded. "Oh, I agree. You have grand shoulders all right and a large head to match. Nevertheless, there is no other choice. Will you but trust me in this?" Unwilling to budge from her spot, she waited for Darrick to enter. "Please," she pleaded.

She swore she heard him grind his teeth before he finally relented. He worked to control his temper as he stepped deeper into the tunnel, squeezing his broad shoulders into the tight confining space. Bracing his legs, he blocked the entrance, motioning Sabine to stop where she was.

"Do not move until I tell you to," he hissed.

"We should be safe here."

"My lady will bend to my will in this," he barked.

After what seemed like an eternity, Sabine could no longer wait. Peeping over his shoulder, she cleared her throat. "You will find a torch along the wall. There will be a bag hanging on a peg next to the torch. It contains the flint and steel."

Her fingers drummed at her hip while Darrick found the torch. They would need it to travel safely into the tunnel. She wanted to find it herself but the dog would not move out of the way. He stood blocking the passage, awaiting his master's command.

Eyeing the dog, she muttered under her breath, "Traitor."

Matilda fidgeted, bumping into legs and stepping on toes. Sabine shifted the baby to her other arm. The goat's milk would turn if they did not get Matilda soothed and milked. "If you would but let me pass, I will locate it," Sabine called out.

"No need. Hold where you stand."

The fire caught at the torch, instantly revealing the tunnel. Built from stone, the walls were carved out ages before. Each smooth stone was trussed with a timber frame to support the vaulted ceiling. The air was musty from lack of use, but it was not damp, as one would expect from an underground room.

Sabine pushed past Thunder and stepped down the narrow stairway. Pausing at the bottom of the steps, she pointed to the right, indicating another passageway.

"That tunnel will take you past the outer wall and to the valley that leads to Balforth."

Sensing Darrick's eagerness to find Nathan, she clasped her hand around his arm. Feeling the tension in his body, she pressed her fingers against his flesh. "There is yet a great deal you should know."

Warmth spread through her veins, flowing through her fingertips. His bunched muscles tensed under her hand.

"More than this network of tunneling?" he asked.

A smile that never quite reached his eyes tortured his lips. She could see that worry filled his troubled soul.

"No need to fear," he said. "I am not so foolish. However, time is running out for Nathan. You know, as well as I, that we must plan carefully. I am tired and hungry and have need of weapons and a safe place for young Chance's keeping."

Sabine drew him into the tunnel that led to the left. "If my father's calculations were correct we'll have everything we need."

Leading him to an arched doorway, she pressed her hand against the keystone in the center of the stone arch. With her weight pushing against the central wedge of stone, the door opened into a cavernous room piled high with various household items. Trunks and bins were meticulously stacked. Alcoves jutted out from the main room, each one containing specific duties.

Sabine stood at the entrance. "I pray that the mice and beetles have not destroyed all the hard work that has gone into storing our belongings."

Darrick paced around the cavern. "Have you everything one needs to run a castle buried in this tomb?"

Sabine nodded. "All but the servants."

Raising one of the trunk's lids, he revealed bolts of fabric neatly tucked away. There were bolts of coarse wool and serviceable linen for the servants. Tossing open another lid, he found brilliantly dyed wool and embroidered silks. Another heavy trunk held furs for lining cloaks. Tapestries, rolled and stacked, hung off the floor to keep the damp from seeping in. Leathers hung from the beams overhead; some were thick and heavy and others soft and supple to the touch.

"Is there clothing that is already sewn? Something that would replace our ravaged clothes?"

Picking his way carefully through the many piles of stores, he explored further into the room. Holding the torch aloft, it revealed more trunks stacked one atop of the other.

Sabine located the stores of candles. Although it was an extravagance, she grabbed as many as she could hold. Singling out one candle, she carefully lit the wick. The flame sputtered. Smoke billowed from the tallow candle. A black tail spun from the wick as the cloud of smoke hallowed her head. Lifting the candle high, the flickering light chased the shadows away.

With extra light, they found Sabine's cradle. Passed down through her family, it was stored with great care in the hope that one day the next generation would use it. While rummaging through the storehouse Sabine brought out a blanket with which to tuck Chance into his new bed. Once Chance was safe in his cradle, Sabine was free to search the tiny alcove concealed in the corner.

Soon, she located the heavy trunk where she had left it many months earlier. Before lifting the lid, she wiped away a thick layer of dust clinging to the top. Afraid of what she might find, she slowly peeked inside. Stuffed within, were folded strips of bandages and jars of healing ointments. With a deep sigh of relief, she leaned against the chest.

Looking overhead, she saw the vials of sweet oils and soothing balms resting on the shelves. Bundles of dried herbs hung from the rafters. Their scent filled the air. She ran her fingers over the dry leaves, releasing their fragrance as she brushed by. Although some had aged beyond their usefulness, she found others that would provide what she required.

The weight of the past few days lifted from her heart. Possibilities were beginning to grow inside her head. Hope built as she surveyed the stores that had been hidden for almost a year. Perhaps her father had thought of everything after all. Even the air was circulating, aided by one of his inventions.

It pained her that he would never know that what others had scoffed at and said was a worthless effort; these treasured stores would now be their salvation. His eccentricity would help them defeat DePierce.

Her thoughts drifted to Taron. Could he still be alive, as Darrick had suggested?

Finding the ale and wine barrels, she cut through one of the seals. Selecting a wine, she poured it into a jug. She was determined to see that Darrick's wounds would heal properly.

"I have found what we need. Have you discovered anything of interest?" she called out.

"'Tis something of a wonder down here."

Sabine watched Darrick's approach. His movements were stiff, restricting his customary grace. Most assuredly, his ribs stung when he moved. She bit her lip, praying that he would readily allow her to administer to his wounds.

He pointed with a dirt-smudged finger, wary of the strips of material she carried in her arms. "What have you there?"

"'Tis only herbs and salves to soothe the sting from the arrow."

Anxious to get her job over with, she nodded to a large, wooden, low-backed chair she pulled from a stack of furnishings. It was placed near one of the torches for better lighting. A small table, where she had meticulously laid out her herbs and ointments, stood in easy reach. Placing fresh bandages carefully on the table, she turned. Offering a peaceable stance, she spread her fingers, revealing that her hands were free of weapons.

"'Tis only a scratch and nothing more," he said.

Sabine ducked her head to keep from laughing at the knight who had changed into a little boy before her eyes. "You know better than I that even a small wound will fester and become tainted."

"Is that correct? And who did you hear that nonsense from?"

"A great knight once told me so."

He sniffed at the jars in her hand. "More than likely a great fool."

"Only if he doesn't do as he is told. The arrow went quite deep and the wound requires washing. I will not have you dying on me, Sir Darrick of Lockwood."

Grabbing his hand, she drew him towards the chair. "Rest here a moment. If we are to rescue Nathan then you'll need rest and nourishment."

Her hands shook as she poured the wine in two goblets, pressing one in his hand. "Perhaps this will help."

He offered a final grunt of protest and drained his cup. She held his gaze. His eyes reminded her of the turbulent water that coursed between her home and Wales. Sometimes it would change color with the mood of the channel. If a storm flew over, it became a dark brewing gray as the mist blew in. On occasion, the bright sun would shine, reflecting a breathtaking aquamarine.

What turbulent colors would churn from his piercing gaze when she poured the wine over his injury? Her mind warred with what she knew was right. Dread lingered, wrapping around her throat.

Even now, she could feel his pain deep inside her heart. She would have willingly taken his injuries upon her person. She could still feel the way his gentle fingers caressed her bruised and battered flesh. His touch had healed more than bodily wounds. He had restored something much deeper. She longed to caress him in return, to cradle his head against her breast. To tell him…

Her thoughts stilled her hand, *When had the need for the warmth of his touch turned into something more? He had become a part of her. Just as Chance belonged to her heart, so did he.*

* * * *

Darrick loathed doing her bidding without complaint, but the woman stood with unrelenting determination. He knew she would not let it go until she had completed her task. If he learned anything about Sabine, it was that she was a stubborn wench. Hesitant, he reluctantly sat down and braced his arms against his thighs, questioning the wisdom in trusting his person to her care.

Wishing the wine would do the trick and numb his senses, he doubted she realized that a small cup of wine would not even begin to muddle his brain. He had purposefully hardened his tolerance to more than battle. He knew his mind was strong against the spirits and his head would be very clear when she started her ministrations. Taking a deep breath, he looked around for something more desirable to capture his attention. Prepared for her assault, he let his thoughts return to the lovely vision of Sabine's fair legs, peeking out from under her skirts.

Cool liquid trickled down his shoulder, sluicing over his heated skin. Darrick flinched when it finally tore its way across the injured flesh. His nerves were awakened by the stinging attack. Born from the need to survive, his automatic reflex was to throttle the wench. He forced his thoughts from the owner of the winsome legs. The minx was inflicting more damage to his body than what he would normally allow.

Determined to ignore the biting torment, he focused on Nathan's rescue and the justice that would be served at the end of his sword. He did not know where his men-at-arms were. It bothered him to have no knowledge of their whereabouts. Leaving them with Rhys in tow had seemed like a good plan at the time. It worried him that in his absence they may have found someone with a larger purse.

Darrick knew that a soldier's alliance was as strong as his purse strings. Times had changed from when he had become a knight. The cost was prohibitive. A man's honor and integrity came at a heavy price indeed. One could not always choose the battle because it was right. Most times the decision to fight for another was based on whether they paid you well, and if you would live to see the next battle.

He was a knight first, but had learned to fight cheek-to-jowl beside the men-at-arms. He knew 'twas the longbow men in mass numbers that were necessary for the victory. Even now, his armed guards served him well and were paid substantially for their service. Perhaps they were waiting for his signal, their loyalty to him still intact.

Sabine finished cleansing his wounds. The soothing motion of her hands relaxed his aching muscles. He swore that if she did not stop soon, he would be fast asleep, lost for good.

Instead, the noxious fumes penetrated his thoughts. They emanated from his back, rising from his body, and wrapped around his head, making his nose twitch with disgust.

Trying not to breathe in the odor, he sputtered through his teeth. "What exactly did you put on me? I reek like I have been dead and buried for months."

Sabine stood in front of him, frowning. He was quick to note that she made a concentrated effort to keep him at arm's length while she wrapped the clean bandages around his ribs and back. She was careful not to get too close to his stench. Keeping her head ducked down, her eyes did not waiver from her handy work.

"Enough! Any more bandages and not only will I smell like a dead man, I'll look like one, too. What did you put on me that gives such an…aroma?"

Sabine shrugged her shoulders and tucked a stray hair behind her ear, nervously nibbling on her frowning lips, mumbling, "An unguent. 'Tis all."

"My lady, I'll have you know I have ridden beside many unwashed men and they have never smelled like this. Not even after they have been on a march for months. Hell's fire," he sputtered. "Even a rotting corpse does not smell this bad."

"'Tis a simple treatment for injured flesh."

He continued to glare, the steel from his eyes as sharp as any blade he might wield. His nostrils flared, quivered, and then finally released the breath he had been holding. He waited, staring at her, counting the ways he would make her pay.

"All right, ungrateful cur," Sabine snapped. "If you really must know, the ointment is made out of sheep's fat and then boiled with bark from an elder tree. It will help you heal and won't allow any more scars to form."

The simple explanation finished, she turned to find fresh air of her own.

Grabbing her hand before she passed, he drew her close. Her nose twitched, her eyes watered, as she shared the unusual fragrance from his body. His enjoyment of her discomfort increased threefold. "It normally does not smell this way, does it?" Carefully scrutinizing her response, he watched the guilty flush wash over her face.

She swallowed, and nodded. "Well, perhaps not quite…as bad. It was stored for some time." Staring at the center of his broad chest, she finally conceded. "Perhaps the lard has turned a bit… rancid?"

Her lips twitched as she tried to control the giggle that threatened to break loose.

Raising his eyebrows, he scowled. The smell was overpowering and he was determined not to endure it alone. Her hands held captive to his chest, he pulled her closer, wrapping his arms around her and drawing her lips to his. He nibbled at her rosy petals as if enchanted by her sweet kisses.

Distracted by Thunder bumping against his legs, he got the feeling the big hairy beast wanted to roll around on top of him. Much like the dog was wont to do when he found a ripe-smelling dead animal.

Breathing through his mouth in the hope of avoiding the stench, Darrick pressed his forehead to Sabine's, wondering what to do with her. "There shall be a price to pay for what you have done."

Sabine pulled back from his embrace. "Quit your complaining. 'Tis nothing compared to the time I had to climb down the latrine hole," she snorted. "The stench filled my nostrils for days after. I thought I would never wash it from my hair."

A shadow passed over Sabine's upturned face. Only moments before, she had been laughing and taunting him. Now he watched the recurring sadness draw a curtain across her countenance.

Her bitter chuckle cut through the rancid air. "Thankfully, no one else could smell it but me. It will forever be imbedded in my memory."

Stepping away from his embrace, she turned, moving quietly towards the stairway that led up to the entrance. The lightness of the moment was forgotten.

"Perhaps the well is still in good repair. I imagine carrying a foul odor around is not something one really wants, no matter how good the cure."

Darrick tried to interpret the bits of information she had dropped for him. He pinched the bridge of his nose, trying to understand what reason Sabine had that would force her to climb into the filth of a latrine hole.

Upon waking, Chance began to whimper, ready for his next meal. The jug filled with milk stood by the cradle waiting for the baby. Darrick was thankful she had already milked the contrary goat. Resourceful woman. He had no desire to wrestle with the thankless beast.

* * * *

Carefully making her way up the steps, Sabine leaned against the outer opening. She moved slowly, half-expecting the smelly man to follow. But he failed to do so. Not that she needed him for anything, of course.

Cool fingers pressed to her temple, her head ached where it had been stitched. He could have stopped her. Or, at the very least offered to get the water, she grumbled to no one in particular. Once filled, it would be awkward carrying the bucket down the stairway. Having to fend for herself for so long, she had forgotten how to ask for help. It did not come easy for her, although, it never really had. She supposed the same was true when it came to trusting someone.

"It serves him right that he'll smell like a rotting animal for a while longer."

Perhaps she should feel a wee bit guilty putting the awful stuff on him, but it really had been done with good intentions. What fun to see his stony countenance slip when the stench had made its way to his nose, burrowing through that cold wall he was always erecting. Her fingers ran across her lips, remembering the way that he had caressed her mouth. If he intended his kisses as a punishment then she would willingly sacrifice a month of Sundays for more.

The cool, moist air brushed past her cheek. The night skies were dark except for the few stars that peeked through the mist. Rolling in for the night, it caused the damp to seep into the thin material of her gown. Perhaps, she too, would be able to bathe and change into fresh clothing. Her old dresses tucked away in a trunk might not be the fashion and perhaps a bit musty but they would be cleaner than the woolen dress that had seen one too many days.

Lifting the bucket from the well she felt the hair stand up on her arms. Someone or something was watching her. Crouching down beside the well, she waited, listening for approaching footsteps. Silence followed, but her skin continued to sizzle. Hugging the bucket to her stomach, she crept towards the shadows that hid the entrance to the tunnel. Barely daring to breathe, she listened to the silence.

Was it man or beast? Fear wrapped around her arms and legs. They refused to move from where she hid. Still hugging the bucket of water, she felt her gown tugged from behind. A large shadow loomed over her.

Chapter 18

Darrick grabbed the hem of Sabine's dress and guided her to the safety of the shadows. Holding her close to his chest, he silently shut the slab of stone behind them. His hands shook as they ran up and down her arms, smoothing her hair from her face. Prying her fingers away from the bucket she still clutched in her arms, he drew her down the stairs.

He piled blankets and furs on the floor to soften the cold stone. Without a word, without a glance, Sabine let him lead her to the pallet. Shivers threatened to take control of her body. "Someone was out there."

Thunder left his post and moved over to lie by his mistress. He pressed nearer, gazing longingly into her face. She dug her fingers into the dog's coat and let his presence soothe her.

"Shh," Darrick soothed. "You're safe. No one will harm us."

He knelt down and lifted her head, placing it gently in his lap. Sabine squeezed her eyes shut. Traces of tears dampened her lashes. When would she close the door on fear and once again know the idyllic life?

Her body began to release the tremors. She relaxed under Darrick's care as he traced her brows with a light touch. Mindful of the bruise above her eye, he slowly followed the curve of her cheekbones to her hairline. He raked his fingers through her long tresses, letting the strands fall slowly to her shoulder.

"Never fear, love," he whispered. "We shall be safe for a while longer. But I think it will soon be time for us to make our move."

Sabine curled her body closer to his, gathering strength from his warmth. She burrowed deeper, head nestled in his lap, she felt secure, knowing he was there to watch over her.

His touch penetrated the chill and brought her body singing to life. She reveled in his caresses, carrying a heated message to her thoughts.

It held desire, sensuous anticipation that would fill her mind and body. Goose flesh pebbled her skin where his touch had set it on fire. Her senses heightened, her body demanded more.

Darrick stroked the base of her neck. Eager for his caresses, she turned, pressing against his hands. Waves of longing surged through her body. Leaning down to cup her breast, he ran his thumb across her nipple. Her body arched toward him. He caught her mouth with his and tugged at her lips as he devoured her kisses.

A soft crying pulled at the back of Sabine's mind. Reality settled, registering that the baby needed her. Shutting the door on the hunger that was clawing to get out, Sabine sat up, dazed from the desire sizzling between them. After rearranging the bodice of her gown, she made a mental note that should she ever marry she would be sure the children had their own rooms.

"Why did he do it?" Darrick asked.

"Who?" she asked, confused at his strange question.

"Your father. How did Sir William know to create an elaborate tunnel system like this?"

Patting the baby's back, she gazed back at Darrick, weighing the mystery of it all. "I never really thought much about it. These tunnels have been around for hundreds of years. He always said the ancients built them."

"I remember it drove my brother mad when father chose to build onto the tunnels. Taron wanted the outer walls updated and fortified with stone. Father would not hear of it. Said the secret to our survival was in the tunnels. Would you believe that there are catacombs in here?"

The babe once again fed and content, she returned him to the cradle. She wrapped her arms across her chest, cupping her elbows. "Father had my mother's tomb buried beneath the castle walls. As a child, I never wanted to come down here."

"How were you able to carry so many supplies down here without anyone noticing? What of your servants? Could you trust them to keep it secret?"

Sabine shook her head. "Before Father disappeared, he felt the need to bring most of the larger furniture down. Using a winch that hung from his private tower, he lowered the items down by himself. Of course, the servants never felt they could voice their opinion but 'tis certain they questioned what was happening to our furnishings. He was always working on something in his tower. His library was above the main storage room and below his private chambers so it was quite easy for him to keep his secrets."

Sabine played with the edges of her sleeve. "The few weeks before Father disappeared, he had been irascible. He had sent for Taron, requesting his immediate return to Clearmorrow. On the night Father left, he received a message that he was needed."

"Where?"

"I don't know. I don't believe he meant to be gone for any length of time. He must have felt that it was imperative to leave without delay."

"Why is that?"

"All of his experiments were left out on his workbench. Some of his books were open to the pages where he stopped. My father was very meticulous in his work. He loved those leather tomes. He would not have been so careless unless there had been an emergency."

"Were there no men-at-arms? No battalion to ride by his side?"

"No, he rode as you, with little desire to be slowed down by others."

"My men took another path. They will not betray me."

"Perhaps. But they'll no doubt be stopped by DePierce's men should they be spotted."

"What of Taron? Did he not see fit to return as your father requested?"

"I received word that Taron was returning. But, after a fortnight, I began to question if something had gone awry. After a few more weeks, I started storing all the supplies I could carry. The last things I stored were my father's beloved books. If Father had felt there was danger, then I wanted to be sure to save what I could and protect our home.

"Soon after, I received a missive from Taron. His instructions were for me to find DePierce in Balforth should I feel threatened in any way. I thought it odd at the time. No one, except I, knew father was missing, and yet Taron knew to arrange for help."

Sabine waited for the criticism she knew would be forthcoming. Yet, Darrick sat in silence. She glanced up. He met her with a reassuring smile and a silent nod to continue.

"Looking back on it, I realize I was ten times a fool." Sabine picked up one of her father's books and turned the pages. "The missive was a forgery. It had to be. At one time, I was furious with Taron for disregarding our family's need. Then, what few guards we had left disappeared the night of the attack on the castle. If truth were known, I was angry with all men."

Sabine returned the book to the leaning stack. "The only other man, who has helped me for help's sake, was Rhys. Funny thing, is it not? First, he helps me escape and then poor Elizabeth, and now you. 'Tis a wonder how he knows to be in the right place. I'll never fathom how he does it."

Darrick sat still, the weary lines on his face tightened. "Tell me again how you know him. The first time was at Balforth?"

Sabine twisted her fingers together, aware that his mood had changed. "Once, I believed so, but now that I have returned to Clearmorrow, the memories flood back. I remember when I was a little girl, seeing someone that looked much like him. The stranger would come to visit and Father would go away with him for days, sometimes weeks at a time. Nandra would become agitated when Father left for long periods. Perhaps my father's disappearance is what drove Nandra to the brink of madness. Given what she said, I suspect that they once shared a love."

Darrick rose and grasped her arms. His gray eyes bore into hers. "I need you to be certain. Are you positive that Sir William knew Rhys?"

"I was a little girl and when he did visit I saw him from a distance. You must admit, his physical appearance is not that of the average caller."

"Sabine, questions have plagued me ever since my arrival to these lands. What was Rhys's real purpose at Balforth? Why should he dare help you and risk DePierce's wrath? Why was he willing to risk it all?" Stilling her protests, he pressed his fingers to her lips and continued. "Hear me out on this final question. How could he have known to send a goat with you?"

She pulled away from his hand. "Heaven help me, I do not know. Maybe he simply likes goats. Darrick, he sent your sister to me! He sent you to help us!"

"Exactly! Why would he do such a thing? He and DePierce's men knew where to find you. How convenient. I admit that I am leery of any more of his friendly help."

"If you suspect Rhys, than you must also suspect Nathan. Perhaps he set us up for destruction and now rests his head comfortably at Balforth."

"I've told you, Nathan would never betray me. But this Rhys—"

She shook her head. "But what purpose would Rhys or Nathan have in destroying my family? Or yours? No, our enemy is DePierce and no one else. He wants our lands and is willing to forfeit all to do so." Sabine pointed out the obvious. "'Tis simply that we are in the way."

Darrick rubbed his temples while he paced the floor. "How do you know this to be true?"

They froze at the sound of scraping coming from overhead. He held his hand up, motioning for silence. Thunder jumped up, his low growl rumbled through the tunnel.

Darrick moved soundlessly, up the winding stairway, alert to the danger of another ambush. Standing at the entrance, he listened, straining to discover who surrounded their hiding place. Sabine stood nearby, having taken the baby from the cradle and now holding him protectively in her arms. Thunder pressed his sleek body against her leg.

Voices carried through the trapdoor. Were they DePierce's men? They called out over the noise of hoofs and creaking leather. The racket of setting up camp was almost deafening.

Darrick gestured for Sabine to place the child in the cradle. Puzzled, she hastened to do as he bid her. Satisfied that Thunder stood guard over the baby, she tied the goat to the handle of a heavy chest. She drifted over to the warmth offered by Darrick's protective arm. Excitement glittered in his gray eyes.

He bestowed her with a lingering kiss that drove all thought and worry from her mind. His hands roamed up her arms until they stopped to knead the base of her neck.

Kissing the corner of her mouth he whispered cheerfully, "'Tis all right, my love. My men-at-arms are here. You and my nephew will find safety at the convent. And I'll set off to get our family back from that devil, DePierce."

His finger brushed her sensitive lips. Tracing her mouth, he sighed under his breath. "I have enjoyed our time together. Perhaps, once peace is settled, we'll make arrangements to explore what could be."

Giving her arm a squeeze, he quietly pushed on the center stone over the doorway and left Sabine standing against the wall. Alone.

She crushed the folds of her gown in her fists. If she could have reached him, she would have dug her nails into his devilish eyes. Thoughts and fears resurfaced from the dark corner of her heart.

She could not believe it, again, she was ten times the fool. A convent? For the briefest moment, she had actually enjoyed his touch. Even with the strangers standing outside, she had trusted him. Doubt burrowed into her thoughts, reminding her that there were strangers nearby. Men who she did not know. Men who could not be trusted. Trying to force the dark thoughts away, she was left wondering about his half-hearted promise. *Never!*

She shoved the unease back. He had another surprise coming if he believed she would hide and wait for his return. No matter what they thought, she would not wait for him to bring her brother back. She would be there by Darrick's side, whether he liked it or not.

Chapter 19

Darrick felt Sabine bolt outside before she made contact with his back. Controlling the desire to throttle her, he put his arm around her waist. Instinctively, he pressed her against his hip. He had hoped she would heed his command and wait. He wanted to secure the grounds with his most trusted men before he brought Sabine and his nephew up from the tunnel.

"Your desire for me exceeds your wisdom," he said dryly. His gaze drifted over the troops, searching for the crow-eyed man.

She stood by his side. Tension radiated from her body. He knew he had made a grave mistake. He should have tied her down. The simple task of accepting an order to stay put would never sit well with Sabine.

Well, no matter, he shrugged, what was done, was done. They stood, unprotected, in front of friend and foe alike.

He observed the reaction of his men. Most of them were surprised to see that he traveled with a female companion. Some gave him sly winks and a few sniggers. Those who had rode by his side while serving King Henry ignored the woman. Instead, they voiced their own concerns regarding Sir Nathan's absence. Threats to the dread DePierce echoed against the charred walls.

Sabine pulled away. "Chance…will need me." She turned to slip through the little doorway.

Darrick nodded, relieved that she was making a docile exit. With her retreat, his woman-hungry men would no longer be able to devour Sabine's beauty with their eyes.

His attention returned to the world that he knew best. Staring intently, he determined the ratio of his men and the numbers that he would need to lay siege to Balforth Castle. The oldest member of his army stood off to the side, waiting to give his report in private.

Darrick walked over, calling out to the gray-headed sergeant-of-arms. "So Krell, some of our men gave up on my return?"

"No, Sir Darrick," he grumbled. "They be riding with that straggling caravan."

"What?" Darrick turned in the direction Krell pointed. A caravan of gaily-painted wagons wobbled up the rutted path. "Hounds of hell. Is that who I think it is?"

Krell chuckled. "'Tis a fine thing to see this bit of news shake your fabled nerves of steel. Yes, Sir Darrick, it does my heart good." He rubbed his battle-scarred hands together. "Where is that scamp, Sir Nathan? Not like him to hide from work. Could use an extra hand in setting up camp."

"He has been abducted and taken to Balforth."

Scratching his chin, Krell looked up from under his bushy gray eyebrows. "It's sorry I am, for taking so long in catching up with you. Had we not made the detour we might have been there to keep Sir Nathan out of trouble. Do they think to ransom him?"

Losing his grip on his patience, Darrick ground out. "What runs through DePierce's mind? That, we will not know until we send men on a scouting mission."

Belying the tension building in his neck, he nonchalantly leaned against the tree. He sucked in a breath as he eased his tender ribcage against the bark. He hated to admit Sabine was in the right, after all. No matter how bad the stench, he should have left the smelly salve on his wounds. He ran a hand over his aching ribs and made certain the bandages did not show.

Wearily resting his head against the rough bark of the spruce tree, he asked Krell, "What detour?"

Scrutinizing the seasoned soldier, he waited patiently for Krell to spill his surprise. He had known Krell for far too long for him not to notice a devilish gleam in his crinkled old watery eyes.

Folding his arms over his weathered jerkin, Krell heeded Darrick's stony gaze. Nodding his head in the direction behind them, he pointed to the thin line that wound its way through the trees. "Had a devilish time getting here. First, that man, Rhys, and his strange ways. He makes some of the men downright nervous when he's around. Then, there's the lady. Begging your pardon, but she's been in tears most of the trip. Worrying and fretting, crying and twisting that scarf. Makes a grown man want his own mother."

Darrick swung around to stare at the train of wagons snaking through the valley. He had to squint against the glare of the morning sun. With its gilded trim, the wagon shone brilliantly in the morning sunrise. He jumped when Sabine touched his arm.

"What fools travel without a care who sees them?"

Forcing a smile at her upturned face, he placed his hand on hers and wrapped his other arm around her waist.

Turning to his sergeant-of-arms, he delivered a long cold stare, "I believe Sergeant Krell would normally agree with you."

His man looked uncomfortable, standing in front of the fair maiden. Even in her plain woolen dress, she stood with a regal bearing. 'Twas not the normal doxy clinging to a soldier's backside. Darrick lifted the corner of his mouth in a half smile. "My Lady Sabine, if I'm not mistaken, you were to go where 'tis safe."

A second later and he realized he should have known she would stand fast to the spot by his side. Obstinate woman. His jaw muscles jerking, he ground his teeth together and worked to discipline his impatience. "Till we find out who or what travels this way, I order you to go into the tunnel."

"Krell," he growled. "I pray your reasoning has not left you completely. When I return from escorting the Lady Sabine to safety, you'll explain this mess you have gotten into."

Grim faced, Sabine dug her heels into the soft ground. She swatted at Darrick's hands. "I'm not leaving until you tell me who rides in those wagons."

Krell chuckled under his breath. "Granted, my lady, 'tis a very serious thing to have my traveling companions rolling through the valley. They are a determined bunch and plan to call attention to all who watch their approach. I'll be relieved to wash my hands of the whole lot of them."

Ignoring the old sergeant and Sabine's protests, Darrick swung her over his shoulder like a sack of grain and carried her to the entrance by the well. He set her on her feet and stepped back before she could direct her pointed foot at his shins.

"Love," he said. "I will not lie to you. I do not know who or what is coming. Remember, no matter what happens, my nephew needs you. If you allow me, I'll do everything in my power to protect the both of you. But you must do as I tell you."

Something in his grim countenance penetrated her anger. He'd give a year's wages to know what he did right. He might need to do it again.

Nodding meekly she turned towards the entrance, then paused. "You won't betray me?"

"You can trust me."

"Please...be careful, Darrick."

"I promise to return for you when it is safe."

Darrick cast his attention on the sergeant and silently impaled him with a glare. Bracing his legs, he waited in stony silence for Krell's report.

The old man pointed to the wagons, his eyes grim, he said, "The odd one. The one they call Rhys. Says you will need the lady's help. Says you have a babe traveling with you." Krell's gray brows arched as he stared at him with a jaundiced eye. "Also heard tell you traveled with an old hermit. Yon mistress does not fit the description. What mischief have you gotten yourself into?"

Darrick bunched the old man's leather jerkin in his large hands. "You go too far, Krell. They draw near and I grow weary."

Krell tapped the angry fists that bunched his tunic. "'Tis Lady Camilla. Your mother."

"Camilla? I am well aware of the woman who birthed me." Mindful to cover the shock that threatened to flood his face, he asked through hardened lips. "Why is she here?"

Krell shifted from one foot to the next. "The baby," he repeated. "Rhys said there was a baby requiring her care."

Darrick could see his discomfort but decided not to go easy on his old friend. The sharp-edged bite of danger sang through his veins. "How did he know?" he ground out between clenched teeth.

"Look here, it'll do you no good to bite my head off. 'Tis not my fault. He felt it imperative we bring her here. He would not take no for an answer. Not even from Lady Camilla. Now if you were inclined to ask me, I would tell you that it would be a lucky man to have the privilege to call her your mother." Holding his weathered hand up to silence his onetime pupil, he continued. "Not that you're asking, of course."

While Darrick watched the caravan slowly make its way up the rocky hillside, he relived the accusations tossed around regarding his parents, absorbing the flashes of pain and tears when his father decided to send his mother away to the convent.

Soon they would reach the outer curtain wall, or at least, what was left of it. He could not stop them if he wanted to. He swore under his breath. Clearmorrow's moat was dry and in disrepair. More the pity, he did not even have a portcullis to lower or a drawbridge to raise. After all, she deserved the same reception he had received from his own family.

Krell sighed deeply and placed his wrinkled hand on Darrick's shoulder. "The little one, Rhys, rides ahead of the rest. Shall I delay him for a time?"

"I wish to speak to him," Darrick said. "Krell, you say the men are uncomfortable in his presence. In what way do they find him distasteful?"

"Well, you know how soldiers are, my boy. Superstitious, the whole lot of them."

"Yes, but a good soldier learns to listen to the quiet voice of danger. What causes their unease?"

"Nothing I can really put my finger on." He held his palm out to stop Darrick's interruption, "and 'tis not his size. Though he can make his body shift, growing taller, if he chooses. Do not scoff! I see that look in your eye, Sir Darrick. I've seen him shift with my own two eyes. I warn you. Be careful of that one. He puts on airs of being a man of the cloth, but a few of the men asked him for a prayer, and he near bit their heads off. Says he's on a pilgrimage and cannot break his vow. Though, I don't know what that has to do with praying over a couple of fools." Krell stabbed his gnarled finger into the air. "Mark my words. If he's a man of the cloth, I will eat my helmet, leather straps, and all."

That creeping feeling of dread now pulsated and tugged at the hair on the back of Darrick's neck. He had to wonder about the soundness of the old warhorse's mind. Feelings were one thing but shape shifting was a matter best left for the clergy. His drifting thoughts were called to attention when he heard Krell's crackled voice go on about his unwanted companions.

"He was hopping mad when you did not show up with the old woman. Said she had cast a spell on you and we would need Lady Camilla to protect the baby from the old hag. So we journeyed to the convent and retrieved your mother."

"Truth be known," he whispered, "she, too, does not care to be with him. Although, she'd never speak ill of the church to anyone." Beaming with pride, Krell added, "She confided her concerns to me. Said he was evil his-self and refused to travel in the same wagon."

"What does Lady Camilla hold against him?"

"I wouldn't know. She has been very tight-lipped; except for the crying, that is. Perhaps you should ask her yourself."

Darrick wondered how well his sergeant-of-arms really knew his mother. Wearily he passed his hands over his face and watched the procession draw closer. "And the men?"

"They feel he overstepped his authority in taking Lady Camilla from the convent but you know how it is with the religious minded. The church is full of their God almighty power."

"Have a care, Krell. There would be some that would call that blasphemy."

"Ha!" he huffed. "He might be on a mission, but 'tis not for the church. He is in search of something. His beady eyes follow every step you take. A man cannot even go to do his private business behind a bush without him knowing what you have been doing. Keep your eyes open and never turn your back on him."

"Is that the weasel that rides this way?"

"Aye, yonder he comes. See him clearly for what he is. Ask yourself, Sir Darrick, how did he know to have us travel here, to this tumbled down pile of ruins?"

Darrick felt the tension intensify as the man rode the horse up to them. As the threatening force drew near, he wondered how Sabine and Elizabeth could have been willing to trust Rhys. On the other hand, Sabine remained unwilling to share all her secrets. How could he trust her too?

Drawing a deep breath, he decided to bide his time. Greed and evil would eventually show its ugly head. You just had to be patient. Trouble was he didn't know how much time Nathan could afford.

Darrick followed the path that wound up the hill. At least Sabine's father had placed the castle in a position to see all who approached. Straining to see past the glare of the sun, he was relieved to see that the caravan did not fly their banners. The flag bearers flanked the gilded wagon along with his other knights.

"Why wagons? Krell, you know 'tis dangerous enough with thieves lying in wait. You may have a heavily armed band of men but you bring unwanted notice with the garishly painted carts and wagons."

Holding his hands out helplessly, Krell shrugged. "'Tis the little one again. Said DePierce would think they were wandering minstrels."

Before Darrick could respond, Rhys trotted up beside them and climbed off the horse. The man appeared taller than the first time Darrick had seen him. It felt an eternity had passed since he last viewed Rhys's battered body lying helpless on the pallet. The man had looked like death was only a breath away.

He most certainly recovered quickly, Darrick mused. No bruises or cuts marked his visage.

He could not say that of himself or Sabine.

The unexplained desire to pummel the creature rose like bile in his throat. Reining in his anger and frustration, he patiently waited for Rhys to explain his actions.

"Young knight," the scrawny man hailed. "We meet again. And the old hag?" he asked, searching nervously, "Is she safe?"

"Alas, the old hag is no more."

"What say you?" he sputtered. "Surely, she yet lives!"

"She lives...but she is not an old hermit, as you well know."

"Ah...and...the babe? It too, fares well?"

Darrick pulled the dagger from his boot and began to play with the sharply honed edge of steel. Speaking softly, he forced the irritating clergy to lean in closer to hear what he had to say. "How did you know about the baby?"

Rhys kept his eyes focused on the light playing upon the steel of the blade Darrick twirled in his hand. Nervously, the clergy tugged on the cowl of his robe, giving his neck more room. "Eh? What's that you say...Oh, well..." he stammered, "I am sure you realize your men talk. Like women, you know. Gossips. The whole lot of them. Devil's helpers. That's what they are." Shaking his ragged head, he clucked. "Must keep a firmer hand to them."

"Perhaps this evening you would do me the honor of delivering a sermon on the evils of gossiping."

"No...no...'twould not be necessary."

Rhys reminded Darrick of the huge crows that hopped about the tree limbs overhead with their shifting black beady eyes, ready to dive on the next crumb of food. The black crow was squawking at him again.

"More discipline is needed over your knights and men-at-arms. That Sergeant Krell is not very agreeable. Not at all. Worst of the lot. I had to explain my plan repeatedly. Not very bright." He tapped his forehead. "Perhaps he needs a bloodletting to release the bad humors from his body. Not sure we can find a barber close by but I have had some training in the art of releasing the tormenting humors." Rhys's crow-like head bobbed and nodded in agreement to no one in particular. "'Tis certain that is what he needs."

Darrick folded his arms across his broad chest causing his flexed muscles to ripple. He knew Krell had heard Rhys's tale and would be enraged at the story he was telling. Catching the look on the sergeant's visage out of the corner of his eye, his lips twitched. "I...ah...thank you for your concern regarding my men. I will be sure to look into everything you say. As for Krell...well, he will have to endure his personal torment for now."

Standing off to the side, his longtime friend's face was turning a blotchy red. The old man's bushy white eyebrows quivered as they drew together. His weathered hand stole to the broad sword he carried on a wide, battled scarred, leather belt at his waist.

He did not need anyone to inform him that Krell was close to running the man through. Purposefully ignoring Krell, he tilted his head reverently towards Rhys. Forcing his jaws to relax into a bland smile, his voice ran smooth as warmed honey. "Please continue and explain your strategy for the defeat of DePierce."

"Here?" he squeaked.

Darrick shrugged, forcing his body to relax. "Is there a reason why we should not?"

Rhys peered nervously around his shoulder, quick to change the subject. "You say the wench is safe? She still lives?"

"Is there a reason that she should not?" Darrick fixed him with a stare that pinned him where he stood. "Tell me, Rhys, why does DePierce want Sabine so badly? Why is he relentless in his hunt?"

Refusing to answer, Rhys's eyes glittered in the sun when he looked up at the towering man. "She brought you here."

"Get back to the questions."

"What's wrong, young knight?" his voiced rasped out. "Do you have so little trust in me? Did I not lead you to the island and to your sister?"

"Not soon enough," he ground out. "My sister's life was lost!"

He itched to shake Rhys until his teeth fell from his head. If he knew exactly what was going on, he would have already hung him from what was left of the crumbling tower. For now, he would have to pretend he believed him and needed his plans. Krell was right in his warnings. The little clergyman was not about spiritual pilgrimages.

"But you knew that already," Darrick continued. "Why did you lead me there? What is it you really desire?"

"Only the blessings of God, my son." A serene smile that did not reach his beady eyes stole across his visage. "Your father always trusted my knowledge and wisdom," he said. "You should know you can trust me after I helped you find Lady Sabine. Now that you know what she hides, I cannot imagine why you would still ask what DePierce wants with her. Not after you have seen what secrets she carries. She has shown you by now. What she stole. Took a great chance. Not very bright. Do you not agree?"

Caught off guard, Darrick worked to shutter his surprise.

Rhys's nose twitched. "Lord DePierce was an outraged man after she escaped from his tower. As you are aware, stealing is against God's commandments. But," he shrugged, "when one needs to take something away from evil, one must do what he must." Feigning surprise, he smirked. "By the look on your face I see that she does not trust you enough to share her little secret. I cannot help but wonder what else she is hiding."

Darrick spun on his heel, his cloak whirling silently about him. Only those who had served with him for many years and knew him well understood the knight's dark mood.

"Krell," he barked. "Have Lady Camilla join me at the well. I believe she has a grandson to tend. Watch the clergyman. I must take care of a few loose ends."

"I am a devout man of the cross," Rhys whined. "What of my plan for DePierce? Am I to be punished for the whore's foolishness?"

Darrick swung past Rhys and the men resting by the water well. "Krell."

"Sir?"

"Keep him quiet. I am certain you will know what to do if he should try to disappear."

Krell flashed him a devilish grin as he grabbed the clergyman by the scruff of the neck. "I'll see to it personally."

Darrick smiled thinly despite himself, and continued, "Make camp by the tower. 'Tis not completely out of the weather but you have a good position to watch all who attempt to enter. We will discuss our strategy for Balforth when I return." With a curt nod of his head, he turned to go into the tunnel.

* * * *

Lady Camilla stood at the well, waiting. His mother. Did she still smell of roses mixed with other sweet flowers?

Staring at her, he saw the signs of aging scattered on the woman he once loved as his mother. Her lowered hood revealed her previously raven mane, now shot with silver and plaited in a neat braid. The years etched her smooth face with tiny wrinkles. Her cheekbones, rosy from the wind, stood out from her pale face. Nevertheless, Darrick noticed her watery eyes had not changed. They still sparkled with unshed tears.

She smiled weakly, her lips trembling from the effort. She stretched her hand out, "Please, Darrick, ignore your hatred for me and take me to my grandson."

Darrick felt he was living a nightmare. When he was a youngster, he had prayed every night that she would reach out and hold him as she once did. But how could he trust her again? His own mother had helped arrange for the marriage between Hugh and Elizabeth. Grabbing the frail wrist she held out to him, he dragged her close. "How did you know there was a boy child born to your only daughter?"

"That horrid little man, Rhys, told me." With her wrist held in his tight grasp, Camilla's voice shook. "He and your men came to the convent. He said Elizabeth was dead. That you were missing but he knew where to find you because he was led by God. He said I was needed. I did not want to travel with him but he said, 'twas at your request that I come."

"I did not request your presence here, nor would I ever. If you are searching for redemption you are looking to the wrong person." Unable to give her the honor of calling her mother, he promised, "Camilla, we will talk later regarding the marriage of my sister to that cretin you and Father chose for her. There is much to answer for. I will leave you with this question. Was the prize so dear that you were willing to forfeit the life of your only daughter?"

Feeling her frail bird-like bones grind against each other, disgusted with his lack of self-control, he flung her hand away. Turning abruptly, he went in search of the only woman he had dared to almost trust. He must speak with Sabine.

Darrick stopped, realizing his mother had not moved from the spot where he left her and he returned to her side. Visibly shaken, Camilla stood with her head bowed. She cradled her wrist in her hand. Sighing deeply, he took hold of her arm and directed her towards the opening. Leading Camilla down the stairway by the elbow, he scanned the dark corners, searching for Sabine.

Chapter 20

Sabine paced the tiny alcove while feeding the baby fresh goat's milk. The cold mood of her knight penetrated the cave faster than the damp air from the mists over the channel. Her steps faltered.

The regal woman he led down the stairs wore a dress of plain wool. Fur adorned the neck. Her hooded velvet cloak rustled as it glided across the dusty stone floor.

"'Tis all right, Sabine. This is Lady Camilla of Lockwood." Darrick's voice shook with the anger that seethed just below the surface. "She has much to make amends for and I am led to believe that this is where she wishes to start. From now on, she'll see to the care of my nephew."

"He is correct dear," the woman whispered. "And although he hates to admit it, I am Sir Darrick's mother, as well." Holding her arms out for the baby, she smiled. "Please, may I hold my grandson?"

Sabine cradled the baby closer to her chest and stood proudly erect. "But Chance has just returned."

She held Darrick's gaze, questioning him if it was truly safe to hand his nephew over to this unfamiliar woman. She could see he struggled to hold his anger in place. He teetered on the edge and she did not want to receive the brunt of his wrath. The unnerving thought that she had yet to tell him everything nibbled at the back of her mind. She prayed she had not waited too long.

Her knees shaking, she fought the fear of handing Chance over to his grandmother. "I beg your pardon, Lady Camilla," she squeaked. "I had not anticipated your arrival. Please forgive me."

"Of course, dear." Camilla nodded. "Why would you?"

Sabine delivered the baby into Lady Camilla's arms. She smoothed the patch of fuzz away from his face, kissing his tiny fingers one-by-one.

"Come, Sabine," Darrick growled, "do not take on so. 'Tis not like you'll never see him again. We are only going to walk the tunnel for a bit."

Grabbing her hand, he led her to a private alcove. His gaze slid over her face, trailing a shimmering path to her breasts. "Or do you have other plans that do not include me?"

Guilt played across her face. Her pink cheeks radiated from embarrassment. Ducking her head, she played with the folds of her dress, searching desperately for an explanation she could give her knight.

She had heard everything. Unwittingly, the men stood above one of the hidden airways her father had built. Not only did it provide fresh air to the tunnel, it also carried raised voices through the opening. She had planned to show Darrick the papers earlier but looking at them brought back painful memories that she did not want to face.

The hurt from Darrick's lack of trust ran deep. The knowledge that he was quick to believe Rhys over her was almost more than she could tolerate. True, she should have shown him what she carried, but that was water under the bridge. She could not change what had taken place any more than she could have changed her mistake in trusting DePierce for help.

Sabine rubbed at the healing stitches on the side of her head. Standing with her back stiff and erect, she held her head proudly and waited for his announcement of hatred. She knew she had delayed far too long. Perhaps their fragile partnership was beyond repair but she had to try to reach the gentle nature that he carried hidden deep inside. The wary look in his eyes stung her heart. He would have trouble believing anything she had to say.

"How can you distrust me after all we have shared?" He raked his hands through his hair. Pain etched his eyes.

"I'm sorry," she whispered. "I should have..." Her mouth grim, she shook her head. Hugging her arms tightly around her body, Sabine walked towards the corner of the alcove.

"What?" Darrick asked. He followed on her heels.

Shoved deep in the shadows stood a heavy chest. Kneeling down beside the iron trunk, she carefully removed the contents, one item at a time. She laid the last bundle upon the floor and stared at it as if it were a threat to her very soul. Silently, she stuck her hand into Elizabeth's dirt-encrusted pouch, and pulled out his sister's silver mirror. Drawing the jeweled dagger hanging from her belted waist, she began to pry at the curled edges. Slipping the blade between the layers of metal, she opened the back. A crackle of parchment shattered the growing silence.

In her hand, lay a folded missive, sealed with a smear of wax and marked with Lord Damien of Lockwood's crest. Her head bowed, she held the missives up for his inspection.

"I should have trusted you with this," she said.

Darrick examined the broken wax seal, and then opened the packet. His thumb traced the words scrawled over the parchment. "This is written by my father." He looked up, searching her face. "How did you come by this?"

"Balforth. I carried them with me when I escaped the tower. I have kept them hidden ever since."

Darrick's voice rasped. "You had them all this time and never felt the need to show me? Could you not trust me with this? Did you not understand that this is my father's mark?"

He strode over to the torch, smoothing the stiff parchment for a better look. He kept his broad back turned to Sabine as he read his father's missive.

"My father wrote to King Henry. He writes of DePierce's plans to destroy Lockwood. He knows you have this. It explains his desperation." Striding over to where she knelt, Darrick tilted her face with the crook of his finger. "All this time, you carried proof of DePierce's deceit?" His voice, hoarse from fighting the war within, broke as he asked, "Why didn't you tell me? How did Rhys know of its existence?"

Although his touch was so light it was barely discernible, she flinched. "If I were in league with Rhys, for what reason would he sacrifice my trust?" She balled her fists at her side, her knuckles white with frustration.

"Darrick, you know as well as I, that Rhys must have another agenda. What, I do not know. He helped me escape the tower. Why he used me to hurt you, I cannot fathom. He was kind and caring when I first saw him at Balforth."

Before Darrick could ask her how she knew of his betrayal, Sabine pressed her fingers to his lips and pointed up to the ceiling. Above their heads were tiny pockets, burrowed into the stone.

"Father had airways built into the rock to allow fresh air to travel in. Sounds travel as easily as the fresh air." She confessed. "I know 'tis wrong of me to eavesdrop on conversations but I heard you talking while you stood with your man by the tree."

"I am once again blessed by the Almighty with another woman that would dare try to convince me with pretty words." His glare burned through her. "Do not be misled, fair Sabine. Do you think I forgive so easily after you chose to keep my father's missive to the king a secret?" His jaw clenched, he bowed deeply again in mock reverence. "I have need of fresh air. I trust you will find much in common with my Lady Camilla."

His mother held out her hand, but he brushed past her as if she were invisible. A sad smile flitted across her face.

Sabine shivered from the cold blast of emptiness. With the back of her hand, she scrubbed at the hot tears threatening to fall. Wishing she could wipe away the hurt just as easily, she straightened her shoulders and busied herself about the cavern.

She could not stop thinking it odd that Rhys would turn against her. He had been the one to show her the tower's weakness. He had directed her towards the island, even caring enough to have the little goat waiting for her. Why would he be the one to speak of the secret papers when it had been his idea for her to take them and keep them hidden?

Foolishly, she had never taken the time to unfold the parchment, let alone read the message within. If truth were known, she thought Rhys sought the mere enjoyment of tweaking DePierce's nose than the papers actually being of value.

Aye, he had played her like a puppet on a stage. He was about something altogether different and she vowed to find out what it was. She would show her knight that he really could trust her.

Lady Camilla broke into Sabine's worried thoughts with a pat to her shoulder. "It will work out dear. Love has a way of doing so."

"Love," she whispered. "You have it all wrong, my lady. He despises me."

Lady Camilla shooed her argument away with a free hand and smiled at the heartbroken maiden. "My dear, I am the best at being on the receiving end of the infamous Lockwood wrath. I have had much practice receiving the disdain he has for me. He would not want anyone to know that he is capable of a forgiving nature. Rest assured that should you ever have him as your champion, he would stand for your honor until he can stand no more. My son's love holds no bounds."

"Your son is incapable of love."

"It is perhaps too late for me. Unfortunately, he believes I lost that right many years ago. But you have a choice to make."

Lady Camilla held her hand up to silence Sabine's interruption. "Go to him, child. Do not let the hour pass without explaining your actions. Force him to listen. Do not make the same mistakes I made when I allowed my pride to rule over my heart."

"But Lady Camilla, how can I make him listen?"

"Please dear, call me Camilla. As to your question," her fingers fluttered gracefully in the air. "Use your imagination, my dear. There are many wonderful ways to get a man's attention without having to scream at him. You are a bright woman. He is definitely attracted to your many...charms."

But above all…" She paused, her gaze boring into Sabine's. "My son needs to know that he can trust you."

Having never had another woman speak so freely, Sabine blushed. How would Darrick react if he overheard them speak privately about his love life?

She bit her lip and smiled. The memories of his warm embrace were much stronger than her fears. Perhaps she would take some of Lady…er… Camilla's sage advice.

After seeing Chance and his grandmother tucked in for the night, Sabine made her way to the top of the stairs. She prayed Darrick did not feel the need to bar the door. Pressing on the door, she found that it gave.

The cool night air filled her lungs. Twinkling stars worshiped the moon with their brilliance.

Darrick's men huddled around a small campfire. By the time she had reached her perch, she was determined to listen to their meeting. Staying in the shadows, she sat down on a boulder that had tumbled from a broken wall. Whether he approved or not, she had to know what strategies they planned. The matter of getting her lands and family back was as much her right as his. She had been a prisoner at Balforth and she would know if Rhys continued to lie.

Chapter 21

Darrick knew he should center his concentration on their preparations. He and his men would be riding out towards Balforth by morning. The battle plans were drawn. The horses were readied. The men awaited his orders to mount up.

Instead, his mind wandered to Sabine ever since the source of his desire had appeared out of the shadows and slipped down beside the men. He had every right to be angry with her, perhaps to the extreme of having her manacled with irons but he could not even draw upon the discipline that had carried him out of unwanted battles. Disgusted with his weakness, he stared at the woman who was always capable of diverting his thoughts from the urgent moment at hand. Even now, his need for her welled up and pressed against his hose, aching for her touch.

She sat with her hands folded meekly in her lap. Her mild attitude gave him pause. 'Twas not in Sabine's nature to give in so easily. What was she up to?

He had the proof he needed to seal DePierce's fate with the king. If his calculations were correct and all went well, his trusted messenger would have his father's missives in King Henry's hands in a matter of days.

In the meantime, he would discover how many prisoners Balforth held in its dungeon and then somehow ascertain exactly who sired his nephew. He prayed it was not Hugh or DePierce. That fact would greatly complicate his father's wishes for an annulment of Elizabeth's marriage. The church would frown on the annulment if a child was involved.

The king would not be willing to anger the church. His wild youth diminished, he had become more pious than his father had ever been. Henry had always treated his subjects fairly. However, ever since the massacre of the French nobles at Agincourt, he had displayed an edge of cold cruelty. He dared not guess his king's reaction to the request.

Filling his lungs with the crisp night air, Darrick gave up trying to ignore Sabine. The damp breeze blew, mussing her hair, and chilling her cheeks. She would surely catch a cold. Despite his efforts, he found himself in front of Sabine, offering his hand. "My lady, walk with me. If you please."

He winced when she cautiously accepted. Her chilled fingers burrowed into his palm. He owed it to her to listen to whatever faulty excuses she may have. Perhaps there was a grain of truth in her offer to prove otherwise. He wanted to trust what she said, but the possibility for betrayal was too great.

The breeze caught his cloak. The swan broach winked at him. Its emerald eye twinkled under the moonlit sky; taunting him, reminding him that he, too, kept secrets buried in his past. The king's Knights of the Swan were an evident part of the mystery he found himself embroiled in. The path of the emblem continued to lead him toward his sister.

King Henry had taken great store in keeping his group of knights secret. So secretive was the order, that they themselves did not know all who were involved.

Darrick suspected someone had uncovered their identity and was using this information to his or her advantage. That knowledge was as deadly as any weapon. And could be wielded by anyone.

They wandered aimlessly past the tumbled down walls. The charred wood and stone blended into the ebony night as they made their way further from the gathering of his men. Stopping by the remains of the keep, he turned his attention on Sabine. He longed to delve into the truth hidden behind her long lashes.

He ran his thumb across the expanse of her palm. Circling her tender flesh, he massaged the point where her pulse beat erratically. Fighting the force that emerged when he was near her, he worked to discipline the desire welling inside his body and tried to regain his grasp of self-control. Her scent mixed with sweet herbs enveloped him in their fragrance.

Releasing her hand, he struggled to clear his head. She held the power of his undoing with only a touch of her finger, the lick of her lips, the caress of her body.

Visions of her breasts tipped with rosy nipples brushing against his chest, heated thighs wrapping around his waist, straining against his body, distracted him from the questions he had thought to put to her. His flesh strained against his willpower. Mentally shaking himself, he tried to release his mind from the heat coursing through his veins. He crossed his arms to keep from wrapping them around her waist and offering to share their warmth.

"Earlier, you wished to explain to me how you came to have my father's missives in your possession."

Wariness flashed back. "You wish to listen?"

Darrick tipped his head. "I urge you to not leave anything out."

"For what purpose? No matter what I say, you'll question every word."

"Speak truth, my lady, and I'll not speak one word against you."

"If I do this, will you promise to listen till I am through?"

He nodded, adding, "But do not think to play me false again. Many times, have I asked you of Balforth. Many times, have you dodged these questions and found ways to turn my mind from your answers. I'll not stand for this again."

"This is your promise? Veiled in threats?"

"'Tis all I am capable of offering."

"Very well then," she snapped. "Listen carefully for I shall not repeat this memory." Sabine closed her eyes, gripped her hands tightly in the folds of her dress, and began.

"When I first arrived at Balforth, DePierce was quite welcoming. 'Twas only after he discovered Clearmorrow was set ablaze that he showed his true color."

Her voice strained against the anguish. Clearing her throat, she continued. "I endured the great pleasure he finds in ruling over those weaker than he. The young maid, given to serve me, was fearful of her lord. She urged that I find a way to leave Balforth in haste.

"Given a room in the far tower, I was allowed to go no further than the first floor. One afternoon I slipped out unnoticed by the guards and peeked through an arrow slit cut along the wall of the tower."

A trembling hand brushed at the straying strands of hair disturbed by the wind. They clung to her face where her cheeks were dampened by a trail of tears.

"'Tis where I saw the villagers. They were huddled together in the black hole. So cold and sad. They awaited a miracle."

Darrick started to wrap his arms around her and offer comfort, but stopped when she flinched as he drew near. She had traveled too far into the painful nightmare he had forced her to relive.

Sabine spoke in a hoarse whisper, her words straining to be heard. "Finding the situation at the castle at odds with his position as my protector, I sought a meeting with him. Had I known that one must first go through his master chambers to enter the solar; I would have refused and found another way. Once I advanced inside his suite, I realized he did not mean for me to entertain him with only warm mead and cakes."

She lifted her head, seeking his strength, urging her to go on with her story. Darrick drew her into his embrace.

She pressed her cheek against his chest. "There, I found my darling maid, lying unconscious from the hands of DePierce's man. When DePierce entered the room, I confronted him with the depravity in which he lived and told him that I would be leaving. He is desperate in need of an heir. I suggested that perhaps 'twas not his many wives who had the difficulty of carrying a child. That it was he who could not sire a child. He...he... informed me that I would soon have a change of heart."

"Is that why he would want Chance so strongly?" He stroked her hair, doing his best to soothe her. If only he did not have to make her relive the pain.

"Perhaps," she whispered. Her fingers stilled their flexing over his jerkin. "When I gained consciousness, Rhys was kneeling before me. My maid was gone. Naught but a pool of blood to mark her presence.

"Rhys told me he would help me to safety and urged me to escape from Balforth. Before I left, he gave me the packet of papers. He said to keep them hidden until they were needed. Then he led me to the latrine hole. I had to scramble down like a rat in the night."

Darrick's brows arched with that last impart of information.

She scrunched her nose. "'Twas disgusting. Yet I was desperate to leave. And that strange man had everything arranged for me. He sent me to the island." She clutched Darrick's arms. "I could not look at the pouch of papers for fear of the memories. For the guilt that it represented."

"Guilt? What say you, Sabine? You did naught to be guilty for."

He crushed her to his chest.

She reared back. His heart thudded beneath her palms. "Don't you see? I did naught but hide. I should have fought for my people."

He pressed her head back to his chest and brushed his lips over her temple. "Had you been somewhere other than the island, my nephew would not be alive. Elizabeth would not have had you to comfort her."

Sabine sank into the warmth of his embrace. The rhythm of his heart beat a cadence of comfort, drawing the tension away. Her nose pressed into his leather jerkin. Sighing, she inhaled his manly scent that mixed with leather and an unusual sweet fragrance of baby. Speaking into the wall of muscles, her voice muffled, she said, "I wish to go to Balforth."

His hand stilled, before he continued caressing her hair.

She nibbled at his searing lips, matching his kisses with hers. Hungry for his embrace, her hands roamed across his shoulders and back mindful of his wounds. Her fingers barely danced across the muscles that rippled under his jerkin.

A sigh escaped as his fingers slid down her neck and kneaded the tense muscles of her shoulders.

"Sweet, sweet Sabine, never fear, soon you'll be able to lay your worries regarding your brother to rest." Reclaiming her mouth with his heated kisses, he continued, "In the morn, my men and I will attack Balforth Castle and bring DePierce to ruin."

"And I shall be fighting at your side. Perhaps it would be best that you put away your horses and once more suffer the tunnels leading to the valley toward Balforth. Without the horses, I am sure we can gain entrance to the castle unseen. Then I'll direct you to..." She stroked his flexing jaw. "Darrick, whatever is the matter?"

"You'll not fight alongside my men." He leaned his forehead against hers and pressed his fingers to her lips to quiet the angry words that were sure to spill. "No," he said again. "My men and I are trained and you are not. You are needed elsewhere."

"What?" Astounded, she pulled away from his arms. "'Tis what you've been trying to force me to do since we first met. I've agreed to face my enemy and fight for my family's honor."

"Your place is here. Stay and tend to my nephew. Those are my orders and you will follow them."

"Lady Camilla is here to do that." Sabine wrenched her arms from his grasp. Setting her chin in a stubborn line, she managed to speak through stiffened lips. "My brother may be rotting in that infernal place. How dare you keep me a prisoner in my own home?" Looking around she shrugged ruefully, "Or at least what is left of it."

Darrick's legendary cold control returned. It slipped back and now shuttered his hooded eyes. He met her accusations with silence.

Pensive, she looked out into the dark, not chancing to risk the briefest glance his way. "Does that traitorous creature ride with you?"

He inclined his head with a brief nod. "Rhys goes with us to lead the way. He has agreed to help us with disguises that will allow my men to walk amongst the village unnoticed. The little one has proposed a plan of attack that just might work."

"So that he can turn on you as he did me? Do you believe the tale he told about that night? He accused me of lying and stealing. Do you honestly doubt my word against his?"

Darrick pushed back the swath of hair that fell across his forehead. "Would that I could leave him here, but I must keep him close by my side. I'll keep watch on him should he decide to betray us. He has knowledge of the castle that you do not and I must gain entrance to that tower."

He reached out to steady her. "I'm doing this for the safety of those who entrust their lives in my care."

Shrugging her elbow from his hand, she spun on her heel. Stopping abruptly, she turned and spoke over her shoulder. "I will be joining you on the ride to Balforth Castle in the morn."

Darrick scooped her up into his arms. "No," he growled. "Even if I have to sacrifice a guard to ensure your safety, you will stay here as ordered."

* * * *

Darrick's long strides carried them over the broken rubble from the destroyed wall. His jaw worked against his teeth, grinding as if chewing on a bone. He was doing his best to keep her delectable backside out of DePierce's greedy clutches. For his troubles, what did he get in return? She served him the idiotic idea that she could scale the walls of the tower and free her brother single-handed. Why could she not accept his ruling to stay behind while he and his men brought DePierce down?

Could she not be honored that he'd listened to her side of the story, giving her full rein in the telling of her tale? He did not want to believe the creature Rhys, but without his disclosure of the missives, they would not be on their way to King Henry. And yet, he wanted to believe Sabine. He was certain she spoke the truth when she retold the ill-treatment she had received from DePierce. Her torment told a tale more horrific than she claimed.

Darrick carried her past the tumbled wall, unwilling to take the chance that she would continue arguing her case outside. Slowly stepping down into the narrow passageway, he held her nestled snugly in his arms.

Sabine wound her arms around his neck. Her breath caressed his skin. Assaulted with desire, his footing hovered over the step.

At the bottom of the stairway, Lady Camilla stood with her grandson in her arms. The sight of the elderly woman holding the babe, dressed more simply than he could ever recall, refocused his discipline. Despite their betrayal, he owed it to his family to set their lives aright. Under his breath, he prayed for a miracle. "Dear God, let Elizabeth be alive."

Sucking in a breath, he slowly released Sabine, allowing her to glide painfully down the front of his jerkin, his swollen member pressing against his hose. Her eyes gleamed in the dim candlelight. He brushed his finger over the pearly crests of her breasts. Golden tresses glided against the back of his hands. He pressed a kiss to the corner of Sabine's mouth and instantly regretted that Camilla stood nearby. He had to leave lest he lose all reason and devour her tasty morsels.

With barely a glance towards the silver-haired woman, he coldly commanded, "Lady Camilla, I leave Lady Sabine in your care. I trust you'll see to it that she stays here to help you with the babe."

He bowed deeply at the waist before heading up the stairs. Tonight he would sleep under the stars with the cold night air, hopefully dousing the fire that threatened to consume him. Needing a clear head, he turned with a brief smile towards Camilla. Brushing a gentle hand over his nephew's downy hair, he lightly kissed the babe's tiny waving fist.

* * * *

Sabine watched his broad back retreat up the stairs and into the shadows. Her pale hands balled at her waist. She licked her bruised lips, tasting the sweetness from their kisses. The sensuous glint in his eyes had dazzled her until she lost all reason. They held promises of sweet release to a desire that awoke with his first gaze of hunger. It burned a path across her skin. When Darrick let down his guard and showed his gentle side, her heart twisted in a bittersweet knot. Here was her hope, her tiny glimmer of proof that he was capable of love.

Willing him to return to her arms, she stood stiffly, feeling an acute sense of loss as the stone door slid shut.

A single sob broke loose. Hiding her face in her hands, she ran to the makeshift bed. Fear and anguish for her knight blanketed her mind. The question kept bombarding her thoughts. What if he was like the others and would never return? After a time, her sobbing subsided to an occasional hiccup now and then.

Thunder trotted over to Sabine and licked away the salty remnants of tears from her cheeks.

Chuckling at the persistent animal, she caressed his smooth muzzle. "Where have you been, my ebony hound? Does your master, the tyrant, demand you stay here too?" She ruffled his thick fur and whispered into his coat. "We'll go together in the morn and present our case, once more, to our jailer."

Chapter 22

Sabine sat in the shadowy darkness of the hidden chamber and listened to the silence. She ran her fingers through the tangles in her hair, smoothing the snarled tresses. Where had Lady Camilla taken the baby?

Where was the familiar rustling of people milling about; the male sound of warriors' clanging steel against steel, the jangling of the metal in the horses' bridles? Even the slightest whisper of conversation would have been a comfort. Instead, the silence cut through the fragile sense of belonging that had developed while she was with Darrick. It was too quiet.

Fear enveloped her with the nagging worry. Had DePierce's mercenaries rode in while she'd slept and taken them away?

After donning the leather belt that carried her jeweled dagger, she climbed the stairs that led outside. Her ear to the door, she heard nothing but the birds singing in the branches.

The slab of stone moved under her hand and the door swung open. The soldiers had deserted their camp.

The faintest of sounds came from the remains of the main tower. She raced toward the tinkling whispers.

Drawing near, she peered around the corner of the broken stone. Her heart pounding in her ears, she gripped her dagger, prepared to take the baby from her enemies. By force, if need be. A gasp caught in her throat.

Lady Camilla sat upon a blanket spread out beside the tumbled fireplace. She fed her hungry grandson, nestling him in her lap. Her cheeks were rosy from the breeze that floated over the knoll. The sun glistened against the streaks of silver in her hair. Chance kicked at his grandmother's hands while she sang sweetly to him.

Sabine gulped down the lump that felt like a small apple lodged in her throat and leaned against the wall. She had forgotten how lonely silence could be. Tilting back her head, she let the sounds of life wrap around her. Chance was safe. She pressed a shaking hand to her throat, and waited for the roar in her ears to subside.

Krell stood guard over Lady Camilla and the babe. Ever watchful, he frowned when he saw her marching up with a gleam in her eye.

Turning to the grizzled old soldier, Sabine tilted her chin. "Good morrow, Sergeant Krell. Where is everyone?" She held up her hand. "Please do not waste my time by telling me not to worry or swear you don't know where your lord has ridden."

The old war-horse scratched his gray beard.

Scowling, he glanced towards Lady Camilla. "You will lower your voice before my lady hears this conversation." His old voice crackled from many years of yelling over the clash of sword and shield in battle. "I'll not have the dear lady start tearing up again."

Sabine snorted. "The lady is made of hardier stuff than that."

"Do you think to keep him from the task of finding Lady Elizabeth and Sir Nathan? The knight knows what he is about. Let him do the job he has trained for all his life."

Her shoulders stiffened with the force of his tongue-lashing. "My brother may be held at the mercy of Vincent DePierce. I'm not a weak-minded, weak-kneed maiden. I would thank you to remember that I want Sir Darrick to succeed as much as you do. But not at the cost of his life."

Sabine swung on her heel, her hands clenched into fists. "Your knight is outnumbered. Against odds, he rides toward DePierce. Without the aid of those he can truly place his trust in, the mission is doomed."

Daring to cross over the border of station, he caught her arms in his gnarled hands. "Do not get any wild notions in your head. Sir Darrick gave orders for you to stay at the castle and wait with Lady Camilla and the babe. I intend to see that you do just that."

Sabine poked at his chest with each word. Drilling home her anger, she snapped out the clipped words that she struggled to keep in check. "By the time this is through, I will have learned patience beyond what any normal human should have to endure. Your master knew I wished to go with him, that I could lead him to the tower chambers. He knew I wished to find my brother."

Biting her lip, she turned away, under her breath, she whispered, "He had to have known…that I needed to see him before he took his leave."

Her hair flew about her head in a boiling cloud of silk. With a flick of her wrist, she snapped the woolen skirt of her gown, walking past the insufferable old soldier. Tearing through the bailey, she headed beyond the broken wall that had once stood as the outer curtain. She took the overgrown path toward the knoll overlooking the valley.

With the breeze ruffling her hair, she nervously twisted her fingers together. Sabine searched the horizon for signs of dust tossed about by the pounding hooves of the soldiers' war-horses. Sabine sighed, her unease increasing by the minute.

Pensive, she nibbled on her lips and ticked off all the items she would need when they received word of their return. She prayed they would return safe and victorious with her love unharmed. And Taron riding by his side.

Wandering aimlessly, she stopped to visit with Camilla and Chance.

Camilla waved her over. "Sit a while, my dear." She raised her face to the sky. "Isn't the day glorious?"

Sabine broke off a piece of meadow grass, and slid it through her thumb and finger. "'Tis a day created for victory," she offered.

Under a veil of long lashes, she peered at Darrick's mother. Was Krell accurate in keeping Camilla uninformed of the dangers her children faced? If Sabine were ever to experience the joy of motherhood, she would never want to be the last to know about those she loved.

The baby kicked against her arm, tearing her mind away from the lingering questions. She smiled down at the little knight who had stolen her heart on the very eve of his birth. He gurgled for more attention.

Resting her finger in the baby's bunched fist, she remembered how wonderful it had been while sharing the baby with Darrick. She marveled at the care that he had shown his nephew. At first, he had offered concern out of honor to his family's name but, as the days blended into one, Darrick carried the infant with him wherever he went. Stroking the babe's cheek, she vividly recalled his wonderful scent mingling with Darrick's leather and sage.

"Perhaps, sir knight, one day you will explain your family to me," Sabine whispered in his tiny shell pink ear. "I think that I was a very lucky maiden to have my family's love to make up for the loss of my mother.

"For you," she promised, "I will always be there. Mayhap, my little knight, your story will be different. Let us pray that your Uncle Darrick returns with your mother."

The baby boy batted at the ribbon she had tied around her neck. Her brother's ring swayed gently between her breasts. Catching the ring, she gently fingered its crest and prayed a rider would come and report that all was well.

* * * *

Darrick shifted in his saddle. Not for the first time did he question the sanity of their plan. Only out of desperation had he listened and agreed to Rhys's scheme.

They were running out of time. The opportunity for surprise had greatly diminished. Even now, the little crow continued with his incessant complaints. Darrick gripped the reins in his wind-whipped hands. His knuckles paled as he strangled the pieces of leather in place of the wretch's neck. How he wished that Krell rode with him. His company would have offered a break to Rhys's constant complaints.

Was it any wonder that his sergeant had fallen into fits of laughter when he thought 'twas a jest that he stay behind? Darrick smiled, shaking his head. The elderly soldier swiftly changed his tune once he saw the order must be followed through. Between Sabine and Krell's angry gnawing, it was a wonder he had any ears left.

By all the saints! For a small man, Rhys's needling voice bore a bottomless hole into his nerves. If the man did not stop his never-ending whining, Darrick was sure to toss him into the next riverbank.

His men kept looking over their shoulders, daring to cast withering glares toward the clergyman, but the pompous wretch did not take heed. The men grew increasingly uneasy as they were forced to listen to Rhys's endless droning. Although Darrick was not a religious man, he knew enough to stop the men before they insulted the church. That line grew increasingly close.

All, but the scrawny boy with hair like straw, threw threats over their shoulders as they rode by the straggling rider. Each threat, a bit more outlandish than the one before.

Darrick shook his head. If not for the lives he hoped to find hale and hearty, he would have dug a hole and buried the man himself. He needed to find the patience to deal with the little man a while longer. At least until he found the prisoners held at Balforth. He could not simply wait out the enemy as he would a normal siege. From everything he had learned, their lives were not to be ransomed but used as carrion for the buzzards.

Eyeing each one of his men, he noticed the number familiar to him. Most had ridden in his service upon their return to Lockwood. They had seen the natural destruction that comes without villagers to work the fields or a trustworthy steward to oversee the estates and household. Ever since Hugh had taken control that fateful day of his father's death, the estate and lands that should have been Darrick's by birth lay unattended. It would take a great deal of work to bring Lockwood back to life. Not to mention the chests of coin he would have to spend.

Darrick's thoughts led to his family, and he was left to marvel at the changes in Camilla. His father's death had taken a greater toll than he would have expected. Her beauty, though still evident, had lost the radiance that drew men to her like bees to flowers. He wanted to hate her. Nor could he trust her. But try as he might to squash it, a glimmer of concern towards the woman who single-handedly turned his father against him, remained. He could not take the chance and leave Camilla unguarded at Clearmorrow. Even though he had given Krell strict orders to be at the lady's side at all times, he could not foretell she would be there upon his return. As it was, he continued to worry.

Darrick absently pressed the palm of his hand on the hilt of his father's swan encrusted dagger. He thought of the secrets he and Sabine found concealed in the handle of the steel and vowed he would not return until every question was answered.

Rhys's whining had increased in volume and length. Darrick swore the man did not even breathe between complaints. He should have allowed Sabine to come along. Thus far, the woman had been quite resourceful in the journey. Instead, he'd listened to Rhys. The plan the crow-eyed man proposed did not include Sabine.

Darrick missed the way she always nibbled on her lips when she was nervous. Last night, the gleam in her eyes, when she thought he was not looking, near put him in the grave. A yearning he could not name caught at his soul. He should have at least awakened her long enough to demand a kiss before he left. A kiss so sweet, the taste of honey was incomparable.

A slight movement to the side caught his attention. The straw-haired boy pulled away from the small band of men. The boy's face tugged at Darrick's memory. His gut tightened.

Krell would never have selected the pinched-faced boy. Not even to fill a squire's lowly position. Nor had Krell mentioned the sorry addition to the band of men when he gave his report. The old man had always been one to make his opinions known. Rare was the time when Krell did not voice his disagreement on a decision. Just so, he was quick to proclaim his verdict on every man.

Darrick's hair prickled. How did the waif come to be in his service, if Krell did not approve it?

He shifted his weight, imperceptibly nudging his mount with his knee. Drawing the war-horse closer to the lad, he watched the scrawny man-child nervously slide his eyes towards the line of trees they traveled past. Thinking that perhaps the young one was afraid of all the useless stories of evil Rhys had been spewing forth, he opened his mouth to offer a few words of encouragement.

With no foreseen reason, Rhys fell from his horse. Obviously, in great pain, howling from the tops of his lungs for all to hear, his shrill voice echoed through the trees. He rolled on the leaf-covered ground. The horse's powerful hooves were inches from his body.

Afraid to touch him, the men nervously scratched themselves while they looked down at the writhing man. Fearing that God's wrath had finally fallen on their heads for all the bad deeds they had promised the little clergyman, they stood helplessly by their mounts.

Making short work of the distance between them, Darrick charged his mount up to the commotion. "See to the horse," he shouted to one of the soldiers milling about. "Find out why the man fell in the first place."

The men drew back allowing him access to the wriggling lump. Darrick bent over the saddle, resting his gauntlet-covered forearm on his thigh. "Rhys, quit bellowing like a prodded cow. You will announce our position. DePierce's men will find us well enough without your help."

Rhys flung his dusty brown cloak off his head. Pushing his shaggy hair out of his eyes, he peeked around the legs of the knight's charger, and peered over to the edge of the trees before glancing up at Darrick.

"Blasphemer!" He howled, pointing a long dirty claw. "I am a man of the cloth and will not fight against your enemies. 'Tis against all that is holy!" he yelled. "I demand to be returned to the safety of Clearmorrow!"

Darrick threw himself out of the saddle in one fluid motion. He stood with his feet planted firmly in front of the cleric's nose. His hands fisted at his hips, he worked his jaw free. Would he go to hell if he throttled the fool?

Losing the battle of wills, he grabbed the cleric by the cowl of his robe and lifted him off the ground. Rhys's feet barely touched the leaf-strewn floor of the forest.

A swift movement of straw-colored hair flashed out of the corner of Darrick's eyes. With their attention drawn towards Rhys, he and his men failed to notice the band of mercenaries moving silently through the shadows until it was too late.

Darrick yelled for his men to take cover as the first arrow struck the earth. DePierce's soldiers circled them, their axes and hammers swinging as they charged.

* * * *

Attempting to focus through the fog of pain, Darrick slowly let out a ragged breath. The wound over his ribs throbbed where punishing fists made short work of their target.

Letting his head drop, he attempted to relieve the pressure across his chest. His arms were stretched tied tightly behind his back.

He strained to see past the blood, shards of crimson light slicing through the shadows. Where were his men? He listened for calls to his brothers in arms. How many had they lost in the attack? Licking his cracked lips, he said a prayer for those that had served him bravely and with honor.

He should have heeded Sabine's warning. The realization that she had known their plan would fail, hit him with a heavy force. Had she betrayed him? His stray thoughts gathered strength, giving rise to doubt.

A pair of brown leather boots shuffled in front of his face. Darrick could have sworn Rhys had a pair of boots much like the ones kicking dust in his face. Shite! They could not be his. They were much too large to match the little man's stature. Weren't they?

He had laughed at Krell's belief that Rhys had the ability to shape-shift. Surely, the bizarre suggestion came from a doddering old fool. He tried to peel away the fog growing in his mind. Struggling through the hazy clouds, Darrick focused on the voices that drifted in and out. Catching snippets of phrases, he labored, trying to decipher their words.

The leather boot caught him in his ribs with a breath-stealing blow. "Let this be a lesson to ya, young one. Here lies proof, women are the downfall of man. Aye, a weak man, just like his father."

Darrick groaned as another blow slammed into his body. This time, the foot was smaller. "This is for my mother."

"That's right, make him pay."

"What do we do now?"

"We let DePierce think he is directing his men, and we take the treasure that is meant for us alone."

"Are you certain 'tis there?"

"Aye, the wench knows where to find the treasure."

Darrick rolled to his side. His shoulder popped from the strain against his arms. The ache in his ribs tore the breath from his lungs. The binding cut into his wrists, taking all feeling from his hands. If only he could wrap them around Rhys neck.

The leather boot struck him in the face, splitting his lip. "Bastard."

"Quiet!" Rhys said.

"How can you be certain that she has it?" the other voice whined.

"Then she'll be praying that she did."

Rhys bent over and grabbed a shock of Darrick's hair, drawing his head back. "How the mighty Knights of the Swan have fallen under my command. Nephew, look upon another defeated knight. Enjoy the retribution for the death of your mother."

The sound of rumbling thunder grew as it pounded into the ground, interrupting the examination.

"Quiet. DePierce's men draw near and it is time for us to take our leave."

Darrick drooped against the hands that caught him up and tossed his broken body onto the wooden planks of the wagon bed. Before the wagon jerked with a start, he strained to catch the cold muffled statement that floated beside him. He squinted through swollen lids. Rhys and that boy.

"Well done, nephew," Rhys said. "Learn well this lesson of the ancient art of deception. With a slight of hand and twist of words, done right, no one is the wiser. And, I'll have Sir William's daughter exactly where I want her."

Sabine! Darrick's soul chilled as he floated into the gray haze, keeping time with the rhythm of the turning wheels.

Chapter 23

Lady Camilla stepped off the last step of the stairway. "I despise the way we must wait for my son's return. I feel like a rabbit running to its warren every time I come down here."

Sabine glanced up from the stack of Sir William's beloved books and attempted to smile. The movement felt foreign as her mouth stretched, tugging at the corners. Having recently shed more tears that morning, she felt too drained to worry about protecting Camilla's precious feelings.

Ignoring Camilla's complaint, she returned to the job at hand and continued to stack her father's books. An odd assortment were piled in the corner far away from the rest. Sabine ran her hands over their embossed covers. Why did Father keep them apart from the others? She carried them to another alcove where they would be safe and out of the way of careless feet.

Tiptoeing past Chance, Sabine glanced over at the baby sleeping. Since her arrival, Camilla had taken over his care and never complained when the baby awoke her and kept her from a full night's rest. For that, Sabine was grateful. She, herself, had lain awake, listening for the returning sounds of men, be they friend or foe.

"We cannot wait any longer!"

Lost in her private thoughts, Sabine jumped and swung around. "I …I beg your pardon. What did you say?"

"I said we cannot stay here doing naught to help the ones we love." Lady Camilla walked with halting steps to Sabine. Her fingers trailed along the tidy piles of leather bound books. She tipped her silver head. "Would you not agree, my dear?"

Sabine picked her words carefully. Unable to look Lady Camilla in the eye, she busied her hands with the random stacking of books.

"Perhaps…" She faltered, fearing she was making a mess of things. "Sir Darrick will return most any day now."

Lady Camilla's forced sweet disposition disappeared with a flash, reminding Sabine that Darrick's temperament was much like his mother's. Her eyes glittered despite the weak lighting of the cave. She batted the air in disgust.

"Dare you consider me as dense as that old codger does?" The regal lady stamped her foot. "I am not a half-wit. I know of the danger they are in."

Unchecked tears welled, threatening to fall down Camilla's cheeks. "Child, I am a full grown woman, wedded to the very brave Lord Damien of Lockwood. I have seen the deadly destruction from steel wielded by that same knight. Many times have I watched him ride out with his men when danger surrounded. And a week ago, my son left in that same manner." Worry etched fine lines at the corner of her eyes.

"Every day," Camilla persisted, "I see Krell searching the horizon. I hear you crying softly in the night. I understand the worry, the pain from not knowing. The emptiness, when they do not sleep safely in your arms." She slid her hands up and down her sleeves. "Men are odd creatures, are they not? They dare to protect those they love by keeping us uninformed of the dangers and worries of their life and yet expect us to act intelligently."

Sabine studied Camilla. Her father always said if one peered into a person's eyes, their true self could not help but eventually peer back. Still yet, nagging doubt tugged at her instincts to trust her sincerity. "How did Rhys know where to find you?"

"Ah, Rhys…well, quite simply dear, he knew Darrick's father." With hurt and anger reflecting, the steely glint flashed from her eyes. "Mind you, I have no proof, but I believe Rhys played a part in convincing Darrick's father that I was unfaithful. He dropped innuendoes, questioning the validity that Darrick was of Damien's blood. My husband forsook our love, believing lies instead of truth."

"The rumors?"

"Based on nothing but outrageous songs sung by bards traveling in Rhys's entourage. 'Tis true, Rhys visited Lockwood Castle the night it was agreed to wed Elizabeth to that miscreant Hugh and the contract was signed."

"He is an odd creature but one would have to be filled with evil to do the things which you speak of."

"You too, have felt the bite of his lies." Lady Camilla grasped Sabine's fingers in her cold hands. "Do not believe 'twas an old man's faulty memory of the night you fled from Balforth. Once again, he weaves and twists the story to suit his purposes. He saw the danger of your union with Darrick.

He separated the strength developing between you and my son. How do we know that he will not turn on my son? Why is there no word of any kind? Aye, my dear, I fear 'tis been too long," she whispered.

"What would you have us do?"

Reduced to tears, Camilla wiped the moisture from her cheek with a shaking hand. Smiling weakly, she shrugged her thin shoulders. "I do not know. I had hoped you would."

Sabine's brows arched. Grinning, she knew that in time, she might grow to care for Darrick's mother, after all. "As a matter of fact, I do have an idea but we will have to convince Sergeant Krell to join us."

"Leave that to me, dear," Camilla whispered confidently, adding an intriguing wink. The infamous, flirtatious twinkle had returned. "I can handle our Sergeant Krell."

Amazed at the transformation of the captivating lady, Sabine wondered if it were any surprise that Sir Damien struggled to bestow his trust in the woman he wed. What a vision she must have been in her younger days, filled with grace and beauty and the skills to bend any man to her whim.

Lady Camilla paced across the stone floor with renewed purpose. "We dare not waste more time down in this damned rabbit hole."

Stopping at the bottom of the steps, her foot resting on the riser, her shoulders rigid with tension, she turned, casting a solemn gaze towards Sabine. "Whatever the plot, I am placing my trust in you that it will succeed."

"Then let us pray it does."

Camilla held out her hand and motioned for Sabine to follow. "Come, we must make haste."

Determined to bring as many healing supplies as they could carry, Sabine ensured each member of the small group carried their share of the load. They had strapped a small satchel of herbs to the goat's back. Not wanting to work her too hard for fear of spoiling her milk, they had purposefully made the load light.

Krell pulled Sabine aside. "This is madness. We should stay. Wait on Sir Darrick and his men."

"And if you are wrong? Will you accept the outcome so easily?"

* * * *

Sabine's shoulders ached as she led Lady Camilla and Sergeant Krell through the underground passage. Her father was unable to complete the restoration of the tunnel. The smooth stone covering the floors and ceiling had long since disappeared behind them. Dirt and cobwebs filled their path.

Ancient tools had chiseled out the catacombs centuries before. They left behind mysteries that her father could not ignore. His treasured books had led him to find the hidden entrance. Had she not used the tunnels to escape that night when Clearmorrow was under attack, she would have never believed that they existed.

She stumbled through the dark with the baby in her arms. No longer asleep, Chance struggled against the blankets bound tightly around his squirming body.

"I'll take him." Camilla reached for the babe. "I fear he's spent so much time in tunnels and caves since his birth. He's likely to grow up thinking he lived in a rabbit warren."

Krell brought up the rear and bore the packs of needed supplies in silence.

Despite their discomfort, they pressed on. Their tired steps carried them through the tunnel.

Stopping for a rest, they readied to make their way out of the tunnel. It hurt her that Krell still believed she had magical powers. Instead of incantations, she would be using the knowledge and skill she had learned from her father. With the sleight of hand and a heavy helping of the mixture of herbs and minerals, she would be able to bring back the wrinkled old hag she had become on the barren island. She wondered how Darrick would react when he saw her covered in her old disguise. Closing her eyes, she prayed they would succeed.

The pain in her stomach increased when she thought of the tower she would have to scale. Their survival depended on her ability to climb back the way she had fled. She had no way of knowing if it remained unguarded. She would have to take her chances on DePierce's arrogance over a simple woman.

Once in the tower, she would have to go unnoticed. If she made it that far, she would don the garments she carried. DePierce would not bother her if she were dressed as a haggard old woman. She hoped she was right.

Sabine toyed with how she would convince the elderly couple to stay behind. Their forced pace through the passageway had been grueling. Their bravery was touching, but they would never be able to scale the tower to the garderobe. Had Darrick been with them, he would have forbidden them to come at all. Or, at the very least, he would have pulled them up by his strength alone.

Nevertheless, he was not. This time, she must help him. Perhaps under guard, but at least he would be more accessible to her than in the tower oubliette. The thought of his broad shoulders, squeezed by the narrow opening of the dungeon, made her shudder. Just having to think about it made her stomach twist wildly. Once she found Darrick, they would search for the others.

She shut her eyes and recalled the warm caress of his lips as he trailed down her neck, resting on her breasts. Her nipples hardened against the memories of the love they had come so close to sharing. Desire, want, need, love, she did not know its name, but it all coiled together in her heart to make a rope that gave her the courage to face her fears.

"Hold tight, Darrick," she whispered. "I am coming!"

Lady Camilla brought over the black bundle she carried and laid it carefully on Sabine's lap.

"Dear, here is my wimple and gown from the convent you asked me to bring." Fearfully twisting her hands in the skirt of the filthy gown, she continued, "I do not understand how you can believe dressing in this dreary costume can persuade others to think you are an old hag. With my fading looks, I for one will have no problem passing for an aged nun. Although I do fear Vincent DePierce will remember me from his last visit to Lockwood."

Lady Camilla bit her lip to control the sob that threatened to echo throughout the cave. "And what will we do with Chance? I would rather see him dead at my hand than allow him to be taken by that man."

Shocked that she would threaten to do such a thing, Sabine cleared her throat. "There is naught that I would not do to see your grandson safe." Seeing the answer to her worries, Sabine continued, "Would that I could stay here with him, but...well, perhaps, you and Sergeant Krell could stay here to keep this entrance secure."

Coming up from behind them Krell stiffened, his rheumy eyes glittered. "No!" he growled. "'Tis enough that I must disregard Sir Darrick's orders. I will not stay behind like a wet pup!"

"Sergeant Krell, 'tis a darling brave man that you are," she soothed. "You serve Sir Darrick best by caring for his family. Promise me, if you do not hear from me in two days' time, you will take Lady Camilla and Chance to King Henry. I am sure word would have reached him by then. You know as well as I, Sir Darrick would wish for those he loves to be under the king's protection."

He caught her fingers in his gnarled hand and bent on one arthritic knee. Bowing his head, he said, "Forgive me, Lady Sabine. I swear to you, I will do as you say. I will protect them with my life."

With tears in her eyes, she looked over the crown of his head, the wisps of silver strands shone in the candlelight. Meeting the understanding gaze of Lady Camilla, she tilted her chin, resolved to be on her way as soon as her disguise was prepared.

* * * *

Her wrinkled hands played with a loose tendril before tucking it under her wimple. Sabine hobbled out of the shadows of the cave and into the light of the fire.

Her companions drew a breath in unison. Sergeant Krell crossed his broad chest in a sign of protection before Lady Camilla could elbow him in the ribs.

Camilla dared him with a dark glare, to say anything untoward about their course of action. After giving the old warrior a blazing stare down, she turned her gaze to Sabine. Her eyes positively glowed as she examined Sabine's disguise.

"My dear! The results of the pastes and powders are amazing. You have become an old woman before our eyes. I can almost bring myself to believe that we are going to succeed in this desperate madness." Holding out a tapered finger, her voiced faltered as she asked, "May I…may I feel your skin? 'Tis so wrinkled. Dry as parchment! Does it hurt, dear?"

Shaking her head, a grin broke out, showing yellowed teeth, stained from age and decay. Sabine lowered her voice in a hoarse, broken whisper. "Aye, 'tis a fine thing that you get to know the feel of this scaly skin. I have decided that you and Krell must wear a disguise, as well. I have another gown and wimple that Sergeant Krell may wear. You may use the gown that you are wearing so long as we cover your hair and keep your face shadowed as much as possible."

Despite Sergeant Krell's protest, she proceeded quickly with her plan. Lady Camilla learned how to carry herself, delving into the short lessons Sabine gave her. She hunched and leaned, tottering about the cave and proved to be an avid student. Sabine showed her how to apply the paste if they should require repairs to their decaying skin.

Despite the growing impatience to find their loved ones, Sabine found she could not hold back the chuckle when Sergeant Krell waddled out of the shadows in his black gown. A mixture of goat milk and fat was used to age to his already craggy visage. His wimple hung askew, hanging halfway off his powdered shaggy gray hair. His large feet tangled in the skirts, nearly bringing him to his knees.

Sabine bit her cracked lips. "Sergeant Krell, I fear if anyone were to come near you, our plan would be sunk for sure."

His scowl deepened at the same speed as his growing ruddy complexion.

"Perhaps, 'tis the rather large sword that hangs at your waist that does not fit the portrait."

"I will thank you to get that notion right out of your head!" he growled. "My sword stays with me!"

Punctuating his point by puffing out his chest in a very manly way, he brought the women almost to their knees in a renewed onslaught of laughter.

Lady Camilla took pity on the sergeant. She placed her hand on his shoulder and leaned into him. "In my heart, I do believe you are the bravest man I know. Aside from my son, of course." She spoke softly in his ear, "Thank you for agreeing to this madness, Sergeant."

He sucked in a breath and shut his eyes for the briefest moment.

Intrigued by the exchange between the two, Sabine wondered if she should speak to Darrick regarding their relationship. She kissed their papery cheeks and gathered her things while they whispered instructions and prayers for her safe return. Their laughter faded against the threat and fear of what they had yet to face.

Chapter 24

To Sabine's dismay, the small doorway that led halfway up the outer wall of the corner tower was blocked. Someone had purposefully piled debris from the castle in front of the entrance. The inhabitants of the castle could not escape if they should come under attack. Did DePierce need to force his people to stay inside the castle wall?

She would have to find another way. The gatehouse would have too many clever traps awaiting an intruder. The drawbridge was up and the portcullis lowered. No one traveled in or outside the gate. It was as she feared. She would have to enter Balforth the same way she'd left it.

She located the open chute, coated with draining refuse from the castle latrine. The first chamber window rose high above her head. It led to a dizzying height. She sat staring at the gaping hole, nausea threatening to overtake her.

After taking a couple of deep breaths, which she immediately regretted, she stuck her head into the hole and began the long climb up the inner wall.

"Ohhhh…" she groaned.

Hand over hand, Sabine grasped the edges of the mortar. She hunted for the ledge of stone that jutted out from the inner wall. Slowly she pulled her body up the latrine chute.

Her footing slipped on the muck. She clawed at the stone. Her nose pressed near the sludge. Her stomach rolled, twisting in a knot. Eyes watering, her vision blurred.

"Obviously, he still does not believe in keeping things clean," she muttered.

Her imagination carried visions of rats and vermin crawling near her head. She shook off the fear before it locked her joints and she inched her way up.

She hauled her chest over the lip of the opening. The sludge clung to her clothes. She could not stomach reeking of this muck. They would smell her coming from the other side of the bailey.

A bucket of water stood behind the privacy screen. She washed off what she could. After changing into the oversized gown and wimple that she carried in the satchel slung over her shoulder, she then adjusted the paste on her face and arms and stuffed the soiled gown down the chute.

They would need to discard the plan to disguise Darrick as a very large nun. Resigned to the change of plans, she shrugged her slim shoulders. His passing as a nun had sounded farfetched anyway. They would have to make do with something else.

Her back pressed against the wall in the corridor, she prayed they did not keep him in the oubliette. Sabine shuffled through the rotting rushes covering the floor. The stench penetrated what little tapestry was left hanging on the walls. Although her memories of Castle Balforth were vile, she was shocked to find the state of the household in such decay. She could have worn the mucked gown after all. No one in the castle would have noticed the smell.

Chunks of mold and lichen clung to the damp walls. Feeling her way through the dark corridor, its decaying foliage stained her fingers. Following the sounds of snoring echoing throughout the hall, she made her way to a row of rooms.

A guard leaned against the door, his forehead propped against his hands that held the long pikestaff. A lonely stand of candles created a smoky halo around his head.

She crept against the damp wall, and prayed he slept deeply. Unable to wait any longer, she brought the heavy candlestand down on the guard's head.

The thud of his falling body echoed down the hallway. Waiting to see that no one came to investigate the noise, she took the fallen man by the dirty boots and tugged him into the room next to the one he guarded.

Sabine trussed up the guard with the ropes from the cot's frame, then shoved a rag in his mouth.

Tiling her head, she listened at the doorway. The castle's tower was strangely quiet. Where had the household disappeared to? She stepped over the fallen pikestaff and began ripping open chamber doors. *Where are you, my love?*

* * * *

Darrick refused to turn his head and look at his tormentor. "Do what you have to do and be done with it. You are beginning to bore me."

The panting drew near. It shuffled towards his cot. He steeled his soul, praying he would be able to endure the treatment they would deal out to him, one more time. He released the air he had sucked in and instinctively held, and prepared for the pain.

A cool hand pushed his hair back from his sweating brow. Fingertips trembled against his fevered skin, dancing across his face. Dazed by the tender touch, Darrick flinched when tiny kisses brushed his bruised flesh. Madness must be eating at his mind. Whatever torture they had devised, he feared they might succeed where their fists had not. He swore he heard his name called out by the sweetest lips that God ever put on earth. Moisture gathered on his dry lips. In thirst, he licked their parched surface and sighed.

"Ah," he rasped, "to die with an angel's kiss raining upon my lips. Could there be a sweeter death?"

"There'll be no dying. Not if I have a say in it."

He willed his mind to turn from the apparition.

"Darrick." The melodious voice, whispered again. "My love." Cool hands turned his head. "What have they done to you?"

Kisses grazed his swollen lids. Darrick searched for words but could not knit them together.

"Do not give up on me!"

A gentle weight pressed into his chest. Darrick peeled his lids open. Sabine? She lifted her head. Tears streamed down her face. The caked paste ran in rivulets, making a mess of her smudged disguise. The pasted on wrinkles and flaking skin was washing away with her tears.

"Hello, angel! What took you so long?" Darrick croaked.

Sabine cradled his head in her hands. "We must make haste."

She loosened the leather bindings to allow his wrists to slip out of the loops. It felt as if an angry swarm of bees had attacked his arms. Darrick groaned as the blood flowed back into his appendages. Salty tears stung the cuts on his face. Ambrosia from heaven. His angel's tender kisses gave him strength to keep fighting against the dragons of death.

"Hush, love! Do not weep for me."

Her face swam before him as he forced his eyes to focus to see her. Instead, a hag sat beside him. From the top of her wimple-covered head to the black habit that belonged in the convent. He let his view slowly slide down slim shoulders.

He recognized the pert breasts that pressed his chest where his heart beat erratically. The fringes of her dark lashes brushed against her smudged scaly cheeks. The unmistakable beauty of her eyes gave her away. Liquid brown and bottomless in depth, they brimmed with tenderness and passion.

"Sabine, my love, is this not how we first met? With me tied up and you in your disguise?"

Sabine pressed her cheek against the back of his hand. "You jest at a time like this? I should be furious with you for scaring me as you have. If you would have heeded my warning and allowed me to accompany you as I suggested we could have kept you out of this mess."

Despite his weakened strength, Darrick bristled against her scolding. "If I had let you come along they would have trussed you up in like manner or you'd already be dead."

"Hush!" She pressed her fingertips gently against his parched lips. "You must lower your voice. The other guards have yet to notice your friend at the room's entrance is missing."

She lifted the bladder of watered-down wine to his lips. "Do you have the strength to leave on your own?"

"Give me a moment and I'll be hale and hearty enough."

He attempted to sit up and fell back against the hard surface of the cot. His harsh breaths betrayed his weakness. Sweat sprinkled his brow as he struggled to make his muscles work properly.

Sabine brushed back the dampened hair clinging to his face. "My darling knight, as strong as you may be, I cannot allow you to help me search for the others." She cut off his arguments. "I brought you bread. Eat. Rest here and gather your strength. The household is barren of all signs of life. I'll be safer if I'm able to move about quickly."

"You must allow me to search for the others," she reasoned. "They're here somewhere. I know it! I feel they are close by. 'Tis not too late!"

"I cannot let you do this." Darrick caught her hand and pulled her closer. "DePierce may decide to pay his respects today. Leave this place!"

Sabine withdrew her fingers and pushed his shoulders back down on the rough planking. "I won't leave until we find what we came for. No one will know that I am here," she promised. "I'll find our loved ones and then return for you. Together, we will get them out of the tower. Agree to this, for this is all I will say on the matter."

Feeling his strength slowly seeping away, Darrick grudgingly agreed to wait and rest. The food had filled his empty stomach. It no longer gnawed at his backbone. The wine, although weak and watery, made him compliant and drowsy. "Aye milady, as you wish. But you must promise to do as I tell you!"

* * * *

Finally, after convincing the stubborn lady, his wrists were retied to the cot in the off chance that DePierce or one of his henchmen would return. He examined her handiwork, ensuring the guards would not notice anything amiss.

Sabine had retied the leather thongs to his wrists. The bag of wine was hidden in her pack. The crumbs of food were brushed off. The trail of flakes from her disguise, swept away.

"Return to me quickly," he croaked. "Already I grow worried!"

After fixing the smudges to her disguise, Sabine leaned over and placed a kiss upon his lips. She murmured softly against his fevered brow, "I love you."

Hearing the rustle of the door shut behind the courageous lady, Darrick whispered to the shadows, "I love you too, angel!"

Chapter 25

Sabine's frustration grew after each empty room. Her nerves were spent from the rolling anticipation. Her hopes shattered with every uninhabited chamber that she entered. She had yet to discover the prisoners' whereabouts. The fear that they may have disappeared forever increased with every step through the deserted castle.

Except for the few sentry guards that stood at the top of the towers, she had failed to see anyone moving about the castle. Where did they hide themselves? What mischief drew DePierce and his men away from Balforth?

There was only one small tower left to search. Dread slowed her pace. This was the last place she knew to search. She skirted the stone structure and pressed her ear to the tower door. If she did not find them here, she would have to fetch Darrick and make their escape without them.

She tested the handle and found it unlocked. She shook her head. 'Twas unlike DePierce. Had he slipped even further away from sanity? Had he murdered every one of them, or had the castle's household silently walked away without his notice?

Mindful of the possibility that a guard might be hiding somewhere in a corner, she waited. Her dark habit blended with the shadows dancing along the floor. Silence greeted her.

She continued down the corridor. The scent of moldering straw invaded her nose. Her lungs burned from the stench of decay. Unable to hold her breath any longer, she held the tail of her wimple to her nose. The rhythmic drip of water echoed somewhere in the distance.

Sabine cautiously turned the corner. Her breath caught. An empty chair sat beside a door lined with iron bars. A short wooden table stood nearby. On top of the rough table lay a set of keys. Shadows quivered from a chunk of candle that had almost burnt itself out.

She peered through the leaded bars and searched for signs of life. The cell, barren of furniture, was hardly large enough to allow a person to lie down, let alone stand upright.

A rustling in the filthy straw drew her attention. Sabine waited, barely breathing, and listened. She feared that nothing more than a rat produced the sound.

One of the mounds shifted and rolled over. Her heart thumped wildly. "Who's there?" she whispered.

The mound responded with a graveled croak and shifted again with a moan. She called out. "Sir Nathan?" The mound of straw shivered.

Deciding to try once more, she called out her brother's name. "Taron, is it you? Taron of Clearmorrow, answer me."

The responding stir of rushes moved her to open the door. With time running out for all of them, the need to find the prisoners pressed her judgment. It demanded a decision.

Sabine entered the cell and knelt beside the lumpy form. A dirty woolen jerkin covered a pair of broad shoulders. They could only belong to a soldier. She carefully rolled the man onto his back.

His long pale hair, tangled with bits of straw, hung across his face. A growth of blonde beard covered his jaw.

"Taron?"

A pale hand wrapped around her throat and yanked her close. "Who's there?" he rasped. "What games do you play?"

Fighting against the hand that cut off her air, blood pounding in her ears, she struggled to break his hold. Cursing at her foolish desire to save them all by herself, she wished Darrick were there to rescue her again. But this time he depended on her to succeed. She clawed at the bony fingers wrapped around her throat, threatening to sever the life from her body.

Kicking out she caught the man in his stomach. He gasped. His hold loosened and his hand dropped to the floor. His body curled protectively around his middle.

Their gasps for air blended into one. Moving as far away from the prisoner as possible, she sat and waited for air to return to her lungs.

From the corner, she heard a whimper. A pair of frightened eyes stared back at her. The other prisoner kept still as a rabbit caught in a snare. Its short breaths slowing. Its eyes widened in recognition, "You! The old woman?"

Sabine stumbled back. *Alive...Elizabeth was alive! I saw her go over the cliff that storm filled night!* Until that moment, she had found it difficult to believe they would find Elizabeth alive.

An arm wrapped around Sabine from behind, pinning her head against the sweat soaked jerkin.

"I believe my lady asked you a question," he croaked out, his speech coming in between gasps. Strength slowly ebbed from his arm.

Sabine recognized her attacker's voice and leaned the back of her head against his shoulder. Did her disguise as an old hag keep her brother from knowing her?

"'Tis I. Sabine."

"Liar!" His arm tightened around her neck. The weakened muscles absorbed what little strength he had left. "My sister was beautiful, smooth of skin and glints of gold shining through her hair. You are an old hag," he snarled. "With skin hanging on your flesh. Scaling like a fish left too long without water; dying in the sun."

"Taron, love. Let the old woman go," Elizabeth pleaded. "Perhaps she has news of our child." Her voice growing stronger, she sobbed, "I must know of his fate."

Stunned into silence, Sabine rocked back on her heels and rested her head against the man that sought to end her life. He talked of her as though she was deceased. Moreover, the most shocking news was the revelation that Chance might be her nephew.

Spinning her about, Taron clutched her shoulders and shook her out of her daze. "Well, woman, what can you tell us?"

Sabine adjusted to the surprises she had received. She cocked her head to one side to stare at the filthy man. It was just like her older brother to be so blind. He could not see that she held the key to their escape. "I think, had father yet lived, he would demand an apology for your sister."

Outrage registered on her brother's face. His arched brows lifted as he glared at her audacity. "You'll not speak of my family in this manner. You will be eating those words while you spend what's left of your miserable life buried with the earthworms."

"Enough," Elizabeth cried.

Sabine tore from her brother's hold and knelt beside her. How frail Elizabeth had become. She should not have tarried, wasting time in tormenting her brother. She should have told him outright who she was.

"Lady Elizabeth, you are right," she said. "I'm the one you knew on the island. Last I saw your son he was doing quite well with Lady Camilla." She cast a withering look over her shoulder at her brother. "I do speak the truth when I tell you that I am Taron's sister."

"You are naught but dried flesh and wrinkles," he said. "My sister died in the fires at Clearmorrow."

"Look closely at me. Look past the old woman's flesh. Do I share an old woman's voice or eyes?"

Taron knelt to stare into her face. His eyes widened, reflecting his amazement. "Sabine. What are you doing here? 'Tis a dangerous thing to be in this nest of vipers."

"Think you I am such a fool that I do not know this? 'Tis assumed that both you and Father perished. For almost a year, I too, have been in hiding. I have been in peril, ever since your messenger directed me to find sanctuary in this miserable place."

He shook his head. "I sent no word to you." He followed the trail where Sabine rubbed her throat. "I almost killed you." He hung his head, burying his face in his hands.

"Taron." Elizabeth wrapped him in her arms, cradling his head to her breast. Their lips slid over each other, clinging to life as they had done to survive for the last year.

Elizabeth pulled away and turned to Sabine. "For over a fortnight have we feared Hugh's jealousy had been directed towards our son. Yet, even more terrifying was our fear that our child was in DePierce's deranged clutches."

Taron patted Elizabeth's hand. "Hugh and his uncle had not counted on our survival. Instead of breaking us, it has forged a bond between our hearts that shall never be broken. We promised that if we must die, it shall be in each other's arms."

Sabine cleared her throat. "There'll be no need of promises of death." Feeling their time slipping away, she added, "I search for a friend of your brother's. Have you heard of another prisoner recently brought to the dungeon?"

Elizabeth turned her attentions to Sabine. "Darrick? He's home from the war with France?"

"He came with his men in search of you and at this moment is also one of Castle Balforth's unlucky guests."

"Does...Darrick...is my brother well?"

"I pray 'tis so. I've been gone for what feels like an eternity." Growing impatient to return to Darrick's side, she pressed for an answer to her question. "I am searching for his long-time friend. Perhaps you know of him?"

"Not Sir Nathan!" Elizabeth cried. "I could not bear it if he was the poor soul that bought us time away from Hugh's torment."

Sabine pressed her bone-thin shoulder. "They captured Sir Nathan less than a fortnight ago. What can you tell me?"

"Naught but that he is being punished for harming Hugh," Taron said. "A fight broke out and Sir Nathan proceeded to break Hugh's neck. Since then, DePierce's greed had turned to madness. So much so, that the men-at-arms guarding our cell left without a trace. For the last week, there has been very little food or water. The beating and torment ceased but we were left here to starve to death."

Sabine took out a small amount of food from the pack she carried. "Luckily, while searching for you, I found some abandoned bread and a bladder of wine lying on a table." Flicking the mold with her thumb, she handled the leather bladder to her brother. "'Tis a bit moldy, and the wine watered down."

Elizabeth cradled the chunk of bread in her hands. "'Tis manna from heaven."

"It appears the castle is almost deserted," Sabine said. "You'll be safer where you are until Darrick and I return."

"No. I shall go with you," Taron argued.

"'Tis unwise to leave Elizabeth. Gather your strength. We'll need to move quickly once I have found Nathan."

"Taron, we must listen to your sister."

* * * *

Sabine followed the landmarks that Taron said would lead her down the corridor. She had yet to see DePierce but she knew that the monster still resided somewhere in the castle. She prayed Darrick's strength was rapidly returning. She would have need of his brawn to get the couple safely out. In their weakened condition, they would be unable to climb down the shaft of the latrine as she had first hoped. How was she going to free them from Balforth?

The narrow hallway grew darker as she walked farther away from Elizabeth and Taron. The light dimming, she wished she could have been able to carry a lamp but they had feared it would draw too much attention to her movements. Not wishing to be seen by DePierce or any of his remaining staff, Sabine heartily agreed.

The hallway led to a small empty chamber. She retraced her steps until her slipper caught on a heavy brass ring in the floor. A trapdoor, large enough for a human, was cut into the stone. She tilted her head. There had to be a way to open it.

A thick rope dangled from the ceiling. She looped the rope through the lead ring and pulled down. The stone began to rise. Her stomach lurched as the fetid air reached her nostrils.

"I beg you," she prayed. "For Darrick's sake. Let Nathan be alive."

Frightened she would have to leave him where he was, should he be dead, she searched the darkened chamber for a way to light the black hole.

Stretching out on the cold stone, she leaned over the edge and peered inside. 'Twas the chamber that her maid had warned her about. The oubliette.

Shaped as a long and very slender cylinder, it did not allow the prisoner room to lie down or rest. Usually, the tortured were lowered down into the hole and held in suspension. The tube, so narrow the poor unfortunate soul would be unable to move their arms, the broader the shoulders, the more horrendous the discomfort. Another rope would lower any food or water he may have received. Or they would leave him to starve.

Sabine hoped DePierce used a hole that did not allow water to seep in from an underground spring. If it did, Nathan may be beyond any cures she or Darrick, might know.

"Darrick, my love, what should I do? If only you were here with me," she whispered.

A pair of pleading eyes blinked against the bright light. White orbs flashed in the dark. They peered up at her from the bottom of the pit, widening once they were able to focus.

She could barely make out the face covered in dirt. His massive shoulders squeezed against the wall.

"Sir Nathan, if you can bear with me, I think we can get you out of here."

The eyes flashed in understanding and blinked back. The weary knight opened his mouth to speak. His jaw worked, but no sound came.

She examined the rope. It was hooked to a pulley system overhead with a metal loop to help it run smoothly through the rings. Encouraged with what she saw, Sabine tried to recall everything her father had explained about pulleys and wenches.

"Listen very carefully," she said. "We don't have much time. I can see they have your arms bound by your side so I'll not ask you to pull yourself up. Can you help get your body up out of there by walking your toes along the wall?"

Speaking softly, she explained, "All I need is for you to brace yourself so you do not fall back down. Can you do this? Are you strong enough to do this?"

Nodding, his face grim, his eyes gleamed with determination.

"If you are ready then, here we go. You should be able to feel the rope grow taught with just a few pulls."

Wrapping the rope around the stone pillar that she found in the corner, she worked the slack rope through the rings. It came easily with the first few tugs, and then Nathan's weight dragged against the rope. Sweat beaded over her forehead. Impeded by the folds of the wimple, she tore it off and tossed it out of the way.

The rope dug into her palms as, hand-over-hand, she worked it around the pillar. Every once in a while, she checked the coil growing at her feet, gauging how far he had traveled the oubliette. Inch-by-inch, Nathan groaned, and he slowly came out of the hellhole.

She could hear his boots scraping every time he got a new toehold. Her shoulders burning, legs quivering, her breath came in short gasps for air. She feared she was about to lose her grip and he would fall back down. She had secured the rope around the pillar and tied it off just as her feet flew out from under her. Air whooshed out of her lungs. She spun around and braced her feet against the column.

"Sir Nathan," she gasped. "You have to brace yourself hard against the wall. I'm not sure how much farther we have to go. I have fallen down. But you have to trust me. If you fall back down, I will not let you stay there. Sir Nathan, can you answer me?"

Unable to hear his response, she secured the knot as best she could and crawled over to the opening.

His auburn hair clung to his head in matted clumps. His dirty face smudged with blood and filth, shined with sweat. Overgrown whiskers dotted his square jaw. Bruised rings circled emerald eyes that glittered against his gray skin. He opened his mouth to speak again but only a rasping sound was released.

Sabine's heart broke for the proud man. "'Tis good to see you. Your voice will be fine in a day or two. Then you will be chewing my ears off and questioning my loyalty to your friend again."

Nathan lowered his gaze in shame.

"Come now," she encouraged him. "Let's get you out of here."

It took a few more tugs until he lay on the floor at her feet. Dragging his prone body to the corner, she dropped the trap door back down. After coiling the rope, she looped it over her shoulder and helped Sir Nathan stand. His weight leaning heavily against her, they walked slowly to the cell where Taron and Elizabeth were waiting.

They stumbled through the cell doorway. Sabine helped Sir Nathan lower to the floor. He groaned as he rested his back against the cool wall. His broad shoulders quivered with exhaustion, making it evident to the three that he had been severely mistreated.

Sabine dropped the rope, then turned to find her brother and Elizabeth staring at the top of her head. "Is something amiss?"

"'Tis your wimple," Taron said. "Where is your wimple?"

Lifting a shaking hand to her hair, she felt for the head covering. "Saints," she groaned. "I must have left it on the floor by the oubliette."

"We shall pray that whatever draws DePierce's attention will keep him busy for a while longer," Taron said.

She cast a glance at her brother. "Are you strong enough to escape this place?"

Determination gleamed from Taron's gaze. He stood, legs braced, hands at his hips. "Try to stop me."

"Give Sir Nathan a bite of food and let him drink slowly of the wine," she urged them. "I must return to Darrick before DePierce or one of his men discovers our escape."

Panic settled in Elizabeth's eyes. Sabine rushed to reassure her. "Darrick and I will return for you. I promise!"

Sabine paused to untie the ribbon that hung around her neck and slipped off the ring with the engraved swan's head. She placed it in Taron's palm. "I believe this belongs to you." Wrapping his fingers around the ring, she kissed the back of his hand.

He covered her hand with his. "So that is how you knew we were being held here."

"Darrick and I discovered your message." Grinning up at his shocked look, she added, "It made it to one of the swans."

Noting that his shoulders stiffened when she mentioned the Knights of the Swan, she smiled up at his frowning visage, and pointed to the two lying in the straw. "Watch over them."

He pressed his fingers against the scaling skin of her wrinkled hand and grimaced at her need to admonish him. "I shall do my best."

Sabine held out her jeweled blade. "Use it if they come after I leave."

"What of your own safety?"

"Do not worry about me. They have yet to discover I am here."

"I don't like it."

Sabine gave his cheek a quick peck and shut the door behind her. She slipped across the bailey yard and raced up the staircase that led to the tower chamber that held her love.

Chapter 26

The weary knight gave a start when Sabine flew to his side. Although exhausted from the ordeal, he much preferred the physical torment to the mental anguish of worry. Relieved that she returned to him unscathed, he allowed her to rain kisses down the cords of his neck.

"We found them, my love." Her soothing hands fluttered over his skin. "All of them. They are waiting upon our return."

Relief came crashing down, nearly undoing his control. He freed his wrist from the leather thongs, wrapping her glorious hair around his hands, the silk bands teasing his fingers. She groaned against his mouth. The movement of her body pressing against his chest wrung a moan of desire from his lips. Her breasts teased his aroused senses. His fingers tangled in her long mane, playing with the curls that waved down to her waist. Smoothing the golden amber strands from her cheek, he cradled her face in his hands. He was enchanted by the simple fact that her disguise was at odds with her shining hair.

Sanity returned, thrusting its way between them. A wave of apprehension swept through him. "Sabine, think carefully. Where did you leave your head covering?"

"Oh...well...there is a bit of a concern regarding that matter. I forgot it in the tower where I found Sir Nathan."

Her teeth caught at tender lips. The movement of her tongue almost tore his concentration away from the problem at hand.

Mentally shaking himself, he spoke with renewed discipline. "Damn it woman, make haste, and cut through the bindings at my feet. We do not have a moment to spare. He'll be in a fury when he discovers Nathan is no longer there."

Sabine stiffened in his arms. "I…I…was only caught up in the relief that you were still amongst the living."

"Not for long," DePierce said from the doorway.

She sawed at the leather straps still imprisoning Darrick to the bed. "Hurry, my love."

DePierce glided over to the cot and closed in. "Ah, young love." His mouth flattened. "How I despise it."

Darrick wrestled against the binding at his feet. Had Sabine loosened them enough to free his legs?

DePierce reached Sabine and wrapped his hands around her throat. He drew her up, forcing her to stand on her tiptoes. Her eyes wide, she clawed at the fingers that held her trapped in their vise-like grip. The lunatic's feral lips parted, baring his teeth. The sparse pale beard that came to a point on his chin glistened with spittle. His mincing steps betrayed the strength that he carried in his body. The madness nearly jumped from his eyes.

"Release her," Darrick yelled. "Come for me. Fight me, instead."

DePierce threw her into the high-backed chair that stood behind Darrick. It hit the wall with a sickening thud. Bile soured Darrick's stomach. For hours, DePierce had sat endlessly in that very same chair, asking where the wench was hiding. All the while, his henchmen plied their hate-filled skills to Darrick's body. But nothing they did then inflicted the pain now ripping through his heart.

"'Tis your fault," DePierce yelled. "You could not just do what you were told, could you? All I asked was for you to be a submissive mistress. Give me a child. Was that too much to ask?"

She flinched at the low menacing tone of his voice. He stepped closer. So close, his legs bumped into her knees. He leaned over the chair. "If your father would have agreed to our marriage as I advised him, we would not have to do this at all."

He dragged his finger down her temple. "Had you married me, we could have united our families. Think of the riches we would have had. How strong our lands could have been."

"Leave her alone," Darrick growled. He kept working the leather, stretching it.

"Your wretched father could not even do what he was told," DePierce continued. "I could have made him a rich man. You and your family would have wanted for naught. But your family destroyed all that I worked for; all that I have sacrificed. I had to make them pay a price."

"No!" she cried.

"Aye, and now 'tis time for you to forfeit your price," he growled. "I took you into my home and you repay my kindness by stealing. That missive was very important to me. Where is it? What have you done with it?"

He pinched her chin. "Men stronger than you have died for it. I know where your father's bones are buried. What price would you relinquish for that knowledge?"

Sabine shook her head in denial. Darrick willed her to look his way. The straps were giving. *Stay strong, my love.*

"Once again your cursed family got in the way. Hugh's lack-wit wife comes to my home and displays her swollen belly for the entire world to see. She made a cuckold of Hugh. Embarrassing my household by carrying another man's bastard. Your brother's bastard. 'Tis a pity, the whore lost the child when she went over the cliff, do you not agree?"

"You are the bastard!" Sabina said through gritted teeth.

"Do not forget, my dear, either way—there is a price I demand you pay. I wonder if your helpless knight can tell me if you taste so sweet." He purred menacingly, running a cold finger over her breasts. "Does your flesh taste like warm honey?"

"No!" Darrick's blood roared through his veins. "Get your hands off her." The bonds loosened. *Still not enough.*

He strained against the bindings until they broke apart. Darrick threw his body on top of their tormentor. Unwinding a leather strip from one of his wrists, he wrapped it around the murderer's neck and tightened his grasp until DePierce's long fingers fell away from Sabine. Escorting the lunatic to the hell that he deserved, Darrick watched the older man's body grow limp.

With great pleasure, Darrick whispered into his enemy's ear. "I have news for you, DePierce. Elizabeth's son lives."

It was the last thing that DePierce heard before he died.

He lifted Sabine into his arms. His legs trembled, forcing him to reclaim the chair. He held her close, kissing the temple where he had placed the tiny stitches, feeling the slight pulse that throbbed against his lips. He kissed the pink shells of her ears and pressed gentle kisses to her eyes. Fearing that he waited too long to tell her of his feelings, he pressed his ear to her breast and listened to the steady heartbeat. "My love," he whispered into the nape of her neck.

Sabine touched the back of his head and ran her fingers through his hair, caressing his neck.

Darrick raised his head from her breast and gazed longingly into the brown bottomless pools. His thumb trailed over the soft curve of her jaw.

Drawn to the sweetness of her full pink lips, he traced her mouth with the pad of his thumb. Pressing his lips to hers, he murmured, "'Tis time we gathered our friends and family."

Laying a gentle hand on the muscular bands of his arm, she stopped him before he moved away. "I love you."

Speechless, Darrick enfolded her tightly in his arms, and silently carried his lady down to the deserted bailey below. His state of mind remained unsettled. Fear of losing her had nearly been his undoing. Did he pronounce his love? What if he were to lose her?

He would become a broken man without her.

Chapter 27

Sabine leaned her cheek against the wood railing of the rickety cart. She huddled with the motley crew of travelers, ignoring the pain as it bit into her flesh every time they bounced down the rutted path. Exhausted from their ordeal, the silent passengers swayed with the bumping wagon.

Had she made such a monstrous mistake? Was the tall broad-shouldered knight, sitting rigidly on the bench, really the same one who had held her in his arms, asking for her forgiveness? Had he truly whispered words of love or had she imagined it? She was certain she had felt his tears caressing her neck, his gentle kisses drawing her from the terror.

Wrapped in the warmth of his embrace she had dared to share the discovery of her love. And he had returned her love with brutish restraint. His stone-cold silence broke her heart.

Sighing, she conceded that his irritating control was only a portion of what made the man. Moreover, she had glimpsed another person hidden under the hardened knight's armor, a gentle, warm-hearted man she had grown to love.

The wagon hit a rut, banging the passengers in the wagon bed together. Sabine glanced over at Darrick's sister. Elizabeth's bruised body was nestled in Taron's protective arms. She gasped with every jolt of the wheel. She lay bundled in one of the few blankets clean enough for use. The linens left behind were threadbare, and riddled with vermin. With all the castle folk leaving in the middle of the night, Balforth had fallen into disarray.

Although weak and much thinner than Sabine remembered, Taron sat tall, stoically oblivious to the torturous cuts and bruises he had received. Always one to go searching for adventure, playing light of anything serious, his eyes were now haunted. Buried deep within were the memories of terror for the lady he loved. Fear had eaten at his pride. He knew the life of his child, and the lady he cherished, had been dangerously close to death.

The request for Elizabeth's marriage annulment was sent to King Henry, but it had yet to be granted. His son, born out of an unlawful union, may yet bear the stain of bastard. However, he and Elizabeth had agreed that they would rather their son be labeled as such than tainted with the DePierce's godforsaken name.

Sabine examined Sir Nathan's hulking body huddled on the floor of the cart. He looked worse for wear. The filth had crusted to his broken body. His shirt and leggings, covered in muck. His matted hair hung in dirty clumps where rivulets of what the jeering guards had laughingly passed off as food and dumped upon his head. Any nourishment he consumed was lapped up like the dog they had called him. Fresh cuts joined the other scars on his knuckles. His muscled arm hung awkwardly from his shoulder where Hugh had dislocated it. Luckily, this was Hugh's final damage before Nathan broke the sniveling cur's neck with his one useful hand. Unfortunately, he was outnumbered and quickly recaptured. After being informed of his nephew's death, DePierce had administered Nathan's punishment with extreme hatred.

The brave knight had reported to Darrick with self-satisfaction that he would willingly endure the pain again. The sight of innocent children and women, held prisoner for the smallest infraction, released from the lower dungeon, was well worth any price that he had to pay. He was able to send them on their way before the few remaining henchmen noticed his escape from the two idiots, Gregor and Spurge. Those two were sure to have mighty headaches. Provided they lived after DePierce caught up with them.

She caught a glimpse of one of the watchtowers. There had been an argument amongst them whether to pull the castle down or let it stand. Elizabeth was the first to disagree, begging to burn it to the ground, pleading to pull the castle walls down stone by stone. Her desire to erase the misery caused by the DePierce family was greater than the natural order of pleasing the king. But Darrick stood his ground until they agreed to let the castle stand, at least until they received word from King Henry to do otherwise.

* * * *

Relief had flooded Darrick's weary limbs when he found the haggard horse and half-rotted farmer's cart. He had imagined he was strong enough to walk beside the beast but soon discovered that he was much weaker than he realized. With his strength seeping away, the tree trunks began to blur together as the cart wove its way around the juniper shrubs.

They moved cautiously through the wooded glen. There were no tracks to tell them where DePierce's men-at-arms had hidden themselves. The tingling that raced up the back of his neck signaled that their safety was a fragile thing.

He gripped the reins and ignored the pain in his stiffening fingers. The failings of his body were an embarrassment to a knight. His hands had been far too slow in freeing his ankles from the bonds. His mind had been filled with desire for Sabine and the way her breasts felt as they pressed against his chest.

It ate at his pride that he had been caught unawares. It was his fault that she had borne DePierce's vile touch for even a moment. He had allowed his discipline to slip. That very same discipline he depended on in battle to keep men and king alive had almost permitted his lady to perish.

He renewed his vow to protect Sabine and, if that meant shutting her out and denying any distracting emotions he felt for her, then he would. He might not be able to give her his heart, but by the saints, he would give her his sword arm. No matter how much it pained him.

Rhys's threats kept echoing in his mind. Sabine's life was still in peril. What did she possibly know that was a threat to the little man?

Where had Rhys hidden himself?

Darrick scanned the forest. Aware of the danger lurking in the shadows, he watched for any slight movement made by man or beast. Concern that the whole army of his men had perished in the ambush increased as they made their way to the tunnel's entrance.

Sabine sat facing the front of the cart. Her head was close to his waist. He could feel the warmth of her body radiating through the cold damp air. No matter what he tried to think about, his mind kept drifting back to the woman. He swore he could feel her breath clear through his leggings, tickling the bristling hair on his thighs. He tugged his thoughts back. *What is she quizzing me about?*

The heat of her deep brown gaze bore through his defenses. He glanced down long enough to see the quick flash of dismay and confusion wash across her face before she ducked her head. By the time she raised it, a look of indifference was pasted upon her visage.

Her lack of interest lasted long enough for her eyes to flash with excitement. "There," she said. Pointing to the shadowed juniper, her elbow caught his injured ribs.

He could not believe what he saw. Incredulous, he swung around to confront the woman who had the vexing way of getting under his skin.

"Who the devil decided to leave a lamp burning for everyone to see?" His gaze shifted to the trees, anticipating another ambush. "'Tis certainly not Krell's way."

* * * *

Sabine watched the three strapping knights walk warily around the empty campsite positioned at the cave's entrance. The men agreed there were signs that Krell and Lady Camilla went against their will. It was with small relief that they did not find a bloody trail to follow.

Her brother, Taron, had left his king's court to search out a missing father and never discovered his whereabouts. His results were to become the prisoner of his family's sworn enemy. Even with his recent escape, he was still a sad-eyed man who she did not recognize. Unable to return victorious with his beloved father, Sir William, he wore the shame of unfulfilled duty like a mantle.

Did Taron appreciate the precious gifts that he did have? Elizabeth's love was evident. It positively glowed from every pore. Her love-filled eyes followed him while he paced the cave. Her adoration flowed over his wounds like warm honey.

The petite raven-haired woman was far gentler in character than Darrick had described. Perhaps the events of the last year had softened her shrewish temperament. Sabine stifled a snort. She could not bring herself to believe her brother brought about this change.

And Taron knew that he had been blessed with an heir. But, having yet to see his son, to hold Chance in his arms, he had yet to understand how wonderful the blessing truly was.

Sabine shifted to peek under the protection of her lashes. It appeared to disturb Sir Nathan Stave that he had been rescued by a mere slip of a maiden, far smaller and weaker that he. Sabine shrugged her shoulders. The lunatics at Balforth may have abused his body, but at least his pride was intact.

She wished Father had been there. Her heart felt leaden, unable to mourn the loss of his passing. She ached to shed the tears that held themselves at bay. If there was more to endure, she feared she would indeed shatter.

She craved the comfort of Darrick's strongly banded arms to wrap around her and tell her everything was going to work itself out. The hungry yearning for his touch increased the pain, for the loss was more intense without his love. Aye, fool that she was, she had set her heart upon his love and came up cold and empty.

Since the death of DePierce, Darrick had distanced himself from her whenever possible. The effort that he put into the cold indifference was intolerable. Did he think she intended to press unwanted advances on his honey-sweetened lips? Or, by all that was holy, force her kisses upon his brow or dare to place his hand upon her breast?

She shook her head. Although she had helped them escape from DePierce, the stubborn man would not think to include her in his plans. Even her own brother had treated her as the pampered lady she once was.

Could they not comprehend that time was gone? A lifetime had passed since her head had touched her pillow. Sabine grimaced at the ridiculous thought. How could she have forgotten that her home lay in ashes? Ashes created by the fire that she had set. That coddled lady had been incinerated, along with the life she knew.

Would Taron ever forgive her? Not for the first time, she wondered how her townspeople had fared. Had they all perished that night? Squeezing her eyes tight, she struggled to stop the returning memories of the people held captive in the tower. Where had they taken themselves to hide? Will this nightmare ever end? *Lord, keep us all in your protection.*

Chapter 28

Darrick despised the tight walls that narrowed into nothing more than rabbit holes. When he stopped to get his bearings, Sabine slammed into his back. Again. For the hundredth time since they had set off towards Clearmorrow.

"Beg your pardon," Sabine clipped out the terse apology. "Perhaps it would help if you made some type of motion before you stopped so abruptly."

Darrick allowed a grunt to escape his compressed lips. For whatever unexplained reason, the sprite's dark mood appeared to be matching his mood. To make matters worse, despite his determination, her slightest touch set off an explosion through his veins. He had to spend the next five minutes concentrating on cooling his blood.

"Really, Elizabeth dear, you need not press so hard." Speaking gently, Sabine explained, "We must proceed slowly. To rush in the dark would be foolish if we cannot see where we are going."

"I do beg your forgiveness." Elizabeth's teeth flashed in the weak lighting and crowded them a bit more, bumping into Sabine's back.

Tension building, Darrick rolled his eyes heavenward, asking for forgiveness for whatever sin he may have committed to deserve a feather-headed sister. With the prayer sent to God above, he said, "By all that is holy, Elizabeth, give way to your impatience. Try to understand that we must travel with quiet and caution."

Only a few short steps later, Elizabeth happened to push Sabine into Darrick's back, again. Her feet tangled with his. Darrick turned to the blonde-headed man behind her. "Sir Taron, would you please see to the women? Try to control them."

Taron snorted at the request. "You think me to control these women? This undisciplined one," he jabbed a thumb at Sabine, "was never one to listen to reason. She has always been a pain in the backside."

Lifting Elizabeth's hand to his lips, he pressed her palm to his heart. "And this fair lady," he whispered affectionately, "has my soul in the palm of her hand." Looking helpless at the angry knight, he shrugged his shoulders. "There is naught I can deny her."

Nathan chuckled at the speech. "'Tis a pretty story that you tell. Aye, perhaps you don't know Elizabeth as well as you may think. I've witnessed the stormy temper she is capable of producing. Although tiny, she can yell the roof down if she chooses. She might be tame right now, but I will wager, if provoked, she still holds a temper."

Darrick bristled at Taron's harsh words directed towards Sabine. He clenched his fists, looking for a face to strike. If Sabine's brother was fool enough to get in the way of his knuckles, then so be it. He fought for control before he caused any damage he would regret.

"Had Sabine listened to reason, she would not have taken her life in her hands to reach us. Nor would she have scaled a tower wall, climbing through the filthy shaft of the latrine. She overcame her fears of Balforth Castle to come and save our unworthy hides." Darrick put his arm around her waist and pulled her protectively to his side. "I, for one, have seen no other to compare. Sister, or no, she's a precious gem and I would thank you to treat her likewise."

Sabine stared up at him. Her face flushed from his praise. He had yet to speak words of love, but he cared for her. She deserved a hundred compliments a day. Turning to press on, he continued to hold her hand as they led the way together.

Elizabeth stopped and held Taron's face between her hands. She kissed his mouth, nibbling on his lips, covering the sharp angles of his face and the lean muscles on his neck. "Thank you," she whispered.

Returning her kisses, he replied, "Anything for you, my love."

"I love you."

"And I, you." Taron placed a kiss upon her forehead. "Now let's go find our son!"

Nathan rolled his eyes towards the ceiling. "Proof that love is for fools. Give me a willing tavern wench anytime over that of the strings attached to a respectable lady." He motioned with his good arm for the couple to move on.

"I hate to admit it, Lady Elizabeth," he said grudgingly, "but if you desired Darrick to drop his icy distance then it looks like your plan worked.

However, let us hope he manages to save his rage for someone other than your Taron's pretty face."

With his shoulder hanging awkwardly in the sling wrapped around his neck, Nathan motioned his bruised body towards them. Although Sabine had tried to slide the joint back into place, his shoulder was nevertheless painful to move.

"Why do you concern yourself now, Elizabeth? You cared naught for Darrick's feelings when Sir Damien had the drawbridge raised. God's teeth! He even went so far as to insult him further by lowering the portcullis, shutting out his only son from your ill-fated wedding."

Elizabeth froze. Her body trembling, she finally unlocked her jaw. "Nathan, you know that I did not have a say in the marriage. No say in my life! Hugh was not even present for the wedding. He was in France. I was forced to say the marriage vows with Rhys standing in as proxy.

'Twas that awful creature that urged the wedding take place quickly.

"He already had Father's confidence. After all, Rhys convinced him that our mother had made a cuckold of him while he was away on the king's business. In the beginning, theirs was a marriage that held no trust, let alone love. If truth be known, I think there were always questions in the back of Father's mind regarding her fidelity."

Walking up from behind, ready to command his worthless troops to move their arses, he overheard his sister's comments. Darrick laid his hands upon her trembling shoulders and turned her to face him.

The hurt continued to pierce his armor. "It took only a few scattered words, rumors that have been repeated as far back as when I was serving as squire." A sad smile, never quite reaching his eyes, lifted the corners of Darrick's mouth. Glancing over at his tired friend, he shook his head. "Leave it, Nathan. 'Tis a long time ago and a wedding I am glad I missed. The future is what concerns us. Place your energies into finding my nephew and mother."

Nathan clasped Darrick's arm. "Aye, right you are. I believe we have wasted enough time on this."

Darrick turned to give Elizabeth and Taron a long hard look, his eyes boring into their souls. "Your son needs you. I have grown attached to the child. It would not please me if he were harmed in any way."

"You dare insult me by doubting that I love my son?" Elizabeth answered. "What else was I to do? I did what I could, praying that his life would be spared. Rhys sent me to the island, confident that Hugh would not find me. He swore I would find safety."

"The trail always circles back to Rhys. Would you not question his intentions when he was the one that placed you in that marriage in the first place?"

He turned to stare at Taron, his temper flared while he threw his accusations at his sister's lover. "And you? Does it not eat at you, worrying where your son is? Although Chance was born out of marriage you'll do right by him and my sister."

Taron drew his back straight and stood as tall as his accuser. "I'll take into account that we're all tired and worried, and will overlook your insulting remarks."

"Darrick," Elizabeth said, "If not for Taron, I would have been lost in despair. But I knew he feared for his father's safety. I urged him to leave Lockwood and continue his search."

"I spoke with Sir Damien before I left," Taron said. "I had begun to fear Rhys suspected there was more to Elizabeth's and my friendship. I urged your father to stop Elizabeth's marriage to Hugh. I thought I had time and that the wedding would never take place. I never anticipated the length of which Rhys and DePierce would take to gain the land. He ensured that DePierce's soldiers knew where to set their trap and take me prisoner.

"Never doubt, Sir Darrick, that I willingly recognize Chance as my son." Shrugging his shoulders, he held out his scarred hands. "My king is bound to agree to the annulment your father requested and like as not consent to the joining of our families."

Darrick glanced to where Sabine stroked his forearm. Her touch distracted him from his fury with her brother.

"Unlike you," Taron continued, "I haven't been blessed with the opportunity to set my eyes upon my son's sweet face." He drew in a ragged breath. "I haven't had the good fortune to count his toes and fingers. Nor have I been able to sit and dream of the future with my family."

Heartache winning over the grip on his emotions, his voice shook, "Imprisoned at Balforth for so long, I quit praying for my life. Instead, I feared for the future of the woman that they brought back to my cell. They dumped Elizabeth on my lap, a shell of the woman who had escaped their tower. She was left without anything to wash the salt staining her festering wounds, and naught to heal the open sore in her soul when she feared our son was left in Hugh's clutches. 'Twas the small glimmer of hope that kept us alive when we knew that Hugh and his uncle did not believe Elizabeth had born the babe before falling to the rocks below the cliff."

Taron folded his arms protectively around Elizabeth. "Tell me, Sir Darrick, how would you have behaved should the brave lady you prayed would escape with your unborn child was returned to you broken and without the babe? A baby, conceived out of love."

Although the light was too dim from the tallow candle that they carried, Darrick did not need to see the anguished couple's faces to look into their souls. He heard the painful truth in their voices. "I…apologize for my accusations."

"Is it necessary for me to point out that we have yet to reach Lady Sabine's cavern?" Nathan broke in. "If so, I pray that you will all lower your voices." He lifted one red wing over his glittering emerald eyes and shared a smile with Sabine.

Ignoring the sharp intake of her breath that echoed through the cave, bouncing off the stone wall, Nathan continued with his observation. "Darrick, do you have a plan should we finally arrive at our destination or shall we stand here and wait for our enemy to find us?"

"Sir Nathan," Sabine said, "unless I am mistaken, we decided at the cottage to forgo the titles for another time. Shall we agree this time as well?"

Nathan bowed deeply at the waist. "My dear lady, I am at your mercy and willing to address you in any way your heart desires."

To which the two other men groaned loudly at his foolishness.

Darrick growled at the shaggy man flirting with the woman he had already claimed as his own. Could his friend not see he had marked her as such?

"Let us be on our way," he barked. "Sabine, put the idiot out of his misery and answer him."

Sabine smiled graciously and curtsied for the large knight. With the help of Sir Nathan's outstretched ham-sized paw, he helped her rise.

Darrick scowled as he watched. Irritation showed through his rigid stance, hands braced at his hips. She was smiling up at his huge friend. A black wave washed over him. Fists curled at his sides.

"My darling Sir Nathan," she purred. "If you would do me the honor of addressing me as Sabine, I would be most grateful."

"Aye, I will, if you promise to warm my heart by forever remembering that I am your friend and confidant for life. You must always call me by my given name."

"Which is that?" Taron grumbled under his breath, "Idiot, or fool?"

Elizabeth covered her mouth with her fingers and forced a frown of disapproval. Moving silently, her pointed elbow connected to her darling's tender side.

Looking to avoid another confrontation, Darrick stopped Nathan from plowing Taron over. "Sabine leads from here on."

"We will be able to rest in one of the smaller alcoves before we reach the main storage room under Clearmorrow," promised Sabine.

* * * *

Their fatigue too much to bear, they finally agreed to stop and rest. Darrick sat with his back resting against the cave wall. Although the cold stone was harder than the little cot he had been tied to for the last week, the freedom it offered was infinitely better. Regrettably, the damp air began to seep into his tired bones the moment he sat down.

Sabine pressed her head into his lap, wiggling to find a more comfortable spot. The heat of her breath penetrated his leggings, tickling the bands of muscles on his thighs. Darrick dared not move. His desire to find her wrapped around his burgeoning flesh was growing out of control. Denying his need, he forced his mind to examine the circumstances in which they had found themselves.

The dark room was barely larger than the narrow passageway. If he were to spread out his arms, he would be able to touch all that lay sleeping side by side. With the dirt packed floors behind them, they were able to breathe a little easier. The dust kicked up by their feet no longer penetrated their lungs. The rock floor made a cold, hard surface to sleep upon, but they were able to make a pallet out of the few blankets and meager supplies Camilla and Krell left behind. At last, the height of the ceiling was taller than he was, allowing his back to straighten. He groaned as he stretched his cramping muscles. He knew his comfort was better than that of his friend.

Nathan had yet to stand straight since they entered the bloody rabbit hole. His massive shoulders brushed along the walls. Wherever a rock would jut out, he was forced to squeeze by. He curled upon the floor, sucking in his muffled groans. His movements were so stiff that it caused Sabine great concern.

Not until she demanded to care for his bandages, did he relent. It took all of their skill to ease the pain from Nathan's wounds. Darrick ground his teeth, slowly clenching his jaw muscles. It was just like Nathan to keep silent regarding the extent of torment he had been put through.

In the time that it took for Sabine to fetch what was left of her ointments and herbs from her pack, Nathan had confirmed what Darrick had already concluded. They pieced together the information Elizabeth and Taron had gleaned while Hugh and DePierce raved at them in fury.

The little man, Rhys, had passed himself off as a devout clergyman, set upon by DePierce's men. In actuality, he was the mastermind behind the plot to destroy all those in his way. For what? A mythical treasure that no one but Rhys believed existed. The blood of those who died may not have sullied Rhys's hands, but he would bear the burden when it came time to judge his actions.

How was it possible that he drew everyone to his plan?

That foul creature made sure he was delivered into DePierce's hands. He had talked of finding Sir William's wench. Fool that the arrogant man was, Rhys did not realize the extent of her intelligence and bravery.

Absently following the path to Sabine's temples, he caressed the side of her head. He brushed her hair out of the way, letting the silken strands fall slowly through his battle-scarred fingers. It tore at his heart to know that she still did not trust him enough to reveal her secrets. He could not help wonder at her reasons, but this time his concern was because of the pain that continued to torment her. Nathan told him he believed she did not know she was a threat to Rhys or that she held any secrets worthy of Rhys's interest. Whether his large friend was right or naught, Darrick swore he would protect Sabine with his life.

Rhys had used Elizabeth and Chance to draw Sabine out of hiding. He knew her honor would bring her back to the rubble that once stood as her home. In his search for his sister, he nearly forgot that he brought Sabine exactly to where Rhys wanted her. Bloody Hell! Even he had been used.

It did Darrick's heart good, knowing that with the deaths of Nandra and DePierce, not everything was going according to plan. Some people could not tolerate the guilt that lay heavy on their spirit. Evil eats at the mind until there is nowhere to turn, except inward, to feast on the soul.

How did Rhys conceal his man-sized body? The kick delivered to Darrick's arrow-shot ribs packed too much strength to belong to the hunched over, frail little man he portrayed.

Krell's words regarding the soldiers' fears, floated back to him. They were sure that he was capable of shape shifting. They swore that when Rhys thought no one was observing his actions they had witnessed the wee clergy grow to a normal-sized man. No longer hunched and gnarled, he would stand straight and tall.

Darrick had ignored his mother's concerns regarding the man. Her mistrust came from more than just not liking the man. The man had torn her family apart and used the baby as a carrot, making Camilla travel with him to find her grandson. How had he known that the baby still lived, yet all the while, keeping this vital information from DePierce?

Had Rhys been manipulating Nandra along with the rest? He would know how to use her insanity against DePierce. The final push over the edge of sanity was not yet evident. Perhaps it was the involvement with the plot against DePierce.

'Twas odd that the people of Balforth had left the castle so quickly. Could it be possible that they had received word that King Henry's army was on their way? He prayed to God that his missive had gotten through. 'Twould take a miracle for the messenger to reach Henry, unless he had already been alerted to the problems rising in this land. In the past, the young king had always kept a close watch on the lands so near the Welsh border where he had spent his youth. But lately the lands of France had held his attention.

Sounds whispered about the alcove. Darrick slowly identified each vibration. Using his keen sense, he was able to isolate the direction whence the sound came. Wide-awake, he listened for the scratching of toenails, the presence of a growling hound. Searching again, he listened for the clipped tones of tiny hooves clicking against the floor. There was no shuffling of human feet. No crying or whimpering of a newborn babe.

Had there been an attack, he was certain his brave hound would have drawn blood. Ripping through as much flesh as his white fangs could tear. Thunder had claimed the right as protector over young Chance. He would not let anyone take him away without a loss of limb. Hell, even that damned goat would have put a dent in an intruder. He, himself, could attest to the truth that Matilda's sharp yellow teeth would draw blood if you pulled her udder the wrong way.

A slow confident smile lifted the corners of his mouth. No, his mother and nephew had not been forced to take to the tunnel. He had missed the signs Krell left behind. There had been a scuffle but no blood trailed through the passageway. He had left the oil lamp burning for them at the entrance. The old codger had tramped down the bushes by the entrance, directing them to enter the cave. Never one to sit idly by and wait, his wily sergeant had discovered something in the tunnel that he intended for his lord to investigate.

The old warrior had been in his family's service ever since he could remember. Darrick was confident he could trust the sergeant's loyalty. He could depend on him to protect those that he held dear with his life. They were hidden away safely. He was certain that Krell was seeing to the care of his mother and nephew.

The knotted ball of string fell away, the tangles loosening as they displayed their secrets. Resting his eyes for just a second, he jumped when a warm hand thumped him on his shoulder.

"I will take the next watch."

Blinking his unfocused eyes, Darrick stared up at Taron. A halo of blonde hair shimmered in the dim light. 'Twas almost the same color as the boy with the straw hair. Clearing his throat, he struggled with handing off the responsibility of their safety. He recalled that King Harry did trust Taron well enough to allow him entrance into the Knights of the Swan. Perhaps he was not behaving fairly towards Sabine's brother.

Wearily, he sighed. "I'll rest for a short time while you stand watch."

"My thanks to you."

Darrick grunted back. "Our lives are in your hands, Sir Taron. Do not fail us."

Chapter 29

As the narrow passageway widened, Sabine's pace increased. Yearning for the light of day to warm her face she raced towards the inner room her father had prepared. She could not wait any longer and refused to heed Darrick's order to stop. She entered the cavern that stored what was left of her childhood home. She could hear him promising to take a strip out of her dainty hide when he got close enough.

Sabine halted.

She placed a shaking hand on the damp wall and leaned against the doorway. Unable to compel her legs to carry her farther into the underground chamber, she felt the walls closing in, forcing her to stay in the god-forsaken tunnel, forever.

The room had been ransacked.

Sinking to her knees, her stomach rolled, threatening to spill its contents. For once, she was relieved that the hunger in her stomach was gnawing at her backbone. A hiccup escaped. She caught the hysterical laughter threatening to bubble inside. The only thing she had in her stomach lately was hunger.

"Sabine," he whispered. His concern was nearly her undoing.

Darrick knelt by her side and pressed her face to the hard plane of his chest. He wiped the hot tears that stained her cheeks with the callused pad of his thumb.

Her sobs echoed against the gray rock while Darrick held her in his arms. Taron pushed through the crowded tunnel, forcing his way around Nathan to peer past Sabine and Darrick.

"Our son. Where is he?" Elizabeth shared "What have they done to him?"

"Be at peace, my love. Our son is not there." Weakened with relief, Elizabeth leaned against Taron's side. He gave her a reassuring smile and wrapped his arm around her waist.

"Not to fear, Elizabeth. Nothing more than a small loss of goods," he said. Darrick tilted Sabine's chin. "See, 'tis only foodstuffs. We'll replace it. Come, shall we see what can be salvaged from this mess?"

Sabine nodded and straightened her shoulders. Whoever vandalized the chamber had poured everything out onto the dusty floor. They had destroyed the treasured stores that she and her father had counted on to rebuild the castle. Her father had taught her to think with a level head and the solution would present itself clearly. Perhaps 'twas due to the unusual exhaustion sapping her strength that no answer could be found She struggling to think and fought the urge to curl up on one of the ripped bags of grain. Darrick warmed the bands of tension in her neck with his hands. She sighed as he kneaded life into her body. His touch ignited the fire coursing through her veins.

Darrick turned to the others and spat out orders to the other two knights. "Taron, find the first available spot in which Elizabeth may rest. She is still weakened from her fall."

Taron nodded and cradled Elizabeth in his arms. He laid her gently on the pallet of blankets.

Pressing his lips against Sabine's hair, Darrick murmured softly, "Sit beside my sister and rest yourself. I will take care of things here."

She lifted an eyebrow. "Think you I shall sit by and watch our supplies be ground under your big feet?"

"Sabine," Darrick growled. "Do as I have ordered."

Pulling away, she patted his cheek and smiled wearily. "I shall once I am through. I am still mistress here, and I have a duty to save what I can. You have your own duties. Go find our family."

Darrick reached out and drew her into his arms. Kissing her forehead, he spoke softly before her released her. "You are a stubborn wench."

Sabine grinned back. "That I am."

Moving about the underground storage room, Sabine randomly picked through the supplies ground into the floor. Each alcove that they had deliberately organized earlier was left in shambles by vindictive hateful hands. Stores of foodstuffs, poured out of the barrels and bags, were frantically tossed about the room. Barrels of wine and ale lay broken and drained of their liquid. Trunks of fabrics and spare clothing were pitched across the room.

The men systematically took stock of what needed to be done. They carefully worked their way through the alcove holding the weaponry. The swords and shields that had been painstakingly stacked were scattered about their feet. Each blade was methodically pulled out of its leather scabbard.

The sharply honed weapons spilled out, their deadly edges scraping against the stone surface. Shields no longer leaned against the wall like miniature soldiers, but were tossed about like jetsam from a shipwreck.

Darrick armed each man with a sword and an extra dagger to tuck inside their boots. They each took a side of the cavern to search for anyone who might lay in wait. Looking for clues, they paced off the cavern. Their voices low, they talked amongst themselves.

Sabine explored the tiny hideaway where she had stacked her father's treasures. She was relieved to find the books were unharmed. The leather bound volumes brought comfort as she ran her fingers over the last book he had been reading the night he disappeared. Her father's presence wrapped around her. She could almost hear his soothing baritone voice explaining the ancient rituals he had just read. He had repeated the myth of the riches buried near Clearmorrow.

Gentle puffs of air caressed her dusty skin; she lifted her face towards the low ceiling, and inhaled. Above her head, the tiny ventilation holes penetrated the earthen layer. They reached out to the blue skies above, carrying wonderfully fresh air. The velvety wisps brushed her skin.

Sabine's breath caught in her throat. Muffled voices leaked through the ventilation.

Their buzzing conversation seized her, threatening to squeeze the air from her lungs. She held up a trembling hand and waved for Darrick's attention.

Their backs to Sabine, the men were unaware of her frantic gestures. They were busily creating a strategy to inform King Henry of the changes that had taken place in the last year. They worried that their men-at-arms had found employment somewhere else. Times being what they were, most knights were forced to become mercenary soldiers for hire. The knowledge that most soldiers found it necessary to keep their families fed was certainly understandable. Gone were the days when a knight fought for his lord no matter the hunger or the conditions of the field.

Darrick voiced his concerns. "I fear my men may have given up all hope of my return. Nor do I know if any of my men survived the attack."

"Do we know the numbers in DePierce's band of thieves?" Nathan asked.

Terror seized her. Were the men stomping above their heads, the same band of men that ransacked the cavern? Sabine shook free of the paralyzing fear.

Her hand bumped against a teetering stack of books piled by her side. She picked up the nearest tome and launched it at his back. "Turn around," she hissed.

Spinning around, his eyes filled with shock. His blade, pulled instantly from the scabbard at his waist, whistled through the air. The other knights gripped their swords, prepared to fight by his side.

His mouth snapped shut, his nostrils flared. "Never do that again, dear love." His skin paled. "I might have harmed you." He stared down at the leather bound volume lying at his feet.

Hooking it with the tip of his toe, he tossed it into the air. One flick of his wrist caught her father's beloved tome with the blade of his sword. Balancing the book on the deadly edge, he held it out for Sabine to take.

She shook her head violently. Pressing one finger to her lips, she pointed over her head. Darrick cocked an eyebrow. Her frustration mounting, she continued to make wild gestures towards the ceiling.

Nathan sidestepped over to her brother and whispered out of the side of his mouth. "Tell me true, there is naught one drop of madness in your family, is there?"

"No!" He hissed back. "Perhaps 'tis a woman thing I have heard tell of. Should wear off in a day or two." He hesitated, frowning at Sabine, "I think."

"Would you two shut your mouths?" Darrick directed their attention to Sabine. "She grows more upset when you continue to talk."

"God's bones," Nathan said. "She's rolling her eyes."

Elizabeth awoke to the commotion and approached the three brave knights from behind.

She slid her hands on Taron's arm. "My dear, can't you see she's trying to tell you to be quiet?"

Sabine shut her eyes. Her body dropped in relief. Finally, she found another intelligent human being in the cavern.

Elizabeth continued, "If you would only but look you'd see that she is trying to warn you that there is something frightening overhead."

"Of course there is." Nathan pointed to the low ceiling. "We are in a damn rabbit's warren."

Sabine threw her hands in the air in exasperation. Perhaps she would retain her sanity if she just simply opened the hidden door to the entrance and held her wrists out for them to take her away.

"Can't you hear them talking and stomping on the earth above us?"

She turned to Darrick, his eyes narrowing as he strained to hear. She stepped closer and grabbed his hand, pulling him to the spot where she had stood earlier. "Listen," she whispered in his ear.

* * * *

Her cool fingers touched Darrick's lips. He caught her hand, and pressed it to his chest. Words choked in his throat, the thought that he had almost gutted the woman he had decided to make the mother of his children, tore at his stomach. He tried to find the words to express the horror he felt. He had barely been able to divert his blade, coming deadly close to striking her down.

All he wanted was to pull her into his arms and wipe the fear from her dark eyes. He nibbled the tender column of her neck. It was just the beginning of so many places he would like to taste again. Her lids grew heavy as she leaned into his caress. Sabine quivered, arching her back, offering her body for him to explore. His tongue danced along her fevered flesh.

The buzzing in his ears grew louder, drawing his attention to the noise above. He cocked his head to one side, forcing his brain to concentrate on the sounds.

Sabine's lids were heavy with passion. Someone cleared their throat from across the room. Her face flushed as awareness returned. Darrick shivered. His hands stilled. He shut his eyes and listened again to the words spoken by the men outside.

Keeping her in his arms, he walked Sabine over to the rest of their group. He motioned for them to move to the far side, away from the ventilation shafts.

"The voices she heard are real," Darrick whispered. "There are small shafts bored into the ceiling."

"Father had them drilled into the rock formations," Sabine added. "Not only does this ventilation system permit fresh air to enter but it also lets voices carry through the rock."

Darrick slid his fingers under her hair. The need to make contact with her warmth drove him to madness.

Sabine scrubbed at her flushed face and made an effort to step away. Darrick was not about to let her go.

"Taron, in case you've managed to forget, Father was a strategist and explorer. He knew the need to protect us would arise. Feeling threatened earlier in the year, he prepared for this exact emergency while continuing to search the volumes in his library."

Taron turned on her. "Little sister, I would thank you to remember that I was on duty, doing the business of our king."

"And what does he do to protect the families when he asks the men to go fight for him in a land we do not need."

"Henry is our king." Taron may have kept his voice low, but it snapped with fire.

"He may be your friend but he has done naught but take my family away. Allowing our home...your home...to come under attack by someone who should have never been given any position of power in the first place. He sold a title to DePierce that should have been earned with honor and bravery, not gold. How much was it that he paid? What more was our king able to conquer for the few measly gold coins that madman fed into his war chests?"

Sabine trembled in Darrick's arms. He was relieved her anger had not yet turned on him.

She swung around to Elizabeth, shaking from the anger that had built up for too long. "Your brother did the same. He left you to fight a war that our country did not need. Even our fathers died because of this."

Elizabeth locked her fingers together and shook her head. "Our father dispatched Darrick to France. Father would not accept him as his true heir but he was willing to let him assume the responsibility to die in his place. Darrick went in hopes of keeping honor affixed to our family's name."

"I went willingly to France to serve my king." Darrick growled at Elizabeth. "By my choice and no others. I earned that honor by the blood and sweat of my brow.

"It serves naught but evil to hold blame to King Henry for what has occurred at Balforth. The death of our fathers was not at the proclamation of our king. They died by the hand of a man that would have found another way to attack, even if we had all been home bouncing babies on our knees. You know as well as I that many a home and title have been lost at the royal court. You must not place the blame of our fathers' death on our king. 'Tis treason what you say, and that, I cannot, and will not, allow! Especially if someone above our heads should happen to hear you."

Sabine shook off his restraining arm. "How soon will the three of you leave to fight in another battle for our king? Will you do so, even after you one day become husbands or fathers?"

She turned on Taron. "You have already fathered a son. Are you so willing to leave him behind?"

Elizabeth backed into Taron until their legs touched and created a protective wall. "'Tis not a fair thing that you ask, Sabine. They have sworn on their honor to uphold our king. I know that as soon as King Henry gets word that we need his help, he will provide for our families."

Darrick tilted Sabine's chin. His soul slipped into the depth of her tear-stained eyes. He understood the terror she felt; left without protection or any means of fighting back. Had he ever heard her laugh freely, without a care or worry weighing on her shoulders?

He had seen her anger surface before. It would simmer for only so long and then like a bubble it would burst, dissipating in a matter of minutes. He had to calm her worries quickly.

This he must accomplish before the king's men caught wind of her dissatisfaction. He too had his own disillusionment of Henry, but the man was still his friend and his king. He had taken a vow to serve him and on his honor as a knight, he was determined to do his duty.

"If the almighty should bless me with a family, I'll do what I must to survive. I'll fight to keep what I've gained."

Tension flowed out of her limbs. He buried his nose in her silken golden mane and breathed in her fragrance. His breath caressed her neck.

"And when there are children running through our castle, I will continue to stand for what is mine. Striving to handle it in the way of my father and of your father. Protecting what is mine. Know that by the good graces of our king and through the courts I would strive for the safety of my family, working towards peace. 'Tis all I can promise."

Sabine gazed up at his stern face and whispered. "But is it enough?"

"That remains to be seen."

Raising his head, he nodded at Nathan. "I recognize one of the voices. King Henry's men stand above. The stairwell leads to a hidden door. Press the stone in the center and it will swing open. Take Taron and Elizabeth with you. They have a much anticipated reunion with their son."

Darrick arched a brow at Sabine's brother. "Sir Taron of Clearmorrow, should our king agree to the union of our families you'll have quite a bit of explaining and coaxing to do with your future mother in-law."

Sabine slipped her hand into Darrick's. He, too, may have thought those same arguments and worries, but to speak them aloud was dangerous in the unsettled times in which they lived. To find disfavor with the king could put them off their lands with no title or means of living.

Chapter 30

As the door slid open with a rush of cool air, Darrick and Sabine listened to the joyous reunion. With much thumping and pounding of backs, the men's voices, filled with concern for their health, carried across the breeze. Darrick flexed his fists, praying that no one else had overheard her angry words. She came from a long line of noblemen. She, of all people, should accept things the way they were without question. He could not understand what she expected.

He shoved the pain back into the corner of his mind, forcing his love behind a wall of indifference. Did she desire they spend their future together?

Even now, he was certain that she trembled with passion from his touch. His need for her grew against his chausses. He shifted, fighting the urge to grab her, press her back to the wall and fill her body with his. He would tend to his heart another time.

Brushing the dampened hair from her brow, he smiled longingly, "You'll want to freshen up, love." Full of yearning, his gaze traveled down her cheek to rest at her breasts. "Shall I wait for you?"

Sabine shook her head. "Greet your mother and the men. I'll be fine. I need a moment alone."

Reluctant to heed her request, he began to move away, allowing that it was necessary to search out his men and hear what news they carried. Weariness hung on her shoulders, drawing them down. He could feel the hurt in her eyes following his back. His foot rested on the first step as Sabine stopped him with her question.

"Do you believe I have shamed my family's name by speaking what I feel? Is it wrong to dream of peace? To long for the villagers to return to the way things were?"

"No, 'tis right to dream of peace, but not at the expense of your family or the king." Grimacing he leaned against the wall. "Do you truly want everything to go back the way it was?"

Sabine sighed, looking down at her hands bunched in the folds of her dress. "No, I suppose not everything," she said. "I would not want to lose Chance."

Darrick returned to clasp her shoulders, his hands kneading her tender neck. A curl had loosened from her braid, nestling beside her ear. It drew his attention to the silken mane. "Is that all you would keep?"

"No," she admitted shyly. She turned to press her cheek against his large hands. The heat of her burned his flesh, igniting a fire raging inside his heart. She tilted her chin, inviting him to kiss the exposed skin.

"Tell me," he whispered. "Aside from my young nephew, what else would you keep from returning the way it was?"

Sabine groaned as tension flowed from her body. He would forever be amazed at her body's response to his touch. Her hands trembled. His heart clenched. He would protect and love her until they grew old together, watching their children and their children's children running wild through the castle bailey. If only he knew that she loved him in the same way.

"Say it," he growled.

He ran his hands along her arms, down to her ribs. Encircling her waist, he moved his hands upward, cupping her breasts, fingers caressing her nipples. The rosebuds pressed against the thin fabric of her gown, pebbling under his tantalizing touch. He drew her into his embrace, whispering his admiration for each part of her delicious body. Gathering her against his warm pulsing body, he pressed her to his growing need, groaning hungrily when she wriggled her delightful bottom, brushing against his heated form. His mouth moved in her hair, his lips brushing her sensitive scalp, causing her to shiver with his breath.

"Would you miss what we have together? Would your body betray you and yearn for my touch? Would you awaken in the middle of the night frantically searching for my heat, your appetite hungering to be set loose from the fires raging within?"

Sabine moved even closer to him, driven by the passion igniting their flesh with raw desire. His ears roared from the life coursing through his veins. With each stroke of her hands, hunger for the woman he'd given his heart to ran shivers down his back.

She matched him, kiss for kiss. Their tongues dueled and danced together, swirling and tasting the sweet nectar.

Darrick's discipline slipped. Her feminine scent, heated with passion, threatened to drive him beyond all thought but one: To have her as his own. But he had nearly failed before. If he let go of his tight-fisted control, his vow of protection would be lost. And he could not give Sabine what she yearned for. She wanted promises of peace and what the future held. All he had knowledge of was learned from the back of his war-horse, broadsword in his fist. He had yet to speak with the king's men and discover King Henry's mood towards his family. He knew naught if his father's name held sway over the king's decisions, or if Henry would keep Lockwood from his care.

He took a shuddering breath. Despite all those arguments, he could not let her go. He wrapped his arms around her and drew her into his arms.

* * * *

His tormented groan was a heady invitation, spreading fire to the core of her soul. Sabine found his eagerness for her touch exciting. He may have said naught of love, but she knew he desired her. As her feelings intensified, her resolve to distance her heart melted in his embrace.

It appeared that he had forgiven her for keeping secrets. His gentle patience allowed him to look past her outbursts and anger that sometimes spewed forth. He cared naught that she read from her father's treasured books, nor that she sometimes had a talent for dressing up in disguises. Even her disastrous family and home did not send him running to the battlefield.

The growing hardened ridge in his chausses brushed against her hand. Swaying into his embrace, she ached for the fulfillment of his lovemaking. Eager for his touch, carrying her to forbidden places, Sabine trailed her hand to the band at his waist. The dark coils wrapped around the pads of her fingers, teasing her senses. He sucked in his breath when she lowered her hand, making a nest around his manhood. Wrapping her fingers around the velvet-sheathed steel, she stroked him as his mouth devoured her neck. His body shuddered, thrilling her with the knowledge that the mere touch of her hand drove him to distraction.

"Slowly, love," he murmured, hoarse with passion. "Your touch burns me to the center of my soul."

Lifting her in his arms, he dragged her across the front of his body. With agonizing care, he slowly brushed the tips of her nipples against the planes of his chest, grazing his burgeoning flesh, letting her body feel his urgent need.

Yielding to the captivating fire, she was drawn into the flame. She feared the intense fire raging inside would incinerate her. Praying for her knight to take her quickly, she tore at his tunic, urging him not to waste another breath.

With deliberate care, Darrick dragged the hem of her gown up her thighs. The fabric left a fiery trail upon her skin. The vision sent waves of passion crashing into her core. He devoured her limbs with hungry eyes and tucked the skirt away from her legs. His strong hands trembled as he brushed his fingers across her center.

Her cheeks heated under his intense gaze. She thought her heart would stop when he suddenly pulled away. Aching from the emptiness where his hands had traveled, she bit her lip wondering what she had done to displease him.

Breathing as one, their passion-filled eyes locked as Darrick pressed a callused finger to her lips, swollen from their lovemaking.

"I have no lands that I can offer you. No name to protect you unless my king wills it. I cannot take—"

"You have but to receive, for I give it freely."

He groaned in anguish when she took his fingertip between her teeth and nibbled on the tender side, pulling it into her mouth. Teasing his senses, drawing him into her embrace, she ignored his denial for her pleasure, nudging him with the tip of her tongue.

Booted heels clattered from the stairs behind them. Nathan called out, "Perhaps you could find time to speak to your men."

Too mortified to look over Darrick's wide shoulder, Sabine ducked her head away from the light caress of his fingers.

A shuddering breath shook his body as he lifted his head. His restless hands stilled against her core. "Out," he ordered Nathan.

Ignoring his warning glance, she let her fingertips tiptoe across the wide expanse of his shoulders. Lightly dragging her nails in circular motions, she dipped past the small of his back trailing to the band at his waist. Keeping her hands out of Nathan's line of vision, she cupped Darrick's taut buttocks, kneading his firm muscles.

Nathan stood at the entrance, a frown plastered on his face as he searched the corners of the chamber for them. His face, flushed, matching his wild red hair. "Finish with whatever you may need to do, Darrick. Sergeant Krell awaits your attention. He must speak with you regarding a matter of great importance."

Sighing, Darrick turned and tipped her chin. "Duty calls me away." He devoured her mouth with one of his knee-weakening kisses until she had to lean against him for support. His hands strayed beside her heated thighs. "But I shall return."

Sabine trembled for completion; her mind, too full of unfulfilled desire to worry about the true reason Nathan sought him out.

Darrick whispered near her ear. "You failed to tell me what else you would keep. Must you make me ask again, in front of Nathan?" he whispered, drawing his lips across her cheek.

Sabine felt the heat rising in her face. She did not know if she would rather kick him in his shins or kiss him breathless. She decided it was much more fun to feel the heat explode inside her body whenever she touched him, than stubbing her toes against his hard booted calves.

Taking up his challenge, she stepped away, keeping out of his reach and sauntered seductively around him, circling her prey. Shoulders drawn back, she thrust her breasts out, inviting his touch. "I would keep you by my side." Her velvety voice stroked his skin, rich and full of promise. "Very, very close, by my side."

"Leave us, Nathan," Darrick said. Once the door slid shut, his battle against the burning jealousy swelled out of control.

He reeled her in until her thighs pressed into his. Her stomach brushed against his aroused state. Pain etched the corners of his mouth. "I would have the woman I take to be my wife, capable of standing proudly in front of my men, commanding the same respect that I receive. I will return for you as soon as I meet with my men."

Sabine gaped at his retreating back. His wife? But he had yet to say those three simple words: I love you. Her fingertips rested on her lips and traced the fiery trail where his kisses had been. She meant only to tease him from the tower he continually tried to erect between them. Rethinking her position, she decided to wait for a few minutes before she began to search him out.

She picked up one of the leather bound volumes. A frown tugged at her brows. It felt as if centuries had passed since she last sat in the solar with her father, trying to remain patient as she listened to his ramblings of the ancient Celtic tribe burrowing their way through the white stone buried beneath the rough land of Clearmorrow. And there were others who had followed in their footsteps. Knights who had gone into hiding and carried their treasures from far off places with them.

Wiping a cobweb that clung to her cheek, she recalled how thrilled he was. He had been so excited, practically giddy, the night he had found an answer to one of the many mysteries hidden in their primitive writings. The diagram had carried him further than the catacomb that held her mother's tomb. The familiar leather tome she clutched to her stomach was his latest discovery. Soon after, her father's disappearance had followed in the wake of his celebration.

Hearing a movement in the corner, she tensed. A rodent?

The noise from the underground creatures increased. Echoes reverberated against the white walls, bouncing down the corridors, muffling her strangled gasp.

She groaned as she hit the floor.

Chapter 31

Darrick swatted at the dust clinging to his leggings while he listened to Sergeant Krell's report. After the first initial greetings from his men, the joy had dissipated. He felt the gnawing need to get back to Sabine's side. He had seen the hurt in her gaze as he left.

Half-listening to Krell, he chewed on his tongue to keep from staring at the garb his sergeant wore. The old man was dressed in a nun's black habit. His battered broadsword hung heavily in his belt, contrasting sharply with the flowing gown. His gray hair stuck out, ruffled by the breeze. Grease stains, running from chest to belly, marred his front where he had wiped his hands. Large dusty boots peeked out from the skirt tangling around his feet while he paced like a caged wolf.

Krell added to his report. "And another thing. I must disagree with your conduct towards Lady Camilla. 'Tis not right to expect her to share the blame of all that has occurred in your family's history."

Darrick grunted in response. Unsure of how to deal with the relationship with his mother, he avoided her path, choosing to skirt around her tent. He purposefully steered clear of the reunion between the two women and Elizabeth's lover.

He did not believe Taron was a bad sort. From what Sabine had said, he had matured during his ordeal as a prisoner of Balforth. Even now, from where he stood, he could see Taron holding his son cradled proudly in his arms. He was introducing Chance to the men milling about, awaiting their lord to address them. Watching from across the remains of the bailey, Darrick warmed to see the strong waving fists catch in Taron's golden thatch of hair.

The bruises on Nathan's face were more evident in the sunlight. Darrick did not want Sabine to come between their friendship. However, he would not allow his friend to make another amorous advance toward the woman he had decided would warm his bed until he was lying in his grave.

Nathan scowled, pushing back his unruly mane and cleared his throat, drawing Darrick's attention to what Sergeant Krell was saying. "Darrick, pull your lusting thoughts away from the woman for a moment."

"Aye, Sir Darrick, we have two soldiers in our midst who have recently joined our forces. They are not from the king's army of men." Krell glanced around, searching the grounds. "Nathan believes he recognizes them. They may be a part of DePierce's marauders but he cannot be certain."

"Sorry, my friend." Nathan rubbed at his temples. "My mind is not as clear as it should be. But look yonder at the two men huddled over by the grove of trees. They stand apart from the rest of the battalion, keeping to themselves. Their nervous movements lead me to believe they are up to mischief."

Darrick stared into the glare of the sun. A low growl rumbled in his chest. "Have the two men brought to me. Move cautiously. I would not want them to flee before I have a word with our two friends."

Krell jerked his head and sent a silent command to one of their soldiers.

Confident that his men would succeed in the capture of their quarry, Darrick folded his arms across his chest and directed a pointed stare at the Krell. "My old friend, you must tell me who your seamstress is. I would know if there is naught that you wish to confess."

Krell ran gnarled hands through the white stubble shadowing his chin. "'Twould be the fault of your cunning young woman you keep hidden in the storage rooms below. She forced me to dress as such," he grumbled. "Said should DePierce's men find us before she was able to secure your release, I needed to disguise that I was the one guarding your mother and nephew."

Krell averted his eyes to gaze longingly at the silver halo that shined around Darrick's mother. Her hair glistened in the sun. "You might thank my Lady Sabine for the good sense to dress Lady Camilla and me as we are. Had we not been seen as two helpless women with an infant, the king's men wouldn't have stopped to help us. I fear we would have had a blade in our backs and then they would have asked questions later. King Henry gave strict orders that while they were awaiting your direction they were to disperse all men from Balforth lands."

He slapped his thigh, the humor twinkling out from under his white bushy wings. "Your hound near took a fair chunk out of one of the puffed up knights that ride for the king. Took five stout men to pull him off."

Cackling, Krell shook his head. "Then the infant cries out and the hound spits the knight out like he was a hot coal burning his tongue. Lies down by the boy, as docile as a lamb."

Darrick mentally counted out the number of gold coins it would take to appease the knight's wounded pride. Half listening to the old codger, he realized Krell was still singing his praises of the fair Lady Sabine. It warmed Darrick's heart that his old friend approved of the woman who would be the mother of his children.

"You may deliver your approval shortly. My lady freshens herself while we speak." Feeling the penetrating gaze that attempted to drill into his soul, he efficiently changed the route of the cross-examination. "I see Lady Camilla fares well in your care. My thanks to you."

Awaiting the arrival of the two men, he observed the rest of his army. Soldiers guarded their encampment, patrolling the perimeter of the crumbling castle. It would take a great deal of gold and time to rebuild the castle and the surrounding grounds, but it would be a rare piece of land to hold. The other soldiers were tending to their horses, seeing to the brushing and feeding of their precious mounts. A worthy knight knew the value of a healthy war-horse.

He was pleased to note the number of deaths amongst his men was lower than he anticipated. Only a few of the wounded were being administered to in the tents erected beside the tumbled curtain wall. It pleased him to see so many had chosen to stay and fight beside him.

After receiving word of DePierce's defeat, the villagers had begun their return from wherever they had been hiding. Their campfires burned in the distance. Krell had reported that they began their pilgrimage during the first night of their release. Sabine would be overjoyed to find that many of the children she feared had not survived were running and jumping in the camp, full of the joy of living.

Darrick smiled, his confidence growing with the knowledge that he still found favor with his good friend, the king. Yet, he knew that their task was not yet complete. DePierce's mercenaries had scattered to the winds and hills, afraid of the retaliation of King Henry's soldiers. If the mercenaries were not stopped, they may never find Rhys's whereabouts.

The soldiers brought the struggling men to where Darrick stood. The commotion caused a stir amongst the camp followers. The crowd pushed to hear if their lord would allow them to listen to the interrogation. Men and women followed behind the two men they recognized as guards, jeering at the vermin that had helped their enemy destroy their homes and their lives.

A foul odor followed the heavyset man. Gobs of grease clung to his scruffy beard. His beady eyes squeezed out from puffing cheeks. He shifted his feet nervously, all the while, the soldiers held onto his thick arms. Mindful of the damp stains that darkened the pits of the stinking man, they attempted to stand downwind.

Darrick poked the tip of his dagger into the fat rolled at the filthy waistband. "I see you have been eating well." Narrowing his icy stare, he pondered his next question. "Are you not DePierce's famous Sergeant Gregor?"

Gregor shook his head, his stringy hair brushing against his rounded shoulders. "No, that wicked lord took all that I had. I would never serve the likes of him." His beady eyes slid along the crowd of villagers, searching for an escape. "He treated me poorly, just like all the others that stand around here."

"Would you have me believe that all these good folk are too ignorant to know their enemy?"

Darrick scowled at the other man who smelled just as bad. "I suppose you would have me believe that you are not called Spurge, by all your friends." He smiled blandly. "I imagine a man of your stature has many friends."

The crusty yellow teeth flashed, "Oh, aye...aye...I'm proud to say I'm one of the favorites in these parts."

The rotund man glared at Spurge and shook his head. Freeing a pudgy elbow, he jabbed it into the scraggily man's stomach.

"That is...I meant to say..." Confused, Spurge scratched nervously at his crotch. "I ...umm...I," he stuttered, sliding his glance over Gregor, silently pleading with him to help find the right answers to their questions.

Gregor's full lips pulled back from his blackened teeth. "Shut yer trap."

"Do not waste anymore of my time," Darrick barked. "I know that the two of you served DePierce and did his dirty work. I heard you arguing between yourselves the night you tried to burn me within the cottage. I would recognize the unforgettable stench your body carries."

He grabbed the scruff of their tunics and shook the two creatures, banging their head together. "You don't have the sense to hide here. Who sent you to spy amongst us?"

Nathan pushed his way closer to the captives. "Let me question them, Darrick. I'll have the answers that we seek in a matter of seconds."

Darrick looked down at the stain of yellow fetid water pooling at the greasy men's feet. "No, my friend, these two aren't strong enough to withstand the tortures that you would put them through." Grinning at Nathan, he added, "Although, when I am done interrogating them, you may ensure I have gleaned all the information that I possibly can." He shrugged. "But remember, I would have them capable of breathing after you are finished."

"Mercy! I beg you," Spurge squealed. "'Twas Sir Hugh's orders to set the cottage afire."

"*Hugh?*"

Spurge shrank out of Gregor's reach. "Just, please"...he stuttered, pointing to his companion. "Don't leave me with him and I will tell you what I know."

* * * *

Spurge's information had brought terror to Darrick's chest: it ripped the air from his lungs. He tore down the stairwell. The heels of his leather boots clattering on the white stone. He frantically searched the corners of the storage room. Rhys had used them all to gain access to the woman and the treasures he believed were hidden in the catacombs. *Sabine!*

Her jeweled dagger lay on the floor next to one of Sir William's beloved books. The intricate pattern of the jewels embedded in the hilt reminded him of the diagram drawn on the pages. The stiff vellum fluttered in the silent breeze blowing through the tunnel. The open door drew the fresh air through the passageway leading to the catacombs.

Darrick entered the tunnel in search of his love. Gaining only a few feet into the hole, the dimming light revealed a pattern of scuffmarks, scratched into the dust on the stone floor. Following their trail, he walked the corridor Sabine had recently revealed. 'Twas where her mother was laid to rest.

A warm hand gripped his shoulder from behind. Taron's voice shook with conviction, brooking no arguments. "I'm going with you," Taron added before Darrick could respond, "You'll not deny me this right."

Darrick nodded his head with a jerk. "Just stay out of my way when I run him through," he growled.

"I understand there are two. I know the one is Rhys, but who is his partner?"

Never taking his attention from the tunnel, he answered stiffly. "It matters not to me. I'll kill them both for endangering her life."

Chapter 32

Sabine's head pounded like it had been struck with the giant battering ram she had seen in Darrick's stockpile of war weapons. Her mouth was as dry as parchment. She prodded her tongue against the dusty rag shoved in her mouth.

Her captors had dumped her unceremoniously in the corner, with no concern for her comfort. Her shoulders ached from the constant strain of the rags binding her wrists. Pulling against the bindings, she was relieved to note her captors had not thought to tie them tight enough to cut off the circulation to her hands. With no outside light, she did not have the means to judge how they had left her in that uncomfortable position. She could only await their return.

Darrick! He would come for her. Once he knew she was missing, he would move heaven and earth to find her.

Her stomach knotted, thinking about the damage they might do to her precious knight. She did not want more pain inflicted to his handsome body. Shutting her eyes, she asked the ancient gods that Sir William had studied, to protect her love. And then she offered her prayer to God. "Please don't allow that creature and his cohort to harm him."

Cursing her negligence for not paying attention to the warning voice inside her head, she leaned back against the cool stone. Where did Rhys and the boy with the yellow hair hide themselves?

The scraggily clothed boy had attempted to stand menacingly over her, constantly fingering the thin growth of whiskers on his chin. Barely visible, his pride and joy was little more than peach-fuzz. His shaggy blond hair stuck out from under his cap like a stack of straw tossed about. She had to fight the motherly urge to shove the dirty hair aside so that she might see his fawn brown eyes.

He had been fairly put out with her for leaving a trail. She had dropped tiny scraps torn from a small book she had tucked inside the pocket of her skirt. Sabine found it extraordinary that his anger had not poured down about her head when he caught her hand with the piece of vellum in it. Instead, he had directed his rage towards Rhys when the older man had struck her. He had yelled at him for hurting her and gently wiped at the reopened wound. Before blacking out, she actually imagined concern for her safety registering on his countenance. The look was somehow familiar.

Sabine could not fathom what Rhys thought he would find in the tiny room by her mother's vault. He kept ranting about the hidden treasure he was sure her father had found. He was furious when she swore she did not know what he was talking about. The only treasures she had any knowledge of were her father's ancient books. Those treasures certainly were not hidden. They stood piled high in the storage room.

She shifted the weight on her hip. The hard lump biting into her backside reminded her that she still carried one small insignificant book that her father kept as a journal for all his great discoveries. Struggling to sit more comfortably before her tormentors returned from their errands, she listened for the approaching footsteps that carried her future.

* * * *

Taron wiped at the moisture dripping from his forehead. "There's another one."

Little bits of fiber glowed against the dim light. "That's my girl," Darrick murmured. "Show me where you are. Keep believing in me, sweetheart."

The empty shadows swallowed all signs of life that might enter the sanctity of the sacred grounds. While Taron ranted, throwing his temper around with youthful exuberance, Darrick searched the bound volume Sabine had been looking at right before she was abducted. He methodically looked for any clues that would explain why Rhys continued to play so ruthlessly at his game.

Darrick cursed his weakness for letting her out of his sight. Memories of their last embrace drew what little common sense he had left. Although the thought of walking around like an idiot for the rest of his life was unmanning, it was far more appealing then to have to exist without her arms and limbs wrapped around his waist. Nor could he live without her love to warm his heart. He vowed, when they finally buried this threat to their families once and for all, he would ensure his beautiful love would have a smile gracing her lips every morning. He would personally see that she found joy in every day of her life.

"I am coming, love," he whispered, praying that she could hear him in her heart. "Trust in me."

The trail of parchment had stopped as suddenly as it had started. When they had retraced their steps, it was no longer there.

"I fear we may not find her in this damn labyrinth," Taron said.

Undergoing the savageries from the guards at Balforth, Taron's endurance was at the end. The bravado he had at the beginning turned to defeat and despair. He leaned heavily against the dampened wall, cooling his fevered brow against the damp surface. His breath came in harsh draws, sucking the air into his lungs. "Never have I been so frustrated with the frailty of my body."

Darrick understood what his future brother-in-law was going through but he did not have the energy to deal with him. Grinding his teeth, he wished Taron had kept to his infant son and stayed in Elizabeth's ministering arms. It would have been wiser to have his hound with him instead of allowing Sabine's brother to join him. It was against all discipline that he knew but he agreed to let him join in the search. He understood it was a matter of love and honor. He prayed that Taron's honor did not come at the price of Sabine's life.

He shot out his hand, silencing Taron's wheezing.

High-pitched nasal whining came from a room that they had missed earlier. Lady Mary's tomb lay inside the tiny alcove off the great room. From the angle where they hid, they could see the layout of the little room. The shape of a swan's back was carved into the ceiling. The lid to her tomb, shaped as the bowed head of a swan. Its long neck curved, the head dipped down gracefully, pointing to another.

The shadows from the torchlight danced eerily across the graceful back of the swan. The smooth stone dipped into the wall, indented where the wings should be. The lid was off, propped against the stone. The head of the swan waited to be laid in place. And beside it, Rhys stomped and raged.

"Empty! That troublesome wench will tell me where her father hid the treasure. I will draw it out of her. By God, even if it's her last breath."

It was plain for Darrick to see that Rhys was no longer a helpless man who prayed for lost souls, urging others to pick up a cross and join his pilgrimage. This man was willing to kill, or better yet, to coerce the weaker minds to do the work for him. It mattered not, just as long as he found what he was looking for.

Perched on the balls of his feet, Darrick was ready to spring out and tackle the crazed clergyman. Taron placed his hand on his arm, stopping him before he thought things through.

Taron's grip was like a vise. "Wait for the right moment. Rhys might be smaller in stature but his strength comes with the knowledge of this maze." Darrick reluctantly nodded.

They kept their distance as they followed Rhys through the twists and turns of the tunnel. He came to a small anteroom jutting off to the side and entered.

Darrick and Taron stood with their backs pressed against the wall and listened. More than once, Darrick almost lost his patience and prepared to charge after him. He was going to smash the rodent under his boot when he heard Rhys's fist strike Sabine. Only the shouted words coming from the skinny boy with the straw-colored hair drew him back.

"I swear, Rhys, if you dare to touch her like that again, I'll break them legs of yours."

Darrick and Taron shared a glance. Why would the boy challenge the older man?

"You'll do good to remember your place," Rhys said. "Lucky for you, I don't have time to teach you a thing or two. I'm going to search out that fresh hole I saw while I was taking a piss. Stay and keep her quiet, hear?"

Sabine motioned wildly, pleading for the young boy to take the rag out of her mouth. Her brown eyes, matching his, widened when he relented and bent over to free her mouth.

"Don't know what that lunatic thinks he's gonna find," he grumbled under his breath as he sawed at the rag with his dagger. "Old William left me nuth'un anyway."

His mouth pinched with regret. "I'm sorry," he whispered. "I didn't know he hurt so many people before he came for me."

The lad bent over, the knife coming even closer to Sabine's precious skin.

Darrick rushed out to stop him. He grabbed the boy's thin wrist, squeezing to release the weapon. The spry youth was limber and could slither around but was out-muscled and out-manned. His wrist bones ground under Darrick's hand.

"No," Sabine cried. "Don't kill him."

Darrick glanced at his lady sitting by his booted feet. The woman he loved and cherished carried fresh bruises around her eyes. A smear of dried blood clung to her temple. He was incensed when he noticed it was the same wound that he had carefully sewn in the tiniest of stitches, ensuring her beauty would not be marred with ugly scars like his.

Wanting to please his ladylove and wipe the terror from her eyes, he reluctantly agreed. "I vow I'll not run the boy through with my broadsword. Not immediately, anyway."

Instead, he smacked the boy's thin wrist against the stone wall. Muscles and tendons crackled under the grinding pressure before he let loose of the blade.

Darrick drew back to strike him.

"Darrick—"

The revenge tasting too sweet to ignore, he let his fist connect with the pale-skinned jaw before seeing to the cause of her renewed fear.

Taron's position as guard was lost in the desire to set his sister free. Fury raced through Darrick's veins. Even the first year squires knew to follow one of his orders. His anger subsided when he saw the determination settle upon Taron's face. He could not fault the man for loving Sabine. God help him, it was impossible not to love the woman.

Taron's hands shook from the effort it took to slice through the threadbare rags binding Sabine's wrist. Darrick worried Taron was about to collapse. They would need all the strength they could muster to carry themselves safely out of the catacombs.

* * * *

Sabine jerked. She gasped from the searing pain as an arrow ripped through her flesh. "Darrick," she cried.

Too weak to move quickly, Taron stared numbly at the blood trickling from her shoulder.

Darrick dove to cover her, providing the length of his scarred back as a target instead of her tender body. He stiffened when another arrow found its mark in the back of his thigh. His leg collapsed with the impact.

"Get whomever that is, Taron," he bellowed.

Darrick glanced at the boy lying on the ground, knocked unconscious. He offered no immediate threat. A shadow shifted. The dim light caught the movement. *Rhys.*

Rhys's thin lips curled in a snarl. No longer forced to bend under the weight of the ugly brown robes, he now stood to his full height and was nearly as tall as the two knights.

"You were my father's friend," Taron said. "Greeted warmly at our castle. Yet you ensured Elizabeth's imprisonment. Almost succeeded in killing our son!"

Bellowing with rage, Taron charged him with an explosion of strength. Surprising the man, he wrestled him to the ground. Their bodies locked in battle, arms and legs struck the hard floor, each man struggling to stay alive. Taron's strength began to slip away. His hands fumbled on Rhys's neck. "Don't lose him, Taron." Darrick yelled. He ripped off a portion of Sabine's skirt. The flow of blood continued to seep through her bodice. He placed the palm of his hand on her shoulder, pressing where the shaft protruded from the wound.

Sabine flinched. Panting against the pain, she smiled up at her love, "I knew you would come."

He stretched his injured leg out and braced his arm across his good knee. "You must hold on, sweetheart," he whispered.

She arched an eyebrow. "Is that an order?"

"Yes, love, 'tis another order."

"I thought as much. I don't mind. Just this once."

He framed her face with his hands. "We are almost finished here, and then I promise we will go home." His thumbs stroked her cheek.

Drawn to the soothing sound of his voice, she asked wistfully, "Home... where is that, I wonder?"

Darrick kissed the top of her silken crown, his lips moving in her hair. "Wherever you are, my love, I am with you, for you have my heart. And, wherever I am, you must be, for I cannot live without you. That, my love, is where home is." He stopped, afraid for a moment she would argue with him. "Is that agreeable with you, my lady?" he asked, daring to hope.

"Aye," she sighed softly, "I am ready for my dark swan knight to pick me up on his mighty wings and carry me away with him."

A soft sigh passed from her lips as her head spun dizzily out of control. Her head throbbed with the pounding in her ears. Her nose felt fuzzy. The walls began to shift. She sighed. Perhaps they had been down in that rabbit hole for so long they had begun to shift their shape into rabbits, after all. Maybe, if she were lucky, her dark swan would be hungry and devour her, one nibble after another.

She pulled her mind from the swallowing depths. Her focus wavered. She peered through the gauzy veil wrapping around her head as Darrick gripped her hand, refusing to let go. "Taron—"

"Must help him." Darrick moved as though his legs were welded to the floor. "Saints' bones," he swore. "'Tis the damn poison." His unsteady legs buckled. Crashing to his knees, he groaned loudly when the shaft bit into his leg, digging further into his thigh.

"Release him, Rhys," he cried.

His eyes glittered from his position above Taron.

"One moment, Sir Darrick of Lockwood," Rhys sneered. "Soon as I finish with this weakling, you are next. And then after she tells me where she's hiding it, I will have my way with your woman."

Raising the dagger he had wrestled from Taron's hand, he readied his aim. Tears burned in the corner of her eyes. Sabine blinked.

The boy lying crumpled on the floor, sat up. The purple bruise where Darrick had struck him had bloomed. After surveying the room, he began dragging his body towards Rhys. He edged closer.

The boy pushed to stand. "'Tis not supposed to be like this," he cried. "I don't want to lose anymore!" He catapulted into Rhys. As he rolled with him, he tucked his knife arm into Rhys's stomach, turning the blade into the soft flesh of his underbelly.

"Sorry, Uncle," he whispered.

Rhys struggled to rise. He bucked the towheaded boy off his back. The crack of the boy's skull striking the wall, echoed across the chamber. Shrugging his narrow shoulders, Rhys looked down at the knife protruding from his gut. Smiling weakly, he whispered into the gray mist of the dead. "Ah, Nandra, I always said Tate came from ungrateful stock."

Chuckling, he did not notice the bow tangled around his feet. He fell onto his stomach, gasping as the dagger plunged to its hilt.

Fierce howling could be heard, cutting into the silence following Rhys's last breath. Shouts echoed across the dark passages as they drew near.

Darrick's hand uncurled, slowly letting the tip of the bow roll out of his fingers. A triumphant smile lifted the corners of his mouth before the darkness drew him behind the blissful black curtain.

Sabine's fingers clenched. *Empty. Darrick. My love. Where are you?* Air leaked through her lips as she slipped into the dark.

Chapter 33

Shrill barking bore into Darrick's head like a broadsword striking his helm in battle. Groaning, he shifted on the fur pallet. Before opening his eyes, his hand searched the bed for Sabine. He needed her by his side. *Where is she?*

When he sat up, the room shifted dizzily. Memories of the small chamber caught his breath. His heart ached as he roared with despair. Did they reach her in time? He planted his bare feet on the ground and swung off the bed.

Nathan found him leaning against the tent pole. He was holding onto the piece of wood as if his life depended on it. And it did. His life depended on finding Sabine. Alive and well.

"What do you think you are doing? Your leg is not yet healed. 'Twas tainted by that nasty poison ol' Rhys liked to use."

Darrick grunted. "At the moment I do not give a damn if the man put piss and tar on it. Where is she?" he rasped.

"Where is who? Do you mean Tate? Sabine's half-brother wants to make amends for the small part he played in Rhys's hands."

Darrick turned on the redheaded giant standing proudly before him, looking hale and hearty. A far cry from when he saw him last.

"Don't play with me, Nathan. You won't wish to know my wrath when I am fully recovered. Tell me you reached her in time. Where is Sabine?"

Afraid of the possible answer, Darrick shut his eyes and waited for the room to quit spinning. "Tell me that she lives."

Nathan finally relented. "Aye, you can see for yourself that she lives."

"If I could do that, I wouldn't be standing here clutching this damn pole, would I?"

"Look yonder."

Darrick opened his eyes and looked past the tent flap. A procession of knights carried his love to the tent.

Nathan snorted. "That stubborn woman was found halfway to your tent. Twice now, I, myself, have found her lying on the ground. I cannot very well stop what I am doing to patch her up every time she falls down, now can I?" Shrugging his wide shoulders, he frowned at his friend. "I have not the time for either one of you. You'll have to take care of each other. I have a castle to rebuild."

The men brought her in and gently laid her down on his cot.

"Sabine." Darrick drew her into his arms. He grazed his lips across her pale forehead, inhaling the precious fragrance that was hers alone. "What were you thinking, my love? You could have caused serious injury to yourself."

Sabine traced the fullness of his sensual mouth with her lips. "What else could I do? My heart breaks when I am away from your side."

Darrick kissed her. He reveled in the sweetness of her lips.

She nipped at his mouth. "Remember, wherever you go, my heart must go with you."

"And wherever you go," he whispered. "I will follow. For you hold my heart in your gentle hands. I will never let you out of my sight again."

"I love you," Sabine said against his mouth.

"'Tis long past that I should have told you that I love you, too. There was a time when I thought I lost you. "

"And now we found each other."

Darrick paused, and started to pull away. "Lockwood is not...I don't know where we will..."

Nathan cleared his voice, reminding them that he still stood nearby. "About Lockwood, Sir Darrick. It appears that our good king has placed Lockwood back into your hands." He bowed low. "Sir Darrick, Lord of Lockwood."

Could it finally be? But without Sabine as his lady, it would be an empty victory. Darrick forked his fingers through her hair and let the golden threads slide through. His next question would prove more difficult than any battle he might wage. "The Lord of Lockwood needs his lady."

"Of this, I'm certain our king would agree," Nathan added from the corner.

Darrick ignored his friend and pressed on. "Sabine, would you be my Lady of Lockwood?"

"Forever and always!"

He drew her close and winced when the wound on his thigh rebelled. "What do you have there, sweetheart?" He plucked at the hidden pocket in her gown. "More secrets?"

"Hmmm? Oh, that," she mumbled against his lips. "'Tis Father's notes regarding the treasure. Can we talk about this later? I do not believe it is going anywhere."

Pulling the leather journal out of Sabine's pocket, he laid it aside. "Yes. It will keep. I have all the treasure I want in my arms."

Nathan leaned over them and picked up the journal. "Perhaps this will sweeten your request from the king."

Meet the Author

C.C. Wiley lives in Salt Lake City with her high school sweetheart of over 35 years and their four wacky dogs. When given a choice, she prefers a yummy, well-written, historical or contemporary romance that is chock-full of hope, love and a Happy Ever After. She believes there are wonderful courageous characters waiting for someone to tell their story. It's her hope that each adventurous romance she writes will touch the reader and carry them away to another place and time, where hopes and dreams abound. Visit her website at ccwiley.com, find her on Facebook at CCWileyAuthor, and on Twitter @AuthorCCWILEY.

Printed in the United States
by Baker & Taylor Publisher Services